MURDER IN St. BARTS

Praise for the author and his works:

"An entertaining outing...Tony and Rock remain an engagingly laid-back sleuthing duo."
Booklist

"... Ripley comes up with a mixture of innovation, some wry commentary of the fads of the day...a grab bag of fun and excitement."
Midwest Book Review

"Ripley pens exciting book of sex, murder, local color."
Oklahoma Tribune

"Ripley combines a fast pace with graphic descriptions...The Body From Ipanema reads like a TV thriller..."
I Love A Mystery

"...Action-packed plot. Recommended."
Library Journal

"Mystery fans will enjoy the clever plot, loopy characters, and sardonic humor."
Booklist

"The action moves right along, dialogue spurts from the mouths of as eccentric a group as you could wish for."
I Love A Mystery

"Wacky characters, liquid prose, frequent humor, and a decidedly light plot place this [Skulls of Sedona] in the fun, breeze-to-read category."
Library Journal

"Skulls Of Sedona is quick and light-hearted and likely to give you a pretty good vibe."
Miami Herald

"...Ripley comes up with a mixture of innovation, some wry commentary of the fads of the day, and just plain old amateur sleuthing in a grab bag of fun and excitement."
Midwest Book Review

"He always seems to write with a sort of tongue-in-cheek attitude...He has that touch of the bizarre, the outre, the silly...Always entertaining to read."
Oklahoma Tribune

"Written in a totally off-the-cuff, bare bones fashion...has a cutting sense of humor."
Midwest Book Review

"The story is light-hearted, sexy, funny and entertaining. Well-plotted, it rises to an amazing finale. The characters are well-drawn, interesting and believable."
The Tribune

"...A mix of mystery, murder and mayhem."
The Chattooga Press

"...A thriller laced with a good dose of humor...it's perfect for an afternoon at the beach."
Island Reporter

"If his books are as good as his songs, I reckon I need to get my act down to the library."
Nightflying

J.R. RIPLEY

Beachfront Publishing

Beachfront Publishing, POB 811922, Boca Raton, FL 33481. Correspond with Beachfront via email at:
    info@beachfrontentertainment.com

    Library of Congress Cataloging-in-Publication Data

Ripley, J. R. date
  Murder In St. Barts / J. R. Ripley.
  p. cm.
  ISBN: 1-892339-55-2
    1. Saint Barthelemy–Fiction. 2. Police – Saint Barthelemy
    – Fiction. 3. Fashion designers – Crimes against – Fiction.
    I. Title: Murder in Saint Barts. II. Title.

PS3568.I635 M8 2003
813'.54—dc21   2002034280

    Printed in U.S.A.   10987654321

Acknowledgments

St. Barts is a very real and very lovely island in the French West Indies. However, this is a work of fiction and I have employed a great amount of creative license in the telling of this tale. Needless to say, any factual errors are my own, and I hope I have kept these to a minimum.

I want to thank the wonderful people of St. Barthelemy for their cooperation and assistance in the writing of this novel. In particular, I wish to express my gratitude to the men and women of the Police Municipale and the Gendarmerie Nationale. They are truly dedicated and highly professional individuals and I have only the highest regard and respect for them.

Merci beaucoup.

I

"I swear, if the sun gets any closer, it'll set the whole sky afire."

Charles turned to face his unexpected visitor. The man had spoken French, but it was not the same French as Charles' own. No, this man with the fiery hair was definitely an islander, Saint Barthelemy born and bred, suspected Charles, or perhaps Saint Martin. Charles was from France; Lille to be precise.

He squinted over the red-headed man's rounded left shoulder and studied the large sky. It was a limitless canvas of blue on the verge of being overrun by yellow, like a square of soft butter melting atop the world.

Charles said plainly, "Yes, the clouds will go first. All brown around the edges and bubbling up like sugar. Then," Charles threw his hands apart, "foof! They'll be burning. Like so many toasted marshmallows."

The red-headed man laughed. "You almost make it sound like a good thing. Tasty, at any rate."

Charles swept a rivulet of threatening sweat away from his brow with the back of his hand before it could strike his unprotected eye. "Maybe," he replied rather enigmatically. "I've a fondness for marshmallows, anyway."

Charles resumed sanding the wind-worn rail. The fine paper seemed to be sanding away as much of his skin as it did the old teakwood.

"Me, too," said the red-headed man, patting his podgy stomach lovingly, for no one to see. "Aiming to make a go of that thing?" The stranger eyed Charles' boat.

It was a work-in-progress. Before Charles had arrived from his homeland and rescued the old craft from limbo, it had been a work-in-decay. He liked to think he was rescuing the craft from an otherwise slow but certain death.

"No," replied Charles. "It's my home."

"You're living on that thing?" The man seemed incredulous.

"In a fashion."

The red-haired man chuckled. "Not high fashion, I'll reckon you that!"

Charles frowned and puffed out his chest. He was quite sensitive about the boat. Everyone he knew was calling him crazy. And now strangers were freely offering up the same assessment without the least provocation!

"Hey, I'm only funning with you, son." He held out a big hand. There were callouses spread across the palm. But the skin was white and dry, a sharp contrast to the sun infused backs which were brownish-red. "I'm Per Ravelson. You can call me Thor. Everybody calls me Thor."

Charles shook the blunt man's hand, or allowed Thor's hand to engulf his own, rather like a mongoose swallowing an egg. He gave his name and took back his fingers.

"Charles, eh? You're new to the island, aren't you?"

"I only arrived several weeks ago."

"Well, we've all got to arrive sometime. Take my

ancestors, for instance. Arrived by schooner from Sweden back in 1847. We've been a family of West Indies seamen ever since."

Charles set down his sandpaper. He glanced at his wristwatch. It didn't look like he was going to be making much progress this afternoon and he'd sorely wanted to finish sanding down at least the port toprail. "You're a ship's captain, then?"

"No, retired." Thor kicked a plastic bucket on the ground near Charles' feet. "You gonna use this stuff?"

"I've some leaks. I'm told it is the best sealant for the job."

Thor laughed. "Well, whoever sold you this junk sold you a load of donkey manure in the same pitch."

Charles picked up the tub and read the recommendations and directions. "It looks proper to me."

Thor grabbed the tub from Charles and tossed it into a metal dumpster near the picket fence that provided some sense of division between the narrow properties on each side.

There was a small explosion.

"Hear that thunk?" demanded Thor.

Charles nodded slowly. He'd paid better than thirty-two Euros for that sealant!

"Well, that there is all that goo is good for—going thunk."

"But—"

Thor held up a hand. "Now, now. I've got some stuff up at the house that will seal this boat up tighter than a witch's arse. When you're ready, I'll bring it by. No charge. I make it up myself. A man's gotta keep busy."

The red-headed man wriggled his fingers. "A man's got to use his hands. Isn't that right?" He slapped Charles across the back.

Charles bent like a sapling, throwing out his arms, fearing he'd otherwise strike the ground chest and chin first.

"Like the way you're using your own two hands, your sweat and blood, to bring this girl back to life." Thor slapped the boat this time and Charles couldn't help but to let out a yelp. He was sure that the boat would collapse, if not the old dry dock as well.

"Really," Charles checked the blocks and boards supporting the boat above the ground, "we'd better be careful, very careful. Don't you agree?" Charles bent and studied the back cradle. Was it starting to lean forward or had it always been tilted that way?

The old man was nodding but Charles was far from certain it had anything at all to do with what he'd said.

"Yes, a man can never be too careful. I can't tell you how many times I've been in and out of Gustavia Harbor. But sure enough, one night back in '72, during an October storm, I'll be damned if I didn't run up on the rocks." He shook his head as though he still carried a good liter of disbelief in his skull, sloshing around like so much island rum.

Philip Denown, the long-time manager of the Idyllique Hotel and Villas, located along the eye-catching Baie de St. Jean, was a man of medium height and medium temperament. His hair was thinning and gray, not a good thing at all as he considered himself a young forty-six years old.

He had a tendency to lean forwards, forever going up hill in the climb of life—and he stood so now as both the quality and color of his hair and his moderate temperament were each being tested by Lily, a lovely student from Paris but for her thick ankles and largish feet, spending a season in between university courses working as the hotel's receptionist.

"Impossible," Denown said. The manager braced the desk and shook it. He couldn't understand the girl. She'd always been a good, hard worker up until now.

Lily grabbed the computer terminal to keep it from shaking its way to the tiled floor. "No," she said in low, conspiratorial tones, "it's true, monsieur. I swear to you."

Denown shook his head. "No, your English is not so good. You've misunderstood the lady, Lily. That's all."

"No, monsieur. Mademoiselle Somers was quite adamant. She said Monsieur Freon was—" a client of the hotel walked into the lobby and the girl's voice dropped like a rock from Point Milou, "dead."

"Impossible," repeated Denown. He turned to the American guest and said in English, "May we be of service to you, sir?"

"I'm looking for a towel—" The guest gestured with his hands, spreading them out and then up as if giving the exact dimensions he had in mind. "A beach towel?"

Denown smiled. "Yes, sir. The cabana near the *piscine*, the pool, is open at this hour. You've only to ask the boy there and provide him with your suite number."

The American nodded. After he'd gone the manager asked Lily where Mademoiselle Somers was to be found.

Lily replied, "She's in the villa with the body."

"This is impossible."

Lily shrugged rather helplessly. "Perhaps I misunderstood . . ."

Denown clicked his fingers, twice in rapid succession. "Or perhaps it is only a heart attack or a fall down the stairs—not a murder at all. Only an accidental or a quite natural death. There is a subtlety between the English words, you understand." He raised a hand, fingers together. "That is, between dead and murdered."

He spoke like a teacher to his pupil. "In English, one can be simply 'dead tired' as well."

"She said murder. . ."

Denown snapped, "*Ma petite*, must you be so difficult?" He shook his fist. "The property is full of guests—rich, powerful and many famous guests. The Idyllique caters to models, moguls and movie stars, who each demand the best services in the world. And now you test my patience!"

Denown trotted down the path between the small gardens that separated the hotel's deluxe cottages from the even more exclusive and pricey villas that rose from the beach up the cliff face. An unstifled sun beat down on him.

The Onyx was the name of the villa that the American designer, Bobbi Freon, had rented for the winter. It was whitewashed like all the others and was located at the east end of the property. It was so named for its black furnishings, from the black leather furniture to the drapes and the bed sheets, all of which were inky black. Even the granite counter top in the kitchen maintained the color scheme along with each of the appliances.

This was Bobbi Freon's villa of choice when on St. Barts. He was a frequent and easy spending guest. If he were dead, this would be most regrettable. Profits would suffer. His bonus, as a consequence, would too.

The manager knocked lightly on the wind-beaten oak door. It was answered quickly by a lovely, tanned woman in a yellow sarong and matching bikini top. Her feet were bare. Her hair was long and dark. She was tall for a woman.

She looked visibly shaken. This, Denown knew, was Monsieur Freon's housekeeper or assistant of sorts—he wasn't sure which and it was not his privilege or place to ask—Sofie Somers.

"Mademoiselle Somers." He bowed. "Lily at reception told me you called with—" How was he going to put this tactfully? "— difficulties?"

Freon's assistant nodded soberly. She looked Denown in the eyes before lowering her gaze to the floor. "Yes, this way, please." She turned her back and walked slowly, silently towards the master bungalow. The two level master suite was across from the kidney shaped private swimming pool in the central courtyard of the villa itself.

There was another bungalow with two bedrooms on the left, while the kitchen, dining and entertaining areas were on the right. The master bedroom was upstairs. The lower half of the cottage faced the pool and contained a sitting area as well as a billiards table and an upright piano.

Sofie Somers paused at the bottom of the stairs, then, when the manager failed to make the first move, preceded Denown upwards.

There was no door, as Denown knew full well. As his head rose above the floor, he saw Mr. Freon's legs hanging off the bed, bare feet touching the ground.

Denown reached the top of the stairs and paused. Mademoiselle Somers stood to the side, her arms crossed, not looking at the bed. Bobbi, wearing only his black trousers, lay sideways with his back against the mattress. His eyes were half open, staring up through the mosquito curtain and for a moment Denown held out a hope that the American was still alive.

But Bobbi Freon's torso was a bloody mess.

Denown had attended a bullfight once, in Mexico, on a private ranch outside Guadalajara owned by one of his frequent guests, where the matador had been gored badly in his stomach. The matador, a young star from Spain, survived with his agony for nearly two hours; just long enough to arrive at the hospital, where he promptly died.

Like the matador, Bobbi Freon, no doubt, had met his match.

2

"Chief! Come quickly! It's Denown. He wants a word with you!"

In his office, on his private line, the Chief of Municipal Police, Didier Lebon, told his wife to be silent a moment. They were discussing the return of their youngest daughter, Violette, just back from high school. As there were no upper level schools on Saint Barthelemy, Violette had been required to attend a school off the island. And now, having completed her higher education had returned to the family home.

The chief's wife, Elisabeth, was concerned for her future.

Why, the chief could not say. Could Violette not simply find a suitable husband and take care of him? Barring this, couldn't she perhaps seek gainful employment? These were nagging questions the good chief wisely refrained from directly raising with his dear wife.

He barked at the officer in the other room. "Philip Denown, manager of the Idyllique Hotel and Villas?"

"Yes, sir." Officer Pisar Mercer stuck his head in the door.

"What does he want?"

"He says there's been a murder."

"A murder," scoffed Didier. "Don't be ridiculous."

"He wants to talk to you. He wants to know what to do." The officer sounded rattled.

"Bah! He's drunk, Pisar. You know Denown. He drinks too much." The chief looked at his watch. "Even for an islander, it's too early in the day for decorum. But that's Philip for you. A drunkard. His father was a drunkard. His grandfather was a drunkard. His own wife," Didier shook his hand, "I hear is a lush. Favors vanilla rum, if you can believe the rumors."

Didier shooed the officer away. "Tell him to get the hell off our telephone. Remind him it is for official use only and to stop annoying us or I will personally issue him a fine!"

"Yes, chief."

Before returning his attention to his wife, Didier shouted one last thing, "Tell him to have a coffee!"

Didier picked up the receiver, surprised to find that Elisabeth was still talking. "Yes, dear. I am sorry. A slight interruption. You heard what? Murder? No, don't be alarmed. Of course there has not been a murder. Only that joker Denown—falling down drunk and it's barely noon."

Speaking of which, Didier's stomach, a rather imposing structure itself, commenced to grumbling. He would have to extricate himself from his wife as soon as possible and head down to the harbor for lunch.

He held the phone an inch from his ear awaiting a moment where he might jump in to cut off the conversation when Mercer appeared at his door dragging a telephone with him. Grateful for the interruption, Didier said to his wife, "I must go, dear. Duty calls. Yes, we shall talk about it some more later." Like it or not, they would talk about it later, on that he had no doubt.

"What is it now, Pisar?"

Officer Mercer held out the phone. "It's Denown again."

"I told you to tell him to buzz off."

"I did, chief. I told him exactly as you instructed. But he's called back again." Pisar pushed the phone forward. "He really is quite insistent."

Didier sighed and picked up the phone on his desk. Two lines were lit. "Which line is he on?"

"Two."

The chief nodded and pushed the button on the telephone for line two. Pisar stood outside the open door, making no pretense of disappearing and quite obviously eavesdropping.

"Listen, here, Denown. We really are quite busy. What? What is it, Denown?" The chief's face paled. "But that is impossible! Have you been drinking, monsieur?"

On the other end of the line, Denown was insisting he was sober. The chief had to admit that Philip Denown did not sound inebriated. Yet, perhaps he only controlled it well? Lebon had known many a drunk who was able to function quite reasonably in social situations without giving himself away.

Still, the hotelman had described a grisly sight. If it was his alcohol-fueled imagination, it was a sick one.

All the while, the hotel manager was rambling quickly and mostly incoherently.

"Calm down, Philip. Calm down. What?"

Denown asked the chief once more what he should do.

"What to do? How the hell should I know what to do, Denown? There's not been a murder here in—" The chief scratched his head. "In twenty years!" Lebon cupped a hand over the receiver and said to Pisar, "What is the procedure for handling a murder?"

The officer only shrugged uselessly.

"Well, go look it up in a book somewhere!" shouted Chief Lebon. "And you, Philip, stay put and not a word about this to anyone. You understand?"

The manager said yes.

"I'll be there soon." The chief of police dropped the phone in its cradle. It clattered out and bounced off the floor, neatly cracking the receiver in two ugly looking pieces.

But this was only the beginning of the chief's problems.

With two of his men at his side, Chief Lebon headed outside for a police SUV. Halfway along, he paused, thence did his fellow officers, reliably as automatons. Lebon had an idea, told his men to wait for him, and rushed back inside the station.

He dialed the Gendarmerie. The Gendarmes had a contingent of ten men headquartered on the road between Public and Corossol. He reached a gendarme and insisted that it was urgent that he speak to the adjutant who was said to be quite busy.

In fact, the adjutant was busy. He was draped in a long, semi-transparent yellow smock, camel hair paintbrush in hand, fingers and palms covered with cream colored paint, attacking a helpless wall in his windowless office.

The Gendarmerie was undergoing restorations and most all of the gendarmes were called up to this active, if harmless, duty. Nonetheless, the adjutant, after some delay, came to the phone.

Adjutant Bruyer, former paratrooper and medaled member of the elite *Groupe de Sécurité de la Présidence de la République*, was a husky man with a good humor. He was also a meticulous man. He picked up the telephone carefully. "Yes?"

He was suspicious. It wasn't all that often that a call came through from the municipal police.

Chief Lebon quickly explained the situation. "There's been a crime. A murder."

Adjutant Bruyer laughed heartily. "Yes, sure. And I hear Basque separatists have stormed the island and declared a new sovereignty. It must be a slow day for you police. What's wrong? Why not go arrest some nudists at the beach? Or are you afraid of the furor you'll cause?"

Saint Barthelemy was very tolerant of skin. The adjutant did not consider this to be a bad thing by any reach of the imagination, neither did most locals and guests to the island.

The adjutant started to say goodbye but the chief kept him on the line.

"Listen, Emil, I'm not joking, man. There has been a murder!"

The adjutant continued to be suspicious. "And just who is it that has been murdered? A twelve year old bottle of brandy, perhaps?"

"No. Quit joking, this is serious."

"Well," said Adjutant Bruyer slowly, still looking for a way out of this potential trap, "if it's murder, it must be one of your locals. No doubt about it. Feuding gotten out of hand. Too much drink and not enough work."

The adjutant had heard all about some of St. Barts' famous feuds, families who had been waging minor wars with one another for upwards of a century. "So, if it's murder you have, I suggest you, the municipal police, solve it. Take care of your own, I always say. *Ciao.*"

"It's a tourist. An American."

"God's truth?" The adjutant squeezed the receiver to his ear. *Merde*, not only a murder but it had to be a tourist? And an American to boot!

There was a pause.

"Yes."

The paintbrush slipped from the adjutant's hand. He attempted to wipe the tops of his paint spattered leather shoes on the back of his pant legs. Bruyer cleared his throat and collected his thoughts. "Are you certain?"

The chief insisted.

"I mean, I could understand if there has been an automobile accident. . ." The roads on St. Barts could be remarkably treacherous, steep and narrow, with drivers speeding willy-nilly past one another, often as not themselves fueled with as much alcohol as their tanks were with gas.

"This was no accident, from what I gather." Chief Lebon explained the call he had received from the manager of the Idyllique Hotel and Villas.

After a silence, the adjutant spoke, "There must be some mistake."

"Let's hope so," said Didier. "Meet me there, will you?" With that he rung off.

Much to his chagrin, the chief arrived at the crime scene first. He waited in the property manager's office, however, while two of his men stood guard outside the entrance of the Villa Onyx. One such officer was Officer Pisar Mercer, being punished by the chief, justly so or not.

Chief Lebon was still angry with Mercer for answering the call from Denown in the first place and not knowing what to do about a reported murder in the second.

An ambulance had been called from the local hospital and a doctor was said to be on his way.

Adjutant Bruyer arrived and filled the room with his presence. Four uniformed gendarmes silently accompanied him. He shook Chief Lebon's hand and then that of a clearly shaken Philip Denown.

"Well, shall we go see this body?" The chief was still hoping this was some sort of practical joke. Tourists sometimes had bizarre senses of humor. And the drunker a tourist got, the funnier he thought he was being.

Philip Denown nodded somberly and led the way.

As they headed up the garden path, Adjutant Bruyer could not help but contemplate the people who stayed here and other expensive hotels like it on St. Barthelemy. Bruyer knew that lodgings in the hotel suites alone cost thousands of Euros per night and the villas must command many times that rate. He could only wonder at how some people had so much. Sadly, this had never been one of his problems.

They arrived at Villa Onyx where the two municipal police officers were idly chatting. They straightened their backs as the officials arrived. Mercer's face betrayed his feelings of having been unjustly chastened. Nonetheless, his back was the straightest of the two.

Outside the front door, Chief Lebon put his hand on the lever, but as he was about to push the door open the adjutant laid a hand on his sleeve.

"What is it?" asked the chief.

"Listen here, Didier," began Adjutant Bruyer, "before we go inside to take a look at this body, don't you think we should settle things?"

"Settle things?" The chief wiped his face with the back of his arm. He was sweating like a pig standing outside here in the heat. He wanted to get inside where it was bound to be cool, dead body or no.

"Yes, like who is going to handle the investigation," explained Adjutant Bruyer, "and the ensuing paperwork."

Chief Lebon ran his left thumb through the short, thick moustache he'd sported since his twenty-first birthday. He considered the moustache a symbol of his manhood. "It is obvious, Emil, that if this is indeed a murder then it is for the Gendarmerie to investigate."

"Perhaps, but you have much more experience with the locals. After all, you men were born and raised here. We in the Gendarmerie only spend three years at a time on St. Barthelemy and then we move on. Myself, I was stationed in Mauritania before arriving at my current post."

"Nonetheless, this sort of crime is your domain."

"Who can say?"

"Why not ask your superior?"

"The lieutenant? He is headquartered on Saint Martin, as you yourself well know." The adjutant tugged at his collar. This nagging heat was sapping him. "Yes, I suppose he must be informed."

"Besides, I expect that this will be a case wherein the procureur will be the man to decide whose duty it will be to solve this crime." The chief looked at the door as if trying to see through to the other side. "If crime there be."

"Perhaps," interjected the hotel manager, Denown, "you will only need to interview the mademoiselle, Monsieur Freon's assistant, and this case will all but solve itself. . ."

"Where is she?" asked Chief Lebon.

"Down at the beach with her children. I told her to await you there, should you wish to speak with her."

The chief nodded.

The adjutant turned up his lip. "Does she speak French?"

Denown shook his head. "I don't think so. Portuguese."

"Portuguese!"

"And English," added Denown.

"A fat lot of good that will do me," said Adjutant Bruyer. "I'd die of thirst on this island if I even had to order a decent beer in English. As for Portugese, it might as well be

Chinese!" The adjutant turned to the chief. "It looks like this will be a job for you, after all, Didier."

The chief smiled and shook his head. "No. I do not think so. I am a Frenchman. It is the only language I know and the only language worth knowing."

The hotel manager watched in horror as the two men debated the taking of the investigation. Denown was quite worried about his own situation, a dead—murdered—body lying in the master bed of one of his best villas! And in the middle of high season!

Denown wrung his hands. Would the blood stains ever come out?

The two officials continued to bicker outside the villa door while Bobbi Freon waited patiently inside.

"Wait a moment," said Adjutant Bruyer with a sudden burst of inspiration. "I've a young gendarme who has only been just sent over a few weeks past from France. As I recall he speaks English quite remarkably. In fact," he scratched his bristly head, "I seem to remember the young fellow had been an English language major before joining up with the Gendarmerie."

"Really?" Didier, whose stomach had been tense with his intestines knotted up like tangled rope, felt his appetite returning. "Who is this man? Is he one of these fellows?" The chief studied the silent gendarmes.

"No. His name is Charles. Charles Trenet. He is off duty today, working on his boat down at the harbor, I expect."

"Well," said Didier, with clear relief, "perhaps he should be summoned."

"Yes," said the adjutant. "I will send one of my men to fetch him. In fact, I believe Trenet should be here when we go inside." Adjutant Bruyer nodded towards the villa. "After all, if he is going to take charge of this investigation, isn't it for the best that he be present on initial examination of the body?"

"You are a wise man, *mon ami.*" The chief shook the adjutant's hand. It was covered with dry splotches of cream-colored paint. "And better still, as police headquarters is much nearer the harbor, in the name of expediency, I will send a car for your young gendarme."

There were smiles all around.

"I would further propose that we adjourn to Philip's office for a drink while we await this Trenet."

"A marvelous suggestion," agreed the adjutant. He barked orders to his men to assist the chief's two municipal officers in securing the perimeter around the villa and in keeping busybodies, nosey tourists and staff far away.

Denown wanted to protest the delays, but then again, a drink did sound like a good idea and a few minutes further wouldn't change things much. The American certainly wouldn't mind. With luck, mused the manager, rubbing his hands together cheerfully, it will be determined that Monsieur Freon had only committed harikari.

Silently, both Chief Lebon and Adjutant Bruyer congratulated themselves on having successfully dodged the responsibility of this criminal matter. After all, this thing—a murder involving a rich foreigner—could be a political and public relations nightmare and a nasty powder keg of lawyers and sleepless nights all rolled up in one ugly barrel. A barrel that could conceivably blow up in both of their faces if they were not most vigilant.

And both men, having enjoyed long careers which had led them to the tops of their professions, knew that when embroiled in such a situation, if the opportunity allowed—as fate had so generously provided in this case in the form of a certain young gendarme—let the new guy do it.

3

"Hey, you! Trenet? Charles Trenet?"

Charles turned away from Thor, whose knack for soliloquy seemed as endless as the sea around them. He studied his caller. It was an officer in an official municipal police vehicle. Had he done something wrong?

Charles nodded once.

"The gendarme?"

Charles nodded a second time.

Thor said with surprise, "You're a gendarme?" He harrumphed, which came off sounding something like a sexually frustrated bull seal might sound on a cold and lonely night. "I should have known you weren't a seaman."

"Well," the officer leaned his arm out the window, "the adjutant wants to see you, pronto!"

Charles said quizzically, "My adjutant?"

"Well, he sure as hell isn't mine. Hurry up, will you? The chief told me to find you as fast as possible."

"But what for?"

"How on earth should I know? Like I said, he's not my adjutant."

Charles inwardly moaned. *Merde.* He ignored Thor's look of contempt. What could he have done, barely a month on the island, to warrant his adjutant calling on him to report immediately and to further warrant the chief of the municipal police to order the fetching?

The officer in the car honked the horn. "Come on, stop daydreaming there and get moving."

Charles tugged at his shirt. "But I'm not even in uniform."

"That's none of my concern now, is it?"

Charles stole a look at himself in the big glass window of the house next door. He was barefoot, wearing a loose pair of khakis which his mother had given him before leaving home and which he had quickly cut off at the knees upon being assigned to St. Barthelemy where balmy was a permanent condition. And his chest was covered with a once white t-shirt that was stained with seemingly every stain producing substance on the island; animal, vegetable and mineral.

His face was equally dirty and there was a streak of varnish along his forehead. His short brown hair looked as tangled as any of the thickets that lined the island's narrow roads.

Charles wiped his hands on the sides of his pant legs. "I'll just get my motorbike." He stuffed his bare feet into his heavy work boots and bent to lace them.

The officer jeered. "Really? When you don't even know where you're going?!"

Charles stood and frowned, feeling stupid. He wiped at his hands with a rag dipped in kerosene.

"Get in now, will you?"

As if to prove the end of his patience, the officer at the wheel gave the car some gas and edged forward several feet, braked, then repeated the process, giving Charles the impression he might take off without the gendarme, leaving him to suffer the consequences.

Charles ran and jumped in on the passenger side having no clue where he was heading or why.

"Where are we off to?"

"You'll see." The officer sped quickly around the corner, ignoring all traffic as he drove backwards up a narrow one way street. They skirted the harbor and headed past the power station.

They'd climbed the mountain that divided the island's main city of Gustavia from the Aéroport de Saint Jean. The driver kept going. Just beyond a cluster of shops in the Village de St. Jean, he pulled into a posh looking hotel along the water's edge.

"Here?" Charles said. Nervously, he fought to wipe the grime from his hands and knees. He reeked of kerosene. He felt hopelessly out of place.

"*Oui.*"

There were numerous official vehicles, belonging to the municipal police and the gendarmerie, clogging up the small parking lot. Charles had never seen so many in one place. In addition, countless tourist rentals squeezed into every available space of land in the vicinity. This was not unusual. Parking tickets were a rare thing in St. Barts. The locals went so far as to leave the keys in the ignitions of their autos while they were away from their vehicles in case someone needed to move them.

"But what are we doing here?"

The officer snorted. "All's I know is that the chief said to fetch you and fetch you I have." He reached over Trenet and pulled the handle. The passenger side door fell open. "Out you go now."

"But—"

He gave Charles a firm yet friendly shove and Charles heard the sound of a car door closing behind him. The officer sped off.

Adjutant Bruyer stuck his head out of the lobby, saw Trenet standing there, and came quickly marching out to meet him. "Ah, Trenet." He glanced at his wristwatch. "That's quick time you've made. Splendid." He shook Charles' hand. The kerosene on Charles' hands mixed with the paint on the adjutant's and he frowned. "The doctor has already arrived. Let's get this investigation started. We'll go take a look at the body now."

Charles' jaw hung open.

"Shall we?"

"Body, sir?"

"Yes, our victim."

"Victim?" Charles gulped. What the devil was the adjutant going on about and what had it to do with him? Two men appeared at the entrance of the hotel, one dressed in the uniform of the municipal police, the other in civilian clothing. They joined up with Charles and the adjutant on the walkway leading towards the villas.

"This is Chief Lebon of the Municipal Police," Adjutant Bruyer said, making the introductions.

Charles lightly shook the officer's hand.

"And this is Philip Denown, the hotel's manager."

Charles said hello once more.

"If you will just follow me," Denown said. He took the post position and the others followed. They arrived at a large villa surrounded by officers and a fellow in a Florida Marlins baseball cap, a white smock and green shorts. Charles wondered if he was a tourist and what his role in the current enigma might be.

"Hello, Martin, how's it going?" Chief Lebon reached out

and clasped the man's hand.

"Fine, if you call being disturbed from my surgery in the middle of the afternoon a good thing," said the man in the green shorts whose name had turned out to be Martin.

"Nice to see you again, doctor," added the adjutant, who'd had occasion to see the doctor on a couple of personal visits of his own.

So, thought Charles, this odd looking fellow was a physician! Curiouser and curiouser.

Chief Lebon nodded and Denown unlocked the door to the villa. The men crowded into the entryway and Denown took the lead once more.

Charles was the last one up the stairs. The doctor was already leaning over the bed when he got to the top. The adjutant put a beefy hand on Charles' back and pushed him forward.

"Ever see anything like it?" Adjutant Bruyer said.

Charles looked at the bloody mess on the sheets. Several lucky mosquitoes were gorging themselves. He had to admit, he had never seen anything like it. "Who is he?" Charles asked weakly.

"Bobbi Freon," explained the hotel manager. "An honored American guest. This was his villa. He always requested it specially when he visited with us."

Charles turned away from the body on the bed, trying to free the image from his mind, but it clung there as firmly as if it had been nailed in place.

"We'll miss him," said Denown, bowing his head.

Charles refrained from asking if there would be a penalty for checking out early. "He was rich then?"

Denown shot the gendarme a condescending look. "Quite."

The doctor, his nose only inches from the red pulpy mess

that was Bobbi Freon's stomach, turned his head and said, "Where's the weapon?"

The chief looked at Denown, who said, "I don't know. There was none that I saw. Perhaps Mademoiselle Somers—"

"Yes, we'll have a word with her soon enough," interjected Chief Lebon.

Adjutant Bruyer called for one of his men to photograph the crime scene. Another gendarme was instructed to check the room for fingerprints while he, Charles and Chief Lebon went about searching the room. Charles was given a pair of flimsy, latex gloves which he struggled to put on.

"What are we looking for?" Charles asked his superior, as he clumsily pulled open a chest drawer that was sticking along one side—something a little simple planing could solve.

"That," said Adjutant Bruyer sounding like an ancient Chinese philosopher, "is the beauty of criminal investigation. We seek the unknown."

Charles turned his attention to the task at hand. One drawer containing four fancy silk shirts, all black, six pair of black undershorts, seven black socks—that was odd. Oh, well. If one was lost in the wash, the victim wouldn't be complaining now, would he?

He crossed to the luxurious bath, half expecting to see a black bar of soap in the shower. Oddly, it was yellow. But the tile was black, as was the counter. Both looked to be marble. The sink, the toilet and even the bidet were black as night. The oversized towels hanging on the rack matched the color scheme, the only relief from the darkness provided by the monogrammed gold letters BF surrounded by a diamond shaped figure in the center of each bath towel. The man brought his own towels to a hotel?

The rich lived in such a different reality, it might as well have been a different world altogether.

Finally, the photographs were all taken and the fingerprints collected and Adjutant Bruyer called Charles to join him at the grand balcony overlooking the bay. The body of Bobbi Freon was being removed.

Charles watched as the corpse was carried out on a stretcher, zigzagging its way along on the garden path below. A lovely sight, thought Charles, too bad Monsieur Freon could not enjoy it.

The adjutant laid his hands on the aluminum rail. "So, we have a murder."

Charles nodded. He felt someone approaching. It was Chief Lebon who'd come up behind him. The hair on the back of Charles' neck prickled.

"How is your English, Charles?" inquired the adjutant.

"My English?"

"Yes, you speak English, don't you?" Chief Lebon said.

"Former English major, correct?" Adjutant Bruyer said, puffing up his chest with a fatherly pride.

"Yes," said Charles slowly, feeling an invisible snare closing around his neck.

"Wonderful!" exclaimed Adjutant Bruyer.

"Splendid!" echoed Chief Lebon.

"Sir?" Charles looked from one official to the other. "What does my speaking English have to do with the murder? And what does Bobbi Freon's murder have to do with me?"

Adjutant Bruyer grinned.

Chief Lebon chuckled.

It was the adjutant who said, "Why, we want you to solve it, of course!"

4

Charles wove his way along a pink hibiscus lined path leading to the beach. This paved pathway turned into a planked boardwalk which veered off to the right and left along the perimeter of the resort property.

An old woman, topless and pale, lay on the nearest chaise. She caught Charles looking at her and raised an amused eyebrow. Charles reddened. "I beg your pardon. Mademoiselle Somers?"

She was certainly too old to be Monsieur Freon's assistant but he had not been able to think of anything else to say. Her bare breasts taunted him and left him feeling uneasy. Charles made a vow to himself never to invite his mother for a visit to Saint Barthelemy. It would be better to visit her in France than to see her here, like this.

"No, sorry."

Charles made to leave.

"One moment. Since you are here, would you mind helping me with the lotion?" Her face turned to a bottle of white tanning lotion on the table beside her.

After a moment's hesitation, in which the sun beat down

on him like a hot drum, setting his nerves on edge, Charles handed the old woman her lotion.

"Could you?" She sat up and gestured with the bottle toward her back.

Charles stammered, "I'm sorry. I am in a bit of a hurry. I have official business."

She shrugged. "Too bad. Come back when you have more time, why don't you?" She smiled lasciviously, laid back and closed her eyes.

The gendarme nodded and hurried off. The beach was teaming with sun worshipers, but one woman stood out from the crowd. She sat on the sand, facing the sea, wearing a yellow bikini top, which she filled admirably, and a matching wrap that swept in a curve over her knees. Her long, dark hair was pulled back into a loosely flowing ponytail. Her eyes were unrevealed, as she wore sunglasses. Her calves were brown and smooth. Two children were playing nearby and the woman called to them.

As sure as he was that this had to be Bobbi Freon's assistant and housekeeper, as had been described to him, he was equally sure that she couldn't possibly hold such a position. There was an air about her. An air of beauty and superiority. And Charles approached her almost timidly.

She saw him coming and held her ground. The breeze off the water seemed to exist solely to provide her comfort as it lightly danced with her hair and sarong.

Panting from traipsing over the beach in his heavy shoes, Charles licked his dry lips.

She raised her head and spoke first. "I'm sorry, I don't have any money."

"*Pardon?*" The aroma of the ocean mixed with a more gentle citrus scent, a scent of lemon and oranges, that seemed to be coming from the woman and Charles found himself taking a deep, appreciative breath.

"I didn't bring my purse." She pushed her fingers through the sand. "There's so much sand at the beach. It insinuates itself into everything. And the sand here is so clingy. So unlike the sand at the beaches in the States."

She hesitated. "I'm sorry. You probably don't understand a word I am saying. My French is very poor, I'm afraid."

Did she take him for a beggar? "You misunderstand, madame, my name is Charles Trenet. And my English, while poor, is serviceable."

"Oh, you speak English." The girl was taunting the boy and the woman gently called for her to desist. When the girl didn't, the woman rose. "*Au revoir*, Charles. You'll have to excuse me. I must take care of my children."

The gendarme stepped into her path. "You are Madame Somers, *non?*"

"You're half correct. I am Mademoiselle Somers. Have we met?"

She was looking at him suspiciously now and Charles spoke hurriedly. "I beg your pardon. No, we have not met. My name, as I have said, is Charles Trenet and I am with the Gendarmerie Nationale." He held out his hand.

She removed her sunglasses, revealing eyes that shined like emeralds seen through diamond lenses. The tiniest of wrinkles appeared at the corners of her eyes which only made her appear even more beautiful. "The police? You're here about—" Her voice trailed off.

Charles nodded. "That's right."

"I'm sorry. I mean, your clothes—" She giggled, then stopped herself. "I thought—I mean, don't you get a uniform?"

Charles looked down at his stained and sweat-drenched shirt. He tugged at it miserably. "Yes. This was my day off. I was working on my boat."

"Again, I am sorry."

Charles begged her to forget about it. "I'm afraid I must ask you about what happened, what you remember, that sort of thing."

"You want to take my statement."

"Yes, that's it."

She took a long look at the two children.

"These are your children, are they not, mademoiselle?" Charles was confused. The manager, Denown, had said that the woman had two children, yet she'd corrected him when he had called her madame.

"Yes, Cleo and Anthony."

"They're lovely."

"Thank you." She touched his wrist and he felt a warm spark. "Why don't we sit over there?"

They moved to a round wooden beach table and sat at opposite sides. An open red umbrella provided shade. The breeze swept Charles in the face, bringing with it a scent of fresh mangoes. Was it her hair?

"You had some questions for me, Charles?"

Charles broke from his reverie. "Yes." He studied her face. There was beauty and pain in those features.

"And, did you say 'Trenet?'"

"Yes," said Charles, prepared for the inevitable.

"Is there not a quite famous French entertainer—"

"Yes, he is also Charles Trenet."

"And are you—"

Charles was already shaking his head. "Related? *Non*. While I bear the same name, I do not share the lineage. My mother and my father were quite mad about Charles Trenet. And as my father's surname was already Trenet, it was no stretch of the imagination to name me Charles.

"They say I was conceived while listening to *Près de Toi, Mon Amour.* When I was a teenager, going through that typical rebellious teen phase, I threatened to change it."

"What would you have changed it to?"

Charles shrugged and said with some embarrassment, "I told my parents and sisters I wanted to be called Django."

Sofie smiled. "Like the guitarist?"

"Django Reinhardt, yes. Better a guitarist than a singer, at least, so I thought at the time. You know of him?"

"Certainly. I grew up in a home filled with the sounds of music. Still. . ." She laid her hand atop his for a moment. "Django Trenet." Her fingers lightly touched down like the near-weightless legs of a butterfly; there for a moment and then gone. "I much prefer Charles."

She sat back, as if taking him all in. "Yes, it suits you. And I think the story of your conception is precious."

"Thank you, mademoiselle." Charles had all but forgotten what he was doing on the beach that particular moment in time.

"Call me Sofie, please."

Charles nodded.

"You're quite young to be an investigator, aren't you?"

"Actually, I am a gendarme, mademoiselle—Sofie."

"Oh, I see."

"Yes. My adjutant and Chief Lebon of the municipal police requested that I take your statement." Charles searched his pockets for the little spiral notebook the hotel manager had given him along with a pen. He opened the pad deliberately, pen poised over paper, attempting to look as official and experienced as he was capable of mustering himself up to be.

"So," Charles cleared his throat, "first." He wet the tip of the pen with his tongue and wrote. "Your name. Sofie

Somers."

She spelled it out for him.

"And you work for Monsieur Freon?"

She folded her hands in her lap. Her children were playing in the surf. "That's right."

"May I ask in what capacity?"

"I am, or was, Bobbi's assistant."

Charles wrote some more. "What exactly did Monsieur Freon do for a living, mademoiselle?

A lovely dark eyebrow lifted. "You are not familiar with Bobbi Freon?"

"I confess, I have never heard the name before today."

Mademoiselle Somers looked amused. "Well, it's a good thing Bobbi is dead, or I fear your statement would have killed him. Bobbi Freon was a fashion designer. Quite famous, actually. His collections are highly sought after."

"Collections?"

"You really are innocent of such things, aren't you?"

Charles reddened. He stammered, "Well, I—"

"Not to worry. I think it's refreshing. Bobbi designed women's fashion. You know, gowns, casual wear, shoes, handbags, the works. His real name, the name he was born with was Robert Frianetti. When he moved to New York from Detroit, he reinvented himself. He became Bobbi Freon because he liked the sound of it, I guess. Anyway, it's worked for him. Made him a star in the fashion world."

"Ah, I see." Charles wrote in his notebook. Bobbi Freon made women's clothing. And he'd obviously made a bundle of money doing so. The hotel manager, Philip Denown, had told him that the Villa Onyx rented for an incredible eighteen-thousand U.S. dollars per week! He'd been sure the hotel manager had been pulling his leg and it had taken some coaxing on the manager's part to convince him otherwise.

"Are you sure you've never heard of him? The company symbol is a gold pyramid. Bobbi loved all that Egyptian stuff."

Charles shook his head. "I am afraid not."

"He was even branching out into men's wear this spring season."

Feeling somehow embarrassed, Charles said, "I fear I am ignorant of such things."

"Oh, well, I'm sure it's not important. I mean, it's only fashion."

Charles changed tack. "When did you last see Monsieur Freon?"

"About an hour ago."

"An hour ago? But that's—"

"Oh, of course. You mean, when did I last see Bobbi alive." She thought for a moment. "It must have been more than two hours ago. Perhaps even closer to three." She rubbed her left wrist. "I'm afraid I'm not wearing a watch. Let me think. It was just before I brought Cleo and Anthony down to the beach."

Sofie rose. "You'll excuse me a moment. I just remembered, the children have missed their lunch and they have not had a scrap to eat since breakfast. Perhaps I should not have said that. You'll think I'm a terrible mother."

Charles shook his head. "Never."

"Then you will excuse me a moment?"

Charles nodded. "Of course. Growing children need their nourishment. Even a police investigation should not prevent this."

The young lady pulled a handbag from its place of concealment. The bag had been carefully rolled up in a beach towel.

She smiled. "I'll only be a minute." Mademoiselle Somers

opened her purse, took out a blue and tan leather wallet, from which she extracted some European currency. She took the money to her children and pointed to the poolside restaurant. The boy and girl bobbed their heads happily and raced off.

So, she had a purse and money.

Upon her return, Charles rose. "You will excuse me for asking, Sofie, but it is my duty to obtain all the facts in a case such as this. Are you married?" He was looking at the children as they approached the waitress with their fists of money.

"No, I am not."

"Divorced then? Is your children's father on the island?" Perhaps Sofie had been having an affair with this Bobbi Freon and a husband, ex- or otherwise, had become jealous. Could not this be a motive for murder?

"Their father is no longer with us, monsieur. He died rather suddenly."

There was no mistaking the iciness of her reply. "Again, I apologize. I know the questions are not always kind, cannot always be kind."

The ice melted and she smiled and touched him again. "That's alright. It was a long time ago. Please, sit."

Charles resumed his seat and his questioning. "You said it was perhaps several hours ago when you last saw Monsieur Freon?"

"That's about right. He was having coffee by the swimming pool."

"The pool in the villa or the hotel pool?"

"The villa's private pool."

"Can you tell me, was he in good spirits?"

"Yes, quite. It was his suggestion that I take Cleo and Anthony to the beach. So, yes, he was in good spirits. I mean, as much as usual."

"How do you mean?"

Mademoiselle Somers shrugged. "Let me explain. Though Bobbi loved coming to St. Barts for holidays, there is always some business going on, phone calls, faxes, you understand."

"Yes, I suppose."

"It was impossible for Bobbi to relax completely. He had what we call a Type A personality. Always on the go, always working a deal."

"Was there anyone else in the villa when you left?"

Sofie gave this some thought. "No, unless the maids were about. It is a rather large villa."

Charles stifled a grunt. Rather large was an understatement when one compared Bobbi's temporary quarters with his own permanent one. Even growing up, Charles had never lived in so expansive a home. He tapped the paper with his pen. "So, is there anyone whom you think might have wanted Monsieur Freon dead? Someone with a motive for his murder?"

Sofie reached in her purse and pulled out a cigarette which she proceeded to ignite with a platinum lighter. "Sorry, I know I shouldn't. But Bobbi smoked and, once in a while, I simply can't resist the urge."

Charles said he didn't mind and didn't understand why the woman had felt the need to apologize. Smoking was commonplace, here in Saint Barthelemy and back home in his native France.

He waited while she took a couple of puffs on the cigarette, then put it out in the sand.

"You were asking if anyone might have wanted Bobbi dead."

He nodded.

"Well, I don't know. He made a lot of money."

Charles waited expectantly.

34

"You can't make a lot of money without making some enemies. I mean, you have to make money off someone, don't you? At someone else's expense?" She was looking at him questioningly.

"I wouldn't know," replied Charles. "That is a moral dilemma I have not had to face." Please, he thought, God, if you are listening, I am up to the challenge. So far, God had not even blessed him with even a small sum from the lottery. It seemed some people were meant to have money, others were not.

Charles continued his interrogation, though he was running out of questions. "Did you notice anything else unusual when you discovered the body?"

"No, nothing."

"And you didn't see anyone?"

"No, no one."

"Why did you return to the villa?"

Sofie tossed her head back, looping her hair back into a ponytail with a violet scrunchie. "I needed to use the toilet. And I wanted to bring some water and snacks for the children."

Charles nodded with understanding and rose. "Thank you, Sofie."

The woman followed suit. "I'm sorry I couldn't be more helpful to you, Charles."

"You have been as helpful as can be expected. I am sorry for your loss."

Sofie lowered her head. "It is a difficult time."

"I'm afraid you will not yet be allowed to return to Villa Onyx."

"But what about our things?"

"Monsieur Denown has arranged other rooms for you. I'm sure you will be comfortable."

"That's fine." She hugged herself. "I wouldn't want to go back in there again, anyway, especially to sleep."

"Have you told the children?"

Sofie frowned. "Not yet. But I shall have to soon."

"Were they close to Monsieur Freon?"

"Not especially. Bobbi wasn't very fond of children. Probably because he liked all the attention for himself and didn't want to share the spotlight, even with kids. Still. . ." she began, "his death changes things."

Charles agreed. A man he had never known had died and from this his own life had taken an unexpected turn.

5

Charles woke with a start and sat up quickly, striking his head on the low beam overhead. The boat rocked back and forth. The pounding was like a gale dashing his small sailboat against the unforgiving rocks surrounding the island that was St. Barthelemy.

White-knuckled, he clutched the bedclothes. Was there a storm? A flood? Had his beloved boat fallen from its drydock and slipped into Gustavia's harbor?

He heard no rain. A banging came from the stern, almost rhythmic, like a drum roll working its way along the hull. There was a muffled shout. Charles pulled on a shirt and a pair of shorts in the dark.

"Hey-a! Hey-a! Are you there, gendarme?"

More banging and the sound of several cans being kicked over and about. Charles swore and stuck his head up over the deck. "You!"

Per Ravelson stood in the dark alleyway near the prow. Red-faced, he swayed like a drunken Father Christmas celebrating the completion of his annual duties. Time to get blind drunk with the elves.

Charles cursed. "Go away!" Then, glancing at his wristwatch and realizing it was nearly two in the morning, and his neighbors were not already so keen on him and his boat which they considered an eyesore, he lowered his voice. "Do you know what time it is? Go home." He waved the old man off. Charles himself made to go.

The old man groaned.

Charles turned. "Quiet."

The old man pushed on the boat and Charles was forced to grab hold of the rail for support. "Stop that!"

"You're a gendarme, ain't you?"

"Yes, so?"

The old man moaned and his face dropped. "I've lost my cat," he mumbled in his beard. "*Mon pauvre petit chat.*"

"You what?" Charles leaned closer. A move he came to regret as Thor opened his mouth and a whisky-scented, alcohol-filled pocket of recycled air blew over his face. He winced.

"I've lost my cat," said Thor glumly.

It was Charles' turn to groan. "Look, it's two o'clock in the morning. You're drunk and I'm tired. Go to bed," he said slowly, but firmly. He pointed toward the hill. Somewhere in that densely packed jungle of houses and apartments was Ravelson's home, he expected.

Thor tried gamely to climb the rope ladder leading up onto Charles' work-in-progress. He made the second rung, twisted, hit the hull with a dull thud and fell back to earth. Painfully, he looked up at Charles. "You're a gendarme. Help me find my cat."

Staying downwind, Charles replied. "I am a gendarme, not a finder of missing cats!"

Thor sat back, landing on a tarpaulin that had been protecting some paint and old tools from the elements. It had to hurt, but he didn't seem to notice. "Ellie, Ellie, Ellie. Elephant is like a son to me," he lamented. "I've never had a real son." He looked imploringly at the young gendarme, his hands spread over his knees.

Charles rubbed his ears. Elephant? Elephant! The old man wanted him to get up and start a search of Gustavia for an elephant? He sighed, slipped into his boat shoes and leapt overboard.

At least it shouldn't take long. After all, how hard could it be to find a lost elephant in Gustavia, in all of Saint Barthelemy for that matter?

Charles touched Thor's shoulder. "Come on," he said. What the heck, he'd humor the old man for a little while. They could walk around a bit. Thor could work off the worst of his drunk and then go home to sleep the rest of it off. Maybe then, Charles could manage to get some sleep himself.

Thor mumbled his thanks and Charles helped him to his feet. Thor wiped his damp nose with the back of his fingers. "I've always wanted a real son, you know." He sniffed.

"I know." Charles rolled his eyes, careful that the old man didn't see. "And this elephant is your pet?"

Thor nodded. "Best friend I ever had. Not counting my wife, of course."

"Of course." They headed up Rue Jeanne d'Arc. There was a lingering smell of garbage waiting to be collected. "Tell me," said Charles, sleepily, lulled by the gentle lapping of the water along the dock's edge, "was this elephant with you when we met?"

Thor stopped in his tracks. A look of astonishment rode his face. "Are you mad, Charles? I ask you, did you see a cat in my arms?"

Charles admitted he had not.

"Following at my heels?"

"No," Charles said, slowly. "Did you see an elephant?"

"What?"

Charles shook his head. "Nothing." The two men had reached Rue Chanzy, the site of the old fort, now a historical museum. There was a small public library upstairs. The streets were quiet, except for Thor's constant calls of "Elephant! Elephant! Time to come home, my son! Elephant! Elephant!"

A scraping sound came from the left. Thor froze. A gray and white cat appeared from the shadows and leapt into the old man's arms. Thor squeezed the cat and kissed its face over and over. The tears of a drunk fell from his eyes. "Elephant, my Elephant." Thor wagged a scolding finger. "Naughty boy. Do you know the trouble you've caused?"

The cat purred.

"Ah, hungry, are you? Well, you'll just have to wait until I get you home, won't you? How's about some milk and cheese crackers?" Without so much as a fare thee well, the old man and the gray and white cat disappeared up the road.

Success! A father and his son reunited. Charles couldn't help laughing. After all, it was only natural that a father do anything for his son—even if that son was a cat.

Charles whistled all the way back to his boat, not caring a hoot whether or not he woke half the town.

"You wanted to see me, Papa?"

"Yes, yes, come in my child." Chief Lebon rose and greeted his youngest daughter, completely oblivious to the fact that his officers were making themselves scarce.

Violette, dressed in a flowing frock the color of burnt sienna gifted her father with a hug and a kiss on each plump, rosy cheek. The dress exposed her shoulders and throat in a discreet yet becoming fashion.

"Sit," said Chief Lebon. Taking his seat behind his big

desk, he examined his daughter with utmost paternal warmth and affection. Violette really was quite lovely, if he did say so himself. She looked rather like that famous French model. What was her name? Laetitia something. And Violette looked quite presentable today. Quite. "So."

Violette smiled. She looked nervously at her hands, then spoke. "What is so special that you needed to see me, Papa?"

Chief Lebon cleared his throat. "Yes, Violette, I have some important papers here that I need taken to the Gendarmerie and I thought, since you weren't busy, perhaps you might run them over as a favor?"

"You want me to take them? Certainly, Papa. But what about one of your other officers? If these papers are important shouldn't one of your men be doing this?"

Chief Lebon shrugged. "You know what a small force I have here. It's been a busy day and all the men have been called away but for the minimum forces who must remain in the station at all times, particularly during office hours." Chief Lebon scooped up a manilla folder from the scattering on his desk and held it out. "Would you mind, *ma chérie?*"

"Well, I suppose—no, I don't mind."

Chief Lebon rose and pushed the folder into his daughter's hands. "Good. Excellent. You know where the Gendarmerie is, don't you? On the road between Public and Corrosol?"

Violette nodded.

"Wonderful." He laid a loving hand across his daughter's shoulders and walked her to the door. "And you must be sure and give it to Gendarme Trenet. That's T-R-E-N-E-T. It's very important." He walked her to her car. "Have you got it?"

"Yes, Papa." She set the folder down on the passenger's side. "I give the folder to Monsieur Trenet."

"Splendid."

Violette waved and drove off.

Chief Lebon rubbed his hands together. Charles was going to make a splendid son-in-law.

Adjutant Bruyer put down the telephone. He was not happy. His conversation with the procureur had not been a pleasant one. This murder was upsetting the whole order of things. It had even slowed the restorations he'd hoped to complete quickly on the building the gendarmes had long occupied. Monsieur Carreau, the procureur, had not been overly pleased with the results of their investigation so far. And he was less pleased with their choice of an investigator.

How had life gotten so fouled up? A posting on Saint Barthelemy was supposed to be a reward, a vacation in paradise. Somehow, that vacation needed to be gotten back on course.

It was going to be difficult. Still, Monsieur Carreau had agreed to let things continue on as they stood, with the understanding that it was Adjutant Bruyer's responsibility to see that the investigation progressed swiftly and accurately. And perhaps, most of all, with a minimum of publicity.

The adjutant agreed that he would do his best and he'd further expressed his faith in young Trenet's abilities. As far as the procureur agreeing to let them continue the investigation went, this came as no real surprise to the adjutant. After all, Monsieur Carreau spent six weeks every year at this time with his mistress, who kept an apartment in the Marais district of Paris.

The adjutant, having seen a photo of the youthful mistress, expected it would take a nuclear winter to alter the procureur's plans during this period.

Then again, if things got fouled up and the procureur felt compelled to return. . .

The adjutant shivered at the thought. He and Chief Lebon must not let that happen.

With long steps, Adjutant Bruyer strode from his semi-private office and made his way to Trenet who sat at a newly fashioned, makeshift desk of his own, two trestles and an old, three-ply wood door salvaged from the garage. Not having a lot of extra space, the simple desk had been stuffed unceremoniously into a dark corner on the bottom floor.

"Trenet!"

"*Oui*, monsieur?"

"How is the Bobbi Freon investigation coming along, then?"

"Well," stalled Trenet, "I've only gotten started, monsieur."

The adjutant folded his arms across his ample chest. "Have you gotten word on the cause of death?"

"I have not communicated with the physician, yet," confessed Charles.

"How about the girl? Have you interviewed the girl-friend?"

"You mean the assistant? I spoke with her yesterday. I have my report."

"Yes, yes." The adjutant waved him off. "I've seen that. I'm speaking of Mademoiselle Patterson."

"Who?" Charles asked weakly.

"Linda Patterson, Monsieur Freon's paramour."

Charles stammered. "I-I'm afraid I am not familiar with her, monsieur."

"Well," said the adjutant turning about on his heels, "I suggest you *do* familiarize yourself with her, Trenet. And you," Adjutant Bruyer called to a lingering gendarme who seemed to be reveling in the youngest gendarme's discomfiture, "see that Trenet gets a proper desk. We've an investigation to carry on!" He clapped his hands together loudly and the gendarme scurried off.

Charles was about to pick up the telephone and ring the doctor when a colleague called for him to come to the front desk. "What is it? I'm quite busy."

"There's a young lady to see you—personally, she says," came Gendarme Simon Brin's reply. Hoots and whistles, from several other colleagues within hearing distance, followed.

Charles reddened and rose. He approached the counter along the front of the office. A young woman stood on the other side. "Can I help you?" he said, somewhat more harshly than he'd intended, an unfortunate response to his mates' tauntings and the adjutant's still fresh chewing out. It was all quite unfair, Charles thought. Everyone getting on his case. He hadn't asked for this investigation, had he?

No, he most definitely had not.

"Charles Trenet?"

"Yes, that's correct."

"Oh, I wanted to make sure. I have something from Chief Lebon of the Municipal Police. I was told to deliver this to you personally, you see." She held out a slender manilla folder.

Out of sight, Simon Brin and a couple of the others were making juvenile kissing noises which Charles hoped the young woman didn't recognize as such. "Yes," said Charles heavily, anxious to get away, "well, you have then, haven't you?"

"Yes," said the young lady, huffily. "I suppose I have." With that, she slapped the folder on the counter and made her exit, muttering under her breath, "What a jerk."

"What?" called Charles.

She turned. "I said, 'you're welcome.'" The door slammed

on her way out, rattling the already weak window frame.

Charles was left with his mouth hanging open. But the laughs were coming from elsewhere. He stuck his head through the hall door. "Oh, shut up, will you!" Two of his colleagues fell down laughing, a gross and childish exaggeration in Charles' opinion, and he stepped over them on his way back to his improvised desk.

He threw the folder down and opened it. Inside, there was a typewritten report of Denown's initial call to the police, ending with Chief Lebon's first interview with the resort manager on his arrival at Idyllique Hotel and Villas. Charles read through it quickly. All in all, it was pretty much useless to him. Old news at best. He'd read the first several pages and decided to skip the rest. Why on earth had the chief of police had this sent to him by messenger?

Charles shook his head and tossed the folder aside. A trifolded, two-color brochure flew out the end. Charles picked it up. It was some sort of police recruitment brochure. How on earth did that get in here? he wondered. This time he tossed the whole useless lot of it in the trash bin.

Jorge Pena lay on the chaise lounge. His fat belly soaked up the sun like a thick slice of French bread soaked up melted butter.

His wife, Elina, topless and barefoot, came from the bar, carrying two martinis, casting a shadow over his face as she halted over him.

He opened his eyes, grimaced at the painful light as his wife stepped to one side, and extended his hand over his thick brow. The villa's broad terrace looked out on the endless sea and the clouds had deserted them this day. A drop of cool water fell from one of the glasses to his thick thigh. He took the glass. "*Gracias.*"

Elina nodded and sat on the edge of the lounger, forcing her husband to make room. She bent her elbow and sipped slowly.

"So, who was that on the phone? Or is it or *he* a secret?" His ire and suspicion were softened by the proximity of her bare breasts, full and ripe as a couple of casabas, a sight which never failed to arouse him.

Elina's lip turned down. She shook her head. "Please, my darling, your jealousy is unbecoming of you."

Jorge waited.

"It was Roxanne."

"Who?"

"Roxanne, the wife of the broker from Milan. You remember?"

He was shaking his head as if to jostle his gears.

"We met them at the soiree the Bells were having at the Carl Gustav last week."

Jorge was shaking his head the other direction now. Yes, that wedding party at the hotel in Gustavia for some money people from the States that Bell was trying to convince to invest in BFE. A bunch of prissy Ivy League types who thought they were way too refined for the rest of the world, himself included. "What did that bitch want?"

Elina had half-downed her martini. "She said that Bobbi was dead." She looked directly into her husband's eyes, not wanting to miss his reaction. She was not to be disappointed.

He bolted upright, spilling his drink down his bare chest. It soaked into his bathing trunks. "What? Freon, dead?"

His wife shrugged. "That's the rumor going around, so she says."

Jorge rose, unintentionally dumping his wife off the end of the lounger. "That can't be true. The bastard can't be dead." He threw his glass over the balcony mindless of where it fell. He turned. "How's it supposed to have happened?"

Elina set her empty glass on the tiled floor and joined her husband at the balcony. Her breasts rubbed against his arm. "She doesn't know."

He gripped her arms and pressed her closer. "You didn't—"

"No," she replied. "Did you?"

6

"Listen," said Denown, running a tired hand through his thinning hair, "I have had word that the gendarme is coming to interview Monsieur Freon's girlfriend."

Lily looked up from her work. "Yes? You mean, Mademoiselle Patterson?"

"Yes, that's the one," replied the harried manager. Linda Patterson had been Bobbi Freon's latest St. Barts girlfriend. Freon had been coming to the island for years and each time he'd brought a different girl. This winter it was Linda Patterson, a fashion editor from the States who, by the look of her, could have had a lucrative career in modeling herself.

"What does this have to do with me?" asked Lily warily. She was getting used to the manager's insidious way of making more work for her by conveniently taking the burden off his own shoulders.

"I want you to-to facilitate matters," Denown explained. "This is the height of the tourist season." He leaned in close and Lily could smell the man's lime and eucalyptus-scented aftershave. "We do not want to upset the guests now, do we? We must maintain discretion."

"I still don't see what you want of me, monsieur."

"I want you to help this Gendarme, oh, what was his name—Treed-Trent?" He clicked his fingers. "No, Trenet. Gendarme Trenet."

"Trenet," repeated Lily, growing bored and wishing the manager would pester some other employee so she might finish her housekeeping report before lunch.

"Yes, be sure that he is discreet in his investigations. I do not want him pestering our clients." Their well-paying clients.

"But how am I to—"

"Shush. I am not finished. According to Adjutant Bruyer, Trenet is to go through our guest records as well, looking for suspects, I expect." He laid an oily hand on Lily's bare shoulder. "Help him along, quickly! The sooner he is done with his work and the police are done with theirs, the quicker things can get back to normal."

Lily shrugged. Except for Monsieur Freon's sudden death, things seemed pretty normal to her. "I will do what I can, monsieur."

Philip Denown suddenly lifted his hand and straightened his back. He gestured toward the lobby doors with his eyes.

Lily followed his gaze. A pleasant young man with short brown hair stood, as if lost, in the entry. He was wearing navy blue short pants and a light blue, button down shirt with blue insignia on the shoulders. The two top buttons of his shirt were unfastened, exposing a matching pale blue undershirt. His name tag, over his right shirt pocket, was too far away to read.

"Monsieur Trenet." The hotel manager strode forward with his hand extended. "How good to see you again." He turned to the desk. "This is Lily. She will help you in any way she can."

Lily ran a hand through her hair, glanced quickly at her

reflection in the bezel edged mirror on the wall opposite, leaned over the desk and extended her right hand. "Lily Vineuil. A pleasure to meet you."

"And you, mademoiselle," replied Charles. He cleared his throat. "I am here to interview Mademoiselle Linda Patterson."

"Yes," said Denown, cheerfully. "I will check her suite and see if she is in." He turned to Lily. "Check that, will you, *chérie*?"

Lily rolled her eyes and picked up the telephone.

Denown asked Charles if there was any progress in the investigation and Charles reported there was not. "I do need to check your guest register."

"Yes, of course. So your adjutant informed me. That is no problem. Lily here will assist you. I must go. There are a great number of duties running a resort, you understand."

"Yes," replied Charles.

Lily set down the telephone. "Miss Patterson does not answer. I can write down her suite number for you if you'd like to check her room anyway."

"No," said Charles. "I'll try later. Though I am curious. Mademoiselle Patterson did not stay at Villa Onyx?"

"No," replied Denown. "She had her own suite. Though Monsieur Freon footed the bill."

"I see. Well, if I could get a look at your guest records in the meantime?"

"Yes." Denown snapped his fingers. "I'm off." He shook Charles' hand. "Lily," he commanded, "please take care of the young officer." With that, the manager hurried out the front as if the Black Plague were on his tail.

"Interesting," remarked Charles.

"Yes," replied Lily. "He's a bit off, but the pay is good so I put up with it."

"I was speaking of Linda Patterson. She is supposed to be Monsieur Freon's girlfriend and yet they had separate quarters. I wonder why."

Lily blushed, then shrugged. "Who knows why the rich do anything?"

Charles laughed.

Lily smiled. He was cute. She glanced at the clock on the wall. It was nearly her lunch time and Philip was gone. . .She hadn't met anyone on the island yet with whom she had really hit it off. Oh, she'd had a couple of dates, but they'd always ended the way they had begun—drearily. Perhaps she should ask this Charles to lunch? He wasn't wearing a wedding band. "Say, Monsieur Trenet—"

He interrupted her. "Call me Charles, please."

She smiled and ran a hand nervously around her ear. "Charles. I was about to have lunch and, well, if you'd care to join me, I—"

A long shadow crossed their path and Charles turned. It was Sofie Summers. She looked striking in a minimalist white bikini. She was alone and heading in the direction of the pool.

"Excuse me," said Charles, hastily.

With that, he turned heel and hurried off. Lily stamped her foot. Men! Why did they behave like such boys?

Charles ran after Sofie. She'd stopped at the edge of the swimming pool where she exchanged a few words with a sturdy looking young fellow with a deep tan who wore nothing more than a navy blue Speedo. The young man nodded a couple of times, glanced at his gold watch and took off in the direction of the villas.

Sofie went to the bar which was off to the side of the pool area and open to the ocean air. She took a free barstool and ordered a drink.

Charles watched as she lit a cigarette and held it to her lips. She turned in his direction and he colored, feeling like a voyeur. He waved and approached.

"Mademoiselle Somers, how nice to see you again." He tipped his head.

"And you, Charles." She patted the stool beside her. "Join me."

Charles sat and ordered a soft drink.

Mademoiselle Somers was drinking something red and frothy with a slice of lime and floating a small, yellow, paper umbrella. "So, were you looking for me?"

"As a matter of fact," stuttered Charles, searching for an explanation, "I did have some small questions that perhaps you may be able to help me with." In truth, he had other duties, but had felt compelled to follow her the minute she'd passed his vision, like the proverbial moth drawn to the flame.

Sofie smiled. "I'll try. What are these small questions?"

"Well, did you know that Monsieur Freon had a girlfriend also staying here at the Idyllique?"

"Of course," replied Sofie. "Linda Patterson. She's an editor with Fashion Life." She took a small sip of her drink and her full lips glistened.

Charles felt himself growing warm and he reached for his cola.

"Is it not odd that they did not share the villa, then?" After all, the place was capacious enough for a harem!

Bobbi's now ex-assistant shrugged. "Not so very odd. Bobbi was like that. He liked to bed them, but not sleep with them."

Charles looked incredulous.

Sofie laughed. "Bobbi was quite unique, inspector."

"I am not an inspector," corrected Charles, "merely a

gendarme."

Sofie puffed on her cigarette and then put it out in a small glass ashtray. She gripped his forearm and leaned close, creating a vision of cleavage that set Charles' head spinning. "Have you made any progress?" she inquired in a low voice. The bar and restaurant were crowded. "Do you know who killed Bobbi?"

"No, I'm sorry," said Charles. "Perhaps this Mademoiselle Patterson?"

Sofie nodded, giving this some thought. "Yes, yes, it could be she. Bobbi treated women abominably, Charles."

Charles already had no doubt about that. Make love to a woman and then send her off to another room to sleep? What sort of a beast did such a thing?

"They had been arguing a great deal since they've been on the island."

"Do you know what about?"

"No." Sofie shook her head. "But it was at times quite heated. Even Anthony and Cleo complained to me of the shouting. Especially when it carried over into the evenings."

Sofie finished her drink and said, her eyes drifting towards the sea, "Bobbi Freon had a way, Charles, of making everyone look good on the outside, but," she added, "he never failed to bring out the worst in people—" She turned her gaze on the young gendarme. "—From the inside," she finished, laying her fingers over her heart.

She looked at his glass. "You haven't finished your drink."

Charles picked up his soda. "Is there anyone else you can think of with motive?"

Sofie appeared to give this some thought. "The usual," she said finally. "Bankers, manufacturers, suppliers, rivals. But if you ask me, love is a stronger motive for murder than money. Passion, Charles, passion is a very strong motivation."

"And does this Linda Patterson perhaps possess enough passion to have murdered her lover?"

Sofie smiled thinly. "I don't know. Why don't you find out?" She swivelled on her stool, turning her eyes on a topless redhead stretched out like a lizard in the sun at the opposite end of the pool, her exquisite body clinging docilely to a tiny wooden ledge jutting out over the beach a meter below.

"That's her? Mademoiselle Patterson?"

"*Oui*. Tell me," said Sofie as she waved to the bartender for another drink, "does she look deadly to you?"

Quite, thought Charles. No matter what the definition, Mademoiselle Patterson did, indeed, look quite deadly.

Sulking, Lily Vineuil, pushed her sandwich aside, as she watched the gendarme first fawning all over that assistant of Monsieur Freon's, a woman ten years his senior with two children no less, and then heading towards that nearly naked American hussy whom Monsieur Freon had been screwing. "Haumph!" She muttered to no one. "Some investigator!"

Lily wondered what she'd ever seen in Charles. She dumped the rest of her food in the trash and headed back to her desk, determined to forget him.

"*Bonjour*, mademoiselle." Charles tipped his head, averted his eyes.

Two green eyes peeked up over a pair of dark sunglasses. Her red hair fell like strawberry licorice candy in cascades that ended somewhere beneath her back. Charles wondered if Monsieur Freon had ever known or consorted with any ordinary looking persons.

"Not now." She closed her eyes, or at least they retreated

behind the screen of her sunglasses. She stretched her arms over her head and locked her hands together.

He said in English. "I beg your pardon?" Charles couldn't help but watch as her breasts moved upwards and closer together in their own unique fashion, as if her maroon nipples were eyes focusing in on him. "You are Mademoiselle Linda Patterson?"

The woman let out a small sigh and sat up. "What is it you want? Can I help you in someway?" Her voice was hard, the very opposite of her body.

The gendarme looked past towards the sea. "I am Charles Trenet of the Gendarmerie Nationale."

"And?" She eyed the young man who by appearance was staring off into space. "You can look at me, you know. Or have I something you haven't seen before?"

Charles colored for what seemed like the umpteenth time that day. "No, mademoiselle." He looked directly at her face. "Though perhaps never in so lovely a—" he hesitated, searching for the right word in English, "form."

Mademoiselle Patterson laughed lightly, obviously appreciating his compliment, and her guard seemed to come down. "Sit," she commanded, patting a space along the wooden ledge beside her.

Charles complied.

"Is this about Bobbi Freon?"

"*Oui*, mademoiselle. I am afraid I must speak to you about this. I'm sure this is a difficult time for you."

"Difficult?"

"You are in mourning, no?" The gentleman and the optimist in Charles kept him from questioning the woman's form of mourning—topless lounging by the pool the day after her boyfriend had met his death.

"Yes, I suppose. If you say so." Mademoiselle Patterson

ran a hand through a tiny puddle of perspiration that had settled between her breasts.

Charles looked pointedly at his notebook. "When did you last see Monsieur Freon, mademoiselle?"

The American woman leaned forward, clutching her calves. "The night before. The night before he died, that is."

Charles nodded and wrote. "How did he seem?"

"We had an early dinner. Some drinks. Some sex." She spoke bluntly. "Pretty normal to me."

"He was not upset in any way or with anyone?"

"No more than usual."

"What is usual, mademoiselle?"

"Oh," she leaned back once more and rubbed her shoulders, "Bobbi never did know how to relax. Even here," she spread her hands, "amidst all this. I mean, he lightened up a bit but business was never far from his mind."

"I see." Charles wondered how such a man, a rich one with a beautiful girlfriend, could spend his vacation in a paradise like Saint Barthelemy concerning himself with any business more than the business of *amour*.

"I must ask you, mademoiselle—"

"Yes?"

"You did not sleep with Monsieur Freon?"

"By sleep do you mean shut our eyes and catch eight hours?"

Charles nodded.

"No. Bobbi liked to sleep alone."

"And so you did not spend the entire night with Monsieur Freon?"

"No. I went back to my room after we—" She hesitated, then said, "—were finished."

"Is there anything at all that you might tell me that would give some indication of who might have wanted the monsieur dead?"

"I'm afraid not. I'll be pretty useless to you in that regard. I slept till about eleven. Called the office in New York. I lounged around my room a while longer than I really wanted, because I thought Bobbi might call to arrange lunch. I don't mind telling you, I got a bit angry that he didn't call. Then I heard he'd been murdered and I felt guilty."

"That is natural, mademoiselle."

"I suppose it is." She rubbed a fresh layer of lotion along her arms. "Wait a minute." She set down the plastic bottle. "I did phone the villa around noon also. Just to see about that—lunch, that is."

"Did you speak to him then?"

"There was no answer. I mean, it sounded like someone picked up the phone, but then the line went dead." She laughed, then turned melancholy. "I had thought perhaps Bobbi had picked up the receiver then set it down again. Wanting to sleep, you know?"

Charles frowned. A man was brutally murdered and there were no answers at all, it appeared. Harikari? And the victim conveniently disposes of the weapon of his own destruction? If only. . .

Charles tapped the notebook with his pen.

"Can you tell me when the body will be released, Monsieur Trenet?"

"I do not know, mademoiselle."

"I suppose the-the funeral arrangements will be up to me."

"You, mademoiselle?"

"Well, we were engaged to be married."

"Then I am doubly sorry for your loss," Charles said.

"And Bobbi's parents are both gone and he had no brothers or sisters."

"I see."

She patted her stomach. "I've given it some thought and I've decided to keep the child, as well. I think Bobbi would want that, too."

Charles looked startled. "Child?"

"Yes," replied Mademoiselle Patterson, "I am carrying Bobbi's child, you know."

"I did not, mademoiselle. I did not." So, Monsieur Freon is engaged to be married to a woman and gives her a child and sends her to another room to sleep! What sort of monster was this Bobbi Freon?

And what sort of a monster had slain him?

7

Charles reentered the cool, windowless lobby. The young clerk he'd met earlier sat behind her desk. Charles approached. She was typing away furiously at her keyboard and did not so much as glance up. He cleared his throat. The young woman continued her typing.

"*Pardonnez-moi*," Charles said. He picked up a photo frame on the desk and turned it around to examine it. It was a black and white photograph of the woman in question, perhaps several years younger, with two handsome persons who could only be her parents, against the backdrop of a beach somewhere.

The young woman snatched it from his hands and replaced it on the desk. "Finished with your investigations, are you?"

"Sorry," mumbled the gendarme. "I have come to inspect your registrations, Mademoiselle. . .Mademoiselle. . ."

"—Vineuil." Lily rose from her desk, grabbed the handle of a two-drawer oak filing cabinet and yanked. "The records are here, monsieur. Help yourself."

Charles looked over her shoulder. The file was near

bursting. "Those are all current registrations? You understand I need to see only those pertaining to guests whose stays overlap with Monsieur Freon's."

"Then you'll have to sort through them, won't you?" Lily left the drawer hanging open and returned to her chair.

Charles stepped behind the counter and ran a finger over the tops of the files. His stomach complained loudly. "I never had lunch," he explained.

"Poor you," replied Lily, keeping her back turned to the young officer.

"Perhaps I shall get some lunch first. The food here, it is good?" What he wanted to ask was if it was very expensive but dignity prevented him. A gendarme hardly had the budget of a jetsetter.

"Quite," answered Lily.

Charles rose, pushed the drawer shut and said, "Then I'll just have a bite and look through your records on my return."

"Suit yourself." He turned out the door and she grinned wickedly.

Several minutes later he was back.

"Back so soon?"

"It seems the restaurant has finished serving lunch and won't reopen until dinner."

"Oh," replied Lily, unconvincingly, "is it that late already?"

Charles, looking somewhat forlorn, returned to the filing cabinet and Lily couldn't help but take pity on him. He was cute, after all. Besides, he couldn't help it if he was a man and behaved like a beast, could he?

"I'll tell you what. I'll go to the cook and have a sandwich done up for you."

"You will? That would be wonderful, mademoiselle."

"Lily."

"*Oui*, Lily." He tapped his skull. "I remember. I would be most grateful."

He smiled at her and she felt her knees go weak. *Ohmygod*, she thought, *what's come over me?* She nervously ran a finger through her hair and told Charles she'd be back soon with something to carry him over until supper. "I'm reasonably caught up in my own work today, as it happens, so I could even help you sort through those files, if you like?"

"You are an angel, Lily."

Jorge Pena slammed the ultramodern phone against the nineteenth century desk then returned it to his ear. "You're my goddam lawyer. You're supposed to help me."

"I am helping you, Jorge. We are all doing the best we can."

"Well, that's not friggin' good enough. Freon's dead and I want control of BF Enterprises."

"It isn't that simple, Jorge. There are other parties involved. You know that."

"Screw the other parties. The business should be mine. Take it."

The lawyer, in his cozy, climate controlled Boston office, rolled his eyes and stifled a sigh. "It isn't that easy, Jorge. You can't just go in guns blazing and take over a legitimate business. This has to be done tactfully, legally—"

"I know, I know," replied the Ecuadoran impatiently. "Dot all the i's, cross all the t's. Well, understand this, Peter, I want a controlling seat on the board. I've pumped millions into this thing and I don't want it all to go down in flames. Besides," he said coldly, "Bobbi should have been forced out months ago, the little scumbag."

The lawyer let this remark pass over his head. Hear no evil, see no evil. And Jorge Pena was evil. "Listen, Jorge, there are all sorts of irregularities going on with Bobbi's business, you know that. I've got people researching Bobbi's personal finances as well as the corporation's books."

"Screw the books. I've offered the others plenty for their shares. Make them sell."

The lawyer replied with as much tact as he could. "The others, as you call them, include a state university retirement fund, several respected bankers and one very nasty Mitch Martinelli who makes Al Capone look like a Keebler elf."

Jorge lost all patience. "Screw Mitch Martinelli! I'll shoot his mother and his mother's mother. Just get them to sell!" Jorge slammed the phone down on the desk once again. This time for keeps.

"Lawyers!" he said, turning to his wife who had come into the sitting room, with a fashion magazine from Paris rolled up under her arm.

She raised a polite eyebrow.

"And what the hell is a goddam Keebler elf?!"

Elina rose and massaged her husband's neck. "They make cookies."

Jorge's face expressed his confusion. "Cookies? What the hell have cookies got to do with anything?"

"I don't know, my darling. You asked me."

Jorge balled his hands into tight, plump fists. "Friggin' lawyers, even when they talk English they make no sense."

He pulled his wife close and squeezed her arms. "Where have you been?"

"I went to the beach."

"I was on the terrace. I didn't see you," he said suspiciously.

"Maybe you just didn't notice."

His lips turned up. "I'd have noticed."

She shrugged indifferently. "I stopped at the hotel bar."

"Trolling for some new toy? Lover boy's barely stopped breathing."

"Shut up," Elina said, pulling herself away and crossing the room.

"What's the matter? Don't tell me you had feelings for that sonofabitch?"

She swirled. "What about you? Have you no feelings at all? A friend is dead. Aren't you sorry in the least?"

Her husband was smirking. "As a matter of fact, no, I'm not. And Bobbi Freon was no friend of mine."

Elina poured herself a glass of brandy.

"He was a piece of meat to me." Jorge chuckled. "Just like he was for you, except that for me he made money. For you, he merely provided a distraction."

"It was your idea I sleep with him in the first place."

He shrugged. "It served its purpose. My company got the contract to manufacture all his stinking ready-to-wear stuff. Made us even richer. Nothing wrong with that."

Her eyes had hardened.

"Hey, I give you credit," he said with a smirk, "you're quite an effective whore, my wife." He tipped his head in her direction.

"Sometimes, Jorge" said Elina, "you are such a barbarian."

She left the room. Unchafed, Jorge poured himself a brandy. A barbarian? Elina had said it as if it were an insult. To himself, it was anything but.

As for Bobbi Freon, the designer might be dead, but he, Jorge Pena, was not through with him yet.

Charles covered his mouth with his hand, muffling a large yawn. The girl, Lily, had brought him a Camembert sandwich, with half a pineapple and a beer. He'd finished each morsel.

The food, combined with the effects of the tedious paperwork, was rapidly putting him to sleep. He wondered if it would be presumptuous to ask the girl for a coffee. He had hoped to be at his boat the rest of the afternoon. He wanted to get started on mending the sails.

"What exactly are you looking for, Charles?"

Charles sat on the tile, cool against his bare legs. "I don't know precisely." He didn't know at all! "Perhaps Monsieur Freon will have been murdered by a guest who may prove to have stayed here."

Lily crossed her legs and turned towards the right, presenting her best side and plenty of thigh. Was it too much? "Saint Barthelemy is a very small place. The killer could have been staying anywhere. And, of course, they could be long gone by now."

Charles tossed a pile of hotel registrations aside.

"Why don't I give you a printout of all the persons who've checked into the Idyllique within the past seven days. Then, if any of these names come up in your investigations, you might have something that can help you."

"Yes, I suppose." Charles seemed unsure, but frankly he had no other plans. And the girl's idea was as good as any. "Yes, that is what I shall do." That should satisfy the adjutant and Captain Lebon. "*Merci*, Lily."

"It is nothing. You know, Charles," said Lily, punching at a few keys and sending some data to the laser printer, "sometimes, the best thing is to clear your mind. How about a walk along the beach? It works for me."

Charles rose and rubbed his sore knees. He took the sheets of paper that Lily presented him. "That's a good idea," he said wearily.

She beamed.

He rolled up the papers and tucked them inside his shirt.

"I'll do just that. *Au revoir*, Lily."

Lily's jaw dropped.

Charles stopped outside the door. "Oh, Lily."

Lily's heart skipped a beat. "Yes?"

"Thank you, again, for all your help." He patted his full stomach. "And the lunch."

Lily clenched her teeth. "Don't mention it, Charles." She spun around, effectively turning her back on the gendarme before he could turn his back on her.

"What are you doing, man?"

Charles turned. It was the same police officer who'd first taken him to the Idyllique on the day of Bobbi's murder. He stood, arms folded, on the walkway between Villa Onyx and the beach. Why did this fellow always appear at the worst of times? "Taking a walk along the beach."

"Taking a walk along the beach?" The officer shook his head in wonder. "When you're supposed to be investigating a murder?" The officer removed his hat and scratched his head.

Charles stammered, "It's supposed to help me think. It was—"

"Never mind," exclaimed the officer. "Just come along will you. You're to go see Martin."

"Who?"

"Martin Duclos."

"Who is he?"

The officer walked quickly and Charles struggled to keep up the pace. "He's a doctor."

"Ah." Charles understood. This was the same Martin who'd been present at the crime scene. "What am I to see him about?"

"Maybe to have your head examined." The officer got

into his car. "You need a lift?"

"I have my motorbike." Charles nodded in the direction of an ancient looking scooter.

"Right. Used to belong to Napoleon, did it?"

Charles opened his mouth to speak but was cut off by the other.

"Opposite side of the harbor. Up the hill. Next to the hospital. Can't miss it." His hand provided the choreography as he spoke. Finished, he drove off in a cloud of dust that left Charles wanting a drink.

Charles found the doctor's office, which did double duty as the man's home, without difficulty. Parking his motor scooter at the doorstep, he entered the fluorescent lit waiting room where he walked up to a small window with an opaque glass partition. He rapped on the screen with a knuckle. The flimsy glass shook in its frame.

A small woman, in a white uniform, slid the window open. The features of her face were squished together like the top view of a quince. "Yes?"

"I am Gendarme Trenet. Here to see Doctor Duclos." He squeezed his nose. The place had that medicinal smell that Charles loathed.

Her pencil thin fingers ran up and down her book. She looked up at Charles. "You don't have an appointment, monsieur."

"I am here to see him about an investigation." Charles didn't know if he should say more than that. The adjutant had been clear that he should maintain every effort to keep the investigation subdued. It wouldn't do to upset the tourists nor even the locals.

"Have a seat, please."

Charles complied, occupying a stiff, cushionless wooden

chair in the corner. A young couple held hands on a small wicker sofa. Charles nodded in their direction. The young man smiled weakly.

A white door opened. The receptionist appeared and Charles rose. She called out for Monsieur and Madame Vandanen and Charles fell back in his chair.

Twenty minutes came and went, then half an hour. The young couple left. Now they both smiled and appeared more relaxed. Charles looked questioningly at the receptionist. She wagged a finger and told him it would be a few moments more.

Five minutes later, Doctor Duclos appeared at the door and motioned for Charles to follow. Charles was led down a hall, through a domestic kitchen—which itself smelled like a medicine chest—and finally to what was the doctor's office. Doctor Duclos retreated behind his desk, put on his reading glasses and opened a folder lying atop his blotter. "You are interested, perhaps, in hearing more about Monsieur Freon's injuries?"

Charles said he was. He opened his notebook.

The doctor shut the file and folded his arms across his stomach as he leaned back in his overstuffed green leather office chair. "The monsieur was stabbed multiple times in the abdominal region."

"Multiple?"

"Yes."

"Can you be more precise, doctor?"

Doctor Duclos looked at him with displeasure. "Certainly, Monsieur Freon was stabbed with a sharp object, with a blade perhaps ten to twelve centimeters long," he held out his fingers, "and several millimeters, even a centimeter, wide."

"A knife?" asked Charles.

"Yes."

"And not a large one."

Duclos shrugged. "No. The type a man might keep in a pocket or on his belt."

"Yes," agreed Charles. "Is there anything else you have learned from examining the body?"

"Your Monsieur Freon had a fondness for liposuction."

"What's that?"

"There are signs that he'd frequently had the fat sucked out of his gut."

"I am unfamiliar with this."

"After injecting a mild anesthetic with adrenaline, the physician inserts small cannulae, tubes, into the fatty regions, such as love handles—as in the case of Bobbi Freon—or perhaps the buttocks—wherever clients like—and suck the fat cells from the area." He held up his finger and twisted it like a drill bit. "The tubes pass through the body creating Swiss cheese-like holes. The smaller the holes, the better. Less chance of noticeable effects this way."

Charles squirmed. He hated the idea of any type of surgery. "Nothing more? That you can tell me about the victim, I mean." He'd had enough about cosmetic surgery. And the very idea of getting one's fat sucked out, that was disgusting!

"Only that Monsieur Freon ate well and exercised little."

That was stating the obvious. "I meant anything that might help us find the murderer."

"I am a doctor, not a detective." He drummed his fingers atop the file. "Still, the angle of the wounds would suggest that in each instance the punctures came in nearly level or from somewhat below." He jabbed the air. "Going slightly upwards, you understand?"

Charles nodded. "So, if Monsieur Freon had been standing—"

"—His assailant would have likely been shorter in stature. Unless the attacker was stabbing upward." Doctor Duclos rose and demonstrated. "It seems rather awkward this way."

And weaker, thought Charles. "How tall a man was Bobbi Freon?"

"Nearly two meters. I'd have to check the report. Of course, concerning the rest, I state only suppositions, not facts." The phone on Duclos' desk chirped. He answered it, spoke brusquely and hung up. He shot the gendarme a look that said 'What, are you still here?'

Charles recalled Sofie Somers' insinuations regarding Mademoiselle Patterson, Bobbi Freon's girlfriend. Even though she was bearing the man's child, she had not appeared to be in mourning. Not in the least. Unless one counted a black string bikini bottom as mourning attire. Even in St. Barts, Charles didn't suppose that was considered appropriate. Perhaps American women were different. "Could a woman have done this?"

The doctor leaned over the desk. "A woman is capable of anything."

"No, I mean would she have had the strength?"

"Even a child can gut a fish. A woman can certainly gut a man. Just ask my wife."

Charles took this for a yes and departed.

8

Chief Lebon was enjoying a leisurely breakfast at home. In spite of the American's murder, things were well under control. And that gendarme, Charles Trenet, seemed a fine young fellow. He dipped his croissant in his café au lait. "You know, *ma chérie*, I was thinking perhaps we should have a small party for Violette."

"A party?" Madame Lebon, turned away from the gas stove and wiped her hands on her gingham apron. "What's this about?"

"It's about welcoming our daughter home," declared the chief. "We can invite everyone you like. Friends, family—"

"Some nice young men?" said Elisabeth slyly. She'd been married to Didier long enough to know his mind and his ways. And they'd gone through the same song and dance with their eldest daughter, Rose.

The chief stood and wrapped his arms around his wife. He playfully kissed her neck. She giggled. "Well, there is a certain young officer I'd like her to get to know."

Elisabeth pushed her husband away. "Officer? Another of your men? You've already married Rose off to your assistant, Pisar. The rest of your men are wary of you. Which one is it?"

Chief Lebon stuffed the remaining corner of croissant in his mouth and chewed. He poured the rest of his coffee down the sink. Munching still, he spoke. "It is none of them, *ma chérie*. He is a gendarme. Newly arrived from France."

"A gendarme? What do you know of him? Of his family, Didier?"

"He is a very capable young man, Elisabeth. Even now he is helping us with the murder investigation of Monsieur Freon."

"Well—"

Lips covered in fine pastry crumbs, he kissed his wife. "*Bon.* You can handle all the arrangements. I'll see that the young man gets an invitation."

Madame Lebon rolled her eyes as her husband headed towards his vehicle. "I don't know how you talk me into these things!" she called. "Violette may not even find him attractive!"

Didier stopped outside his car, door open. "Nonsense. They've already seen one another. You've nothing to worry about."

Elisabeth closed the door to the kitchen and returned to her cooking. While her hand stirred the pot of chicken stew with curry sauce she was preparing for dinner, her mind occupied itself with thoughts of Violette's upcoming party. Elisabeth's daughter, Rose, was seven years Violette's senior, married to a professional, and already had given her five grandchildren.

With good fortune on their side, Violette would do the same. Of course, Elisabeth must inquire about this Trenet's family. Her daughter could not marry just anyone. Even if he was a gendarme.

"How much?"

"How much?" He paced the edge of the cliff nimbly. Heights had never frightened him.

"You want money, don't you?"

He paused, taking a look at the rocks below. Sometimes he wished he could do one of those majestic dives, the kind those fellows in Acapulco were famous for. "It isn't about money."

She laughed.

He turned, angry and hurt. "It isn't. It's about more than money. I want to be somebody. Bobbi promised me that. He promised he would make me somebody."

Sofie shook her head sadly. Why did so many people think you had to have notoriety to be a somebody? "*Bien.* Fine. Bobbi promised you a modeling contract. I can do the same. You only have to keep quiet about what you've seen."

His well-fashioned brows came together. "Can you do that? Help my career?"

"Of course." The ocean breeze threw her hair against her face and she thrust it back. "I will, for all practical purposes, have control of Bobbi Freon Enterprises. Do we have an agreement, monsieur?" She approached the cliff edge and held out her hand.

The young man beamed. "Deal."

Adjutant Bruyer pulled his young gendarme into his office. "How's it going, Trenet? Have a seat."

The outer windows were open yet that didn't keep Charles from becoming intoxicated from the paint fumes. The adjutant had just given his office a second coat of saffron colored paint an hour before.

Charles sat before he could fall in a dizzy heap. "Not badly, Adjutant. I have found a name, a couple of names actually, which appear on the Idyllique's guest register and also appear on Monsieur Bobbi Freon's list of business associates.

"Really? That is interesting." The adjutant kicked his feet up atop his desk. "Have you spoken to these persons? Have you taken their statements?"

"*Non*, monsieur. They are a Jorge Pena and Elisabeth Pena. They both occupied rooms at the Idlyllique on the night before Bobbi Freon was killed. They are man and wife and yet they occupied separate rooms. Madame Pena checked out quite early on the morning of the monsieur's murder and Monsieur Pena himself checked out at nine-forty a.m."

"They checked out at separate times? How odd."

"Indeed. They had separate rooms."

Adjutant Bruyer sat up straight. "That is quite odd, Charles. Have they left Saint Barthelemy?"

Charles shrugged. "I am awaiting word from Customs."

The adjutant was already shaking his head. "You must go immediately, in person. A response could otherwise take days." He tapped his index finger on his desk. "You must personally point out the significance and urgency of your request." He leaned back in his chair, thinking. "Check the airport and the harbor."

"*Oui*, monsieur." Charles rose. "If the Penas were involved in Monsieur Freon's killing, they might have departed on a private yacht, without a permit."

"All the more reason you should be hurrying along then, isn't it, Charles?" He shooed the young man away and turned on the radio. Painting was a very calming activity and it was all the more so with some gentle music to accompany the labor. He would do the crown molding in white semi-gloss.

Charles drove first to the harbor. He could grab a quick

lunch at one of the cafés, check with the customs agent to see if Jorge and Elina Pena had come or gone by boat. He could also stop at his own little sailboat and apply a coat of varnish to the aft deck. It would be reasonably dry by evening and the day would not be a complete loss.

Charles parked his scooter on the grass along the fringe of the large public parking lot at the harbor's edge. There was a small café nearby where the food was good and not too dear. Before dining, he popped into the Customs office located at the waterfront. "I am Gendarme Charles Trenet. I am inquiring as to whether or not a Monsieur Jorge Pena and/or Madame Elina Pena have come or gone by boat."

The Customs agent, a gaunt fellow with a flat face and a dark brown tan, pushed a small pad of paper and a pencil stub over the counter. "Jot down the names and I'll look into it."

"It is quite urgent," explained Charles. "It concerns the recent murder of the American."

The agent looked unimpressed. He thumbed through a stack of loose message papers next to his computer. "Pena, Pena. . .seems to me we've already had a request for that information."

"Yes," said Charles. "That was from me. An official request of the Gendarmerie, actually."

The customs agent placed his hands on his hips. "Then why are you asking again? You think we've nothing better to do and so you would double our work?"

Charles knew better than to answer.

"I've a ferry due from Saint Martin in no more than a quarter of an hour. I've got to process all those passengers, don't I? They'll all be pouring out like rats from a sinking ship. Every one of 'em in a hurry—every one of 'em expecting to be first. Wanting to get on with their pricey vacations."

He stared the gendarme down. "Or shall I ask them to all wait for the esteemed Monsieur Charles Trenet to complete his investigations?"

"I realize you must be quite busy," Charles replied, trying to calm the obviously short-tempered agent. "However, the information is, as I said, quite urgently needed." Charles added humbly, "I'd be most grateful if you could help me out. The adjutant was most adamant that I obtain this information as soon as possible. It could reflect on our murder investigation—"

The agent looked past Charles. He looked at his watch. "*Zut*, they're early." He scurried from behind the counter, brushed past the gendarme and opened the door.

"What about my information request?"

The customs man grinned. "You know how to use a computer?"

"Yes," answered Charles with some hesitation.

"Well, help yourself then, why don't you?" He slammed the door shut on his way out to the dock.

Charles shook his head. Some people would do anything to get out of their work even to the point of expecting someone else to do it for them. He glanced at the computer. It was some foreign type. Himself, Charles was more used to typewriters, like the old one out at the Gendarmerie.

Once again, Charles cursed the innate sloth of his fellow man. Well, so be it. He would ask Adjutant Bruyer to send along one of his colleagues to search out the information he needed. After all, he had other, more pressing, matters to attend to himself. And if he didn't eat something first, where would he find the energy?

Well fed and with his boat in order, Charles returned to his assigned task. The Aéroport Gustav III, named for Sweden's King Gustav III who had been gifted the island by King Louis XVI in exchange for free-port rights in Gothenburg, in 1784, was a small, but modern facility and even boasted air conditioning.

Charles welcomed the cool burst of air as he strode inside searching for the Customs office which was located just inside the passenger waiting area. After several tries, he found a middle aged woman, with short brown hair swept back in a manly fashion, who offered her help.

She led him to a pleasant office and opened a file. "You say, Jorge and Elina Pena?"

"That's correct, madame," replied Charles. He sat in a comfortably stuffed chair, sipping a cold bottle of Perrier which the good woman had offered him. This was the life. Perhaps he'd joined the wrong branch of public service?

"They occupy a villa in Anse des Flamands. Villa Hyde-White." She turned to Charles. "You are familiar with Flamands?"

"Not particularly, *non*, madame."

"The *Hotel Isle de France?*"

"*Non*, madame."

"Well, Villa Hyde-White is the largest villa at the beach. You really can't miss it. The walls are white, as the name seems to imply—so's the roof. Though it is actually named for the Englishman who built it, a fisheries owner in England. Trout, I think. The family owned it for years, until his widow sold it off.

"It's largely rented out now through one of the agencies, though if you haven't got a couple of million Euros in your account, don't bother inquiring of it for your next holiday. It even has its own tennis court. If you get lost, you've only to ask someone—at the hotel, for instance. They'll set you on your way."

She set her elbows on the desk, laced her fingers together and rested her chin atop, looking expectantly towards Charles who was still installed in his chair, his own hands wrapped around his half full water bottle. "Is there anything else, monsieur?"

Reluctantly, Charles rose and set his drink in the waste can. So much for air conditioning and chilled refreshments. "*Non*, that is all. Thank you very much, madame."

Charles returned to his motor scooter. His shirt was becoming damp once more. He'd always been a quick perspirer. Oh well, the ride to Anse des Flamands would dry him out and clear his head—which thus far was clueless as to the identity of Monsieur Bobbi Freon's murderer.

Villa Hyde-White was indeed impossible to miss. With its imposing white walls and tremendous size, it was the largest private villa in Flamands.

Approaching on his loud, rusting and oft-battered Vespa, Charles felt more than a little intimidated. A dirty, brown mongrel nipped at his heels and he was unable to outrun it, though he tried to shoo the creature away with his foot. Only when the dog gave up the chase, was Charles free of him.

Charles stopped at the gate, pressed an electronic button attached to a small all-weather speaker and gave his name.

A woman, a local by the sound of her, asked what he wanted.

"I am with the Gendarmerie. I wish to speak with Monsieur Pena."

There was a long pause. When she returned, she said, "The monsieur is not home."

"Then I would speak with Madame Pena, please." Charles

tugged at his collar. The heat was unbearable this time of day. He waited while there was another very long pause.

The mechanical buzz of the electric gate caught him off guard. Charles started up his Vespa and hurried through before it could swing shut on him. He followed a long, narrow, flower-lined drive up to a broad courtyard and wondered at the amount of fresh water it must take to maintain them in such glowing health.

A black LandRover was parked outside the closed three-car garage. He climbed off his scooter and raised his hand to the exquisitely carved doors. The doors depicted the Tree of Life and must have taken an artisan quite some time to create.

A woman in a crisp maid's uniform answered. She was small, with a thick neck and wore equally thick-soled white shoes. There was a pink-handled feather duster tucked into the ties of her apron.

Before Charles could open his mouth, she put him in his place. "Madame will see you on the patio. She is quite busy. You may have five minutes." She held up five stiff fingers.

Charles stood, dumbstruck, wishing that for once he could invoke even a modicum of respect.

"Well?" She waved him in.

"Yes, of course, madame." Charles stepped over the threshold.

"Uh-uh." The housekeeper scowled and pointed at his feet. "Your shoes, please. Just mopped the marble. Can't have all that dust marking it up now, can I?"

Charles gingerly gripped the doorframe, removed his shoes, sighed inwardly on noting there were no visible holes in his socks, laid his shoes at the doorstep and followed the housekeeper into the foyer.

The high-ceilinged hall was every bit as chilly as a meat locker. The cold radiated up through his feet and goosebumps rose on his arms and legs and even the nape of his neck.

Charles studied his surroundings with some interest. The villa was richly furnished and the paintings on the walls looked like originals and were probably quite valuable; though some abstracts looked like the stuff he used to produce when he was six years old. Perhaps he should have insisted his mother hold on to them—they could have been worth a bundle today to folks such as these.

The housekeeper led him across the house and out to a grand patio that offered a commanding view of Anse des Flamands, an area renowned for its beautiful beach. This was the first real look Charles had had of it. Golden sand stretched out in a long, soft crescent. The sea was a brilliant blue. How he wished his own little sailboat was ready. He could skirt along the coast here enjoying the view from the opposing side.

Tourists and those lucky foreigners with getaway homes on St. Barthelemy paid handsomely to live on the beach or on the steep hills above it. Charles wondered if any locals could still afford such a view. The Penas must be rich indeed.

Madame Pena stood near the end of the marble floored patio. She held a stainless steel watering can in her hand. She wore a white cotton dress sheer enough to show that it was all that she wore. It was a sharp contrast to her chocolatey skin. Her black, shoulder length hair was tied up in tight braids, the type that American actress, Bo Derek, had made world famous back when he was only a boy. She didn't look older than twenty-five and was, perhaps, a good head taller than he himself.

"Yes?"

Charles stopped short and bowed. "Charles Trenet, madame, of the Gendarmerie. I would like a word with you about Bobbi Freon."

She cocked her head and studied him as though he were an interesting insect spotted in the brambles. He felt a rivulet of sweat roll under his collar.

Finally, she nodded. "Yes, the poor dear."

She upturned her watering can over the edge of the balcony, letting the contents spill down the hill. Apparently the concept of rationing water was as foreign to her as it was to most of the tourists on the island.

"Come, sit, Monsieur Trenet." Madame Pena called for her housekeeper. "What would you care to drink, Charles?"

Charles looked at the housekeeper who seemed to be eyeing him with disdain. "Perhaps an ice tea?" Charles said, slipping into a teak chair in the shade of a large green umbrella.

Madame Pena laughed. "Iced tea? No," she patted his arm, "you must have something stronger. A man must drink, musn't he?" She turned to her housekeeper. "Anna, how about two of those pineapple thingies like you made for us yesterday afternoon?"

"*Oui*, madame." Anna shot Charles a look and quickly departed.

"Now," said Madame Pena, pulling a second chair up beside the one Charles occupied, "how can I help you, Monsieur Gendarme?"

Her frock, unbuttoned to the solar plexus, provided yet another distraction. Charles forced himself to look out at the sea. He cleared his throat, clearing his mind in the same time. "You stayed at the Idyllique the night prior to Bobbi Freon's death, did you not, madame?"

Madame Pena seemed to give this some thought. "I don't know. I suppose—"

"Your name is on the register, madame."

She laughed. "Oh, yes. What was I thinking. Yes," she laid a hand on his forearm, "I did check into the Idyllique that night. I'd had too much wine," she confided. "I had been watching the races at a little bar in the Village St. Jean. I have a weakness for French wine, Bordeaux, in particular. I got a little carried away and I was afraid to drive home. You know how treacherous the roads are around here and there are no streetlights at all."

"That is true, madame."

"So, then I walked up the road and checked into the Idyllique. It's lucky they had a room."

The housekeeper, Anna, came and set two yellow drinks, in tall sweating glasses, on a small table between them, then quickly departed.

"*Salud!*" Madame Pena said, raising her glass.

"*Salud.*" Their glasses clinked and Charles took a tentative sip. "Delicious."

"Yes. Anna's quite a marvel. I wish she'd come home with us."

"Where is home, madame?"

"We've a penthouse in New York and a big spread in Guatemala, outside the capital."

"Guatemala?"

"Yes, that's where I'm from. Jorge has family there, also—an uncle—though Jorge is himself from Ecuador. We spend a fair amount of time down there. Jorge likes to keep an eye on the factory. Jorge likes to keep an eye on everything."

"Factory?"

"Jorge owns a clothing manufacturing company."

"I see." Charles took another drink, thinking that if he had a wife as alluring as Elina Pena, he'd be keeping a close and admiring eye on her. "Tell me, madame, did you see

Monsieur Freon at all, that night?"

"No, no, not at all."

"Can you tell me where your husband is, madame?"

She shrugged. "Who knows? I rarely do."

"Can you tell me when he will return?"

"Sorry. I do not know where Jorge is or when he is coming back."

"An interesting way to live, Madame Pena."

"It suits us."

Charles nodded. He believed it did. "Are you aware that your husband also took a room at the Idyllique on the night in question?"

"What? I mean, of course. Jorge didn't know I'd already paid for a room. I called him to tell him I didn't feel safe to drive and so he said he'd come out to the hotel and spend the night there as well. I suppose he thought I'd be waiting for him at the bar or the pool or something.

"Anyway, he ended up taking a room without realizing I'd already gotten one for us. With the prices they charge, Jorge was furious to be paying for two rooms, I can tell you!"

"I can imagine," replied Charles. "Your husband had a business relationship with Monsieur Freon?"

"That's right. Jorge is on the board of BF Enterprises and his factory produces the entire clothing line."

"Quite a beneficial relationship then."

"Yes. I don't know what will happen now that Bobbi is dead."

Charles commiserated. Though he couldn't see that the Penas would be doing much suffering. They certainly wouldn't be out on the streets begging for food anytime soon. "How would you portray your husband's relationship with Monsieur Freon?"

"Why, Charles," said Madame Pena with a sly grin, "are

you, perhaps, suggesting that my husband had something to do with Bobbi's murder?"

"Not at all. Yet, I am afraid it is my duty to ask the questions that might raise the answer to who is responsible for this man's murder, madame."

Madame Pena swirled her drink. "Well, they were both businessmen. To be sure, they fought. But it was always business. Sometimes they disagreed about the means. But," she said, pausing only to sip, "they always agreed on the ends."

"The ends, madame? What exactly are the ends?"

"Why, money, of course." Madame Pena finished the last of her drink and set her glass down gently on the silver-topped table. "Would you care for another, Charles?" She ran a finger along his arm.

"*Non, merci.* I must be going, madame." Charles rose.

"Such a shame."

She held out her right hand and Charles felt compelled to kiss it. "One last thing, madame, what was the name of this bar in which you watched the races?"

Her brow creased. "Why, I believe it was Le Bayou. Why?"

"Just doing my duty, madame. Please tell your husband that I would speak with him. He may leave word for me at the Gendarmerie, if he wishes."

"I will, Charles."

Charles bowed and took his leave.

Elina Pena watched him go out of the corner of her eye. She didn't like questions. And this gendarme asked lots of questions. "Anna!" She clapped her hands and the housekeeper appeared, kitchen towel in hand. "Bring me another."

"*Oui*, madame."

9

The Village de St. Jean is a small commercial center, second only to Gustavia itself, with many shops and eateries which attract the locals and tourists alike.

Le Bayou was not hard to find, in fact, it was quite easy. Though he had never been inside, Charles had passed by many times. Le Bayou occupied the center of a western-style shopping plaza along the popular Baie de St. Jean.

Charles parked his scooter alongside a wide collection of motorbikes and cars. Le Bayou appeared to be a very popular establishment.

He strode up to the L-shaped bar and ordered an anise. A television set, hanging from a wall in the corner, displayed a soccer match.

A small group of locals had gathered at a table near the center, hunched over an outspread newspaper, discussing racing results and consulting their racing forms.

Charles' Ricard arrived and he added a modicum of water to the anise, pouring judiciously from a glass carafe with the emblem of the sun on its face. He liked his anise strong, not overly watered.

The waitress, a quick moving bee of a woman with her hair pulled back tightly behind her head asked him if he wanted anything else.

"No, nothing now. However, can you tell me if you were working on the twelfth?"

The waitress wiped the counter with a spotted white towel. "I work everyday."

Charles sampled his drink. It was perfect. Even without a measuring spoon, he knew to a milliliter precisely how much water to add to his anise. It was a gift. "Do you know a Madame Elina Pena?"

The waitress stared at him blankly.

Charles gave a description.

The girl shrugged. "I've seen her about."

"On the twelfth?"

"Maybe."

"I need you to be more precise than maybe." Charles smiled.

"Then you should have been here on the twelfth, monsieur."

Charles laughed. "*Touché*, mademoiselle. Still, it would be most helpful if you could try and remember."

Her eyes pushed together. "Has she done something wrong?"

Charles swirled his drink. "Not that I know of."

A man sitting alone at a table outdoors shouted for a beer. The woman filled a glass with Stella Artois and departed. She gave the gentleman his beer then stopped off at the table where the racing fans held court. She whispered something in one fellow's ear.

The man, tall and thin, with a pleasant face, fighting to keep his hair, by offsetting this increasing loss with a small, dark moustache, rose, rubbed out his cigarette and crossed the crowded room. He leaned against the bar beside Charles.

"You are asking about Madame Pena?"

"Yes," replied Charles, holding out his hand. "Officer Trenet. I am investigating the recent murder of Bobbi Freon. And you are?"

"Ah, yes. The American." The fellow reached behind the counter, deftly retrieved an open pack of smokes and lit up. "I'm Gilles." He shook Charles' hand. "I run this place." He offered the pack of Gitanes to Charles, who declined.

"Were you here on the night of the twelfth?"

"I'm always here."

Charles nodded. Was there anyone who wasn't always at Le Bayou. "Do you recall if Madame Pena was in? Watching the races?"

Gilles picked up the nearest open bottle of French burgundy and poured himself half a glass. "To your health."

Charles raised his glass and drank.

"Sure, they were here." Gilles rubbed his mouth with the back of his arm.

"They? Her husband was with her?" This was interesting, considering Elina Pena had stated she'd spent the evening without her husband and only phoned him upon checking into the Idyllique. Still, why would she lie about this matter? And why would they then take separate rooms at the Idyllique? How very odd.

"No," said Gilles, shaking his head as if it was all too obvious. "Her and that gay American."

"Gay American? What does this mean?"

"You know, the dead fellow."

"Bobbi Freon?" Charles pressed his hands against the damp counter. This could be important.

"Yeah. The fellow was gay. I recognize the type."

"What?" Charles had no idea what this Gilles was

implying.

"You know, a gay guy. Liked the boys."

Charles looked confused. "You are saying that Bobbi Freon was a homosexual, monsieur?"

"He designed women's clothes, didn't he?" Gilles mashed his cigarette into an empty wine glass. "He must have been gay. I mean, don't get me wrong. Nothing wrong with that at all. Guy made a lot of money. Good for him. I'm only stating the obvious—" The barman let his thoughts trail off.

"And Monsieur Freon came here with Madame Pena?"

"That's right."

Charles paused to digest this information. What had Elina Pena been doing with Bobbi Freon? The obvious? Having an affair? It was plain that the bar owner was mistaken about Freon's sexual leanings, after all, Mademoiselle Patterson was carrying his child.

Had Bobbi Freon been straying? If so, both Elina Pena and Linda Patterson had possible motives for killing him.

"Can you tell me how long they were here?"

"Who knows? I can't keep track of the bloody customers' comings and goings, can I? I've got a busy restaurant to run. Come by tomorrow night. The special is mussels and french fries. Ten euros."

"Perhaps I shall. Is there anything else that you can remember about their behavior that night?"

Gilles laughed. "Like everybody else. They ate, they drank. They smoked. They laughed." He slapped the gendarme on the back and Charles slipped from his stool. "Same as always."

"Always?" said Charles, as he resituated himself and set his drink out of harm's way. "Madame Pena and Monsieur Freon have come to Le Bayou before?"

"Of course, they have," said the bar owner, drawing

himself up proudly. "Where else is one going to go on this island?"

Charles knew better than to engage in that particular argument. He thanked Gilles for his time, laid some money on the counter, including a small tip for the barmaid, and left.

Charles went straight to the Idyllique Hotel and Villas which was practically across the street. He left his motor-scooter at Le Bayou. It was a beautiful, warm night for a stroll.

Lily Vineuil sat behind the reception desk once again. That was good. Lily was always such a helpful girl. "*Bonjour*, Lily," Charles said. "How are you this evening?"

Lily looked up from the fashion magazine she was reading. She looked at Charles impassively, determined to keep a calm and disinterested demeanor. "*Bien.*" She wet her finger and turned the page.

"Working again, I see."

Without looking up from an advertisement for Italian leather handbags she could never afford on her meager salary, Lily replied. "Yes, Yvette begged me to fill in for her to-night."

"Too bad," said Charles, determined to be friendly.

"It's not a big deal. We close reception at eleven normally."

Charles leaned over the desk and hovered. "I see."

She arched her eyebrows and looked up. "Was there something you wanted, monsieur?"

"Well, actually, yes, there is something."

She stretched her hands across the desk. "Well?"

"Were you working the night before Monsieur Freon's body was discovered."

Lily rolled her tongue over the inside of her cheek. "Yes,

I think so. Yes, I'm certain I was." Her fingers worked over the keyboard. "*Oui*. It's here in the schedule. I was in the office from five to eleven."

Charles pulled out his notebook and began writing.

"Are you accusing me of murder now, Gendarme Trenet?" Lily rose. "Do I need an alibi, as you say?" She held out her slender wrists. "Would you like to slap the cuffs on me now?"

Charles was taken aback. A passing pair of young lovebirds, their arms wrapped possessively about each the other's waist, gave him a puzzled look. He reddened deeply. "*Non. Non*, mademoiselle." He waved at her. "Please, Lily, sit."

The girl glared back at him, huffed and sat down heavily in her chair.

"I apologize if I have in any way upset you or given you any reason to believe that I suspect you of such a horrible crime." Even while Charles was speaking, he was wondering if the poor girl had lost her mind. What was she ranting and raving about? Poor girl, probably overworked.

"Really, Lily. You must believe me. I am only trying to discover what you might be able to tell me about Elina Pena and her husband on that night—Tuesday, the twelfth."

Charles realized his own heart was pounding and he didn't know why. He grabbed a chair from the opposite wall and placed it in front of the reception desk. "Can you help me?"

After a moment, Lily broke the difficult silence. "You already know they had rooms here. And you know when they checked out. What are you looking for exactly?"

"I'm not sure. There's something odd about the situation."

Lily shrugged. "I don't know how I could be of help."

"What time did they check in?"

"I didn't check Monsieur Pena in. I do remember the madame, however. It was fairly late." She turned to the computer once more. "Elina Pena checked in on the twelfth at approximately ten-forty." She did some more searching. "It was after midnight when her husband booked a room."

"How did he do this if the reception is closed?"

"There is a telephone on the wall outside the door. Late arriving guests can pick up the phone."

"Then what?"

"They are connected straight to the manager's apartment."

"Monsieur Denown."

"That's right. He lives on the property."

"I see. So he registered Jorge Pena."

"Yes."

"I will speak with him about that later. Lily, is there anything you can tell me about Elina Pena?"

"No, not really. I didn't even know who she was before she checked in. I mean, I'd seen her around the bar and restaurant before, but she'd never taken a room."

"Is that unusual?"

"No, many come to dine or drink here. The restaurant and bar are open to all, not only paying guests of the hotel."

Charles sighed. "Madame Pena was with Bobbi Freon when she checked in?"

"No." Lily looked surprised. "She was alone."

"Are you sure?"

"Certainly. Why do you ask?"

Charles wasn't sure he should be sharing privileged information about a murder case with a civilian, but it was nice to have someone to talk to and so he said, "Madame Pena was seen leaving Le Bayou with Bobbi Freon the night before his death."

Lily straightened. "I see."

"Yes," said Charles. "In fact, they'd spent the evening together at Le Bayou."

"Ah." Lily grinned. "And you think she and Monsieur Freon—"

"It would seem likely. Though according to the manager of Le Bayou, Monsieur Freon preferred the company of men."

Lily looked amused. "Utter nonsense. I can tell you that from personal experience."

"You mean, you—" Charles wanted to ask if she'd slept with the American but didn't know how to phrase it diplomatically.

Though Lily would have liked nothing better than to make the callous young gendarme jealous, she couldn't bear the thought of anyone, even Charles, thinking she'd slept with that sleazy American moneybags, and so Lily came to his rescue, shaking her head. "No, no. Nothing like that. He made a number of passes at me."

Lily shut her magazine. "I told him he was wasting his time. I mean, he wasn't exactly my type."

"Not to mention he was engaged to be married," put in Charles.

"He was?"

"Why yes, to Linda Patterson."

"Her?"

"Yes, didn't you know? She's a guest here."

"Of course, I mean, I realize she is a guest here. Bobbi had been paying for her room." She scratched her jaw with a finely manicured nail. "It's funny now that you mention it."

"How so, Lily?"

"I'm not sure. But I seem to remember Mademoiselle

Patterson coming into reception that night."

"You mean the night before Bobbi Freon was murdered?"

"That's right. I was registering Madame Pena." She leaned back in her chair as if attempting to reconstruct that night. "She came in. I asked her if I could be of any assistance. She said no. Said she only wanted some brochures."

"Brochures?"

"Yes. She said she was interested in taking a cruise around St. Barts. They're quite popular with the guests."

"Then what?"

Lily shrugged. "That's all. I pointed out where the brochures could be found on the shelf over there." Lily pointed to a wooden rack toward the back. "Madame Patterson grabbed a couple, I think, and then left."

"And there was no sign of Monsieur Freon?"

"None at all." She leaned forward. "It's funny, though."

"What?"

"The way those two women looked at one another, you know?"

Charles shook his head no.

"It's a woman thing, I suppose. But if you ask me, those two looked as if they would have liked to murder one another." Lily tilted her head and laughed. "I wouldn't have been wanting to stand between them, I'll tell you that, Charles. If looks could kill. . ."

If looks could kill. Yes, Charles himself had seen that look. Often. And lately. "Tell me, Lily," he asked, "when was the last time you yourself saw Monsieur Freon?"

"I hadn't seen him for days, to tell the truth. It isn't as if he had much reason to come to reception and I hadn't seen him in the restaurant or by the pool, that I can remember, of late. It's not surprising when you consider he had a full-size villa at his disposal. A full kitchen, a private pool."

"Yes, I see what you mean."

"I did speak to him, though."

"Recently?"

"Funny. Now that you mention it, it was the day he died. He rang up the office."

"What? Do you remember what he said?"

"He told me that he was expecting a visitor and to be certain the gentleman was given directions out to the villa." Lily leaned back, rolling her tongue around the inside of her cheek once more. "Oh, and he wanted me to ring him back when the gentleman was on his way."

"Lily," said Charles. "Why did you not tell me this earlier? Did you get a name for this visitor? He could be our main suspect!"

Lily was shaking her head. "No, Charles. Don't get excited. You see, he never showed up. So, I guess I never thought it was important enough to mention."

Charles sighed. "I see. Still, what was this man's name? Do you remember, Lily?"

"Of course. It was—" Lily frowned, then clicked her fingers. "Bell! It was a Monsieur Bell."

"Bell. Bell. Now where have I seen or heard that name before?"

Lily shrugged. "I really wouldn't know. Well, if there is nothing else?" She rose.

"No, nothing for now." Charles stood.

"I am going to take my dinner break now." She placed a placard on her desk which stated for guests to ring the manager's extension for assistance in her absence. "*Au revoir*, Charles." With a wave of her hand, she was gone.

Charles stomach grumbled like an old man on the losing side of a pétanque match. He'd only had a sandwich for lunch and nothing since. Why hadn't Lily asked him to join her?

He hesitated in the doorway. Perhaps he would join her anyway? Would she mind? He could always take a table to himself. No, he decided, the entire situation might make the girl uncomfortable and she'd been very kind and most helpful to him.

Dejected and hungry, Charles returned to his motorscooter. The sounds of laughter came from Le Bayou. Charles took a small table in the corner of the covered patio and ordered a beer which was brought to him by a tall blonde in a tight, sleeveless white dress with a sweetheart neckline.

Charles opened his notebook on the tabletop and read from beginning to end. Nothing. He read again, this time more slowly. He found what he was looking for. A group headed by Roberto Bell was listed as holding a large interest in Bobbi Freon Enterprises. And apparently this Monsieur Bell was also on Saint Barthelemy.

Charles studied the menu, picked out the cheapest selection—a tomato salad and a small loaf of bread—and ordered another glass of beer. He would find Monsieur Bell tomorrow.

On his way home to his tiny and cramped, land-bound sailboat, Charles motored past the Idyllique Hotel and Villas. Most of the lights were off now. The island itself was a dark netherworld.

Charles glanced at his watch, keeping a one-handed grip on the handlebars. It was past ten. Lily would still be on duty. Probably sitting at her desk, perhaps reading a magazine.

He considered stopping, not anxious to return to his small and lonely quarters. He slowed at the turn which led into the parking lot, then veered back out onto the main road.

What reason could he give for stopping by so late? What pretext?

Inside, at her desk, Lily lifted her head as the sound of a motorscooter coming up the empty road echoed through the open foyer. Was Charles coming back?

She checked her reflection in the computer screen and straightened her blouse. But it was for nothing as the sounds of the motorbike grew closer then diminished in the distance, leaving her alone once more.

10

"Charles Trenet of the Gendarmerie Nationale." Charles showed his credentials to the tall, hirsute gentleman standing behind the elegant counter at the Carl Gustaf Hotel. He was wide shouldered and narrow hipped, reminding Charles of a wooden nutcracker.

The Carl Gustaf, named for Sweden's king, was situated on Rue des Normands, in the hills above Gustavia and held a commanding view of the harbor. It was also one of the chicest and most expensive hotels on the island—a virtual showplace of Italian marble and Greek columns. Not that any of the lodgings on Saint Barthelemy were cheap by Charles' measuring stick.

The man Charles approached had short black hair, swept up and back from his head. His face showed no emotion. "How can I assist you, young man?"

"I am looking for a guest of yours, a Monsieur Roberto Bell. I am informed that he is staying at your hotel."

The elegant gentleman nodded. His brown eyes looked Charles over. "He is a guest. What is your business with him, Gendarme Trenet?"

"That is police business, I am afraid."

The elegant gentleman examined his own glossy, well-manicured fingernails. "Monsieur Bell and his wife are here with us to celebrate their honeymoon, gendarme. It is our duty here at the Carl Gustaf to ensure their happiness."

Charles replied, "Nonetheless, as I said, it is necessary that I speak with Monsieur Bell on official business. Is he in his suite?"

Without directly answering the question, the elegant gentleman said, "I shall phone Monsieur Bell. The decision will be his."

Charles clenched his fists and kept his mouth shut. The elegant gentleman went into a private office. Through the glass, Charles watched him pick up a phone, dial and, after a moment, begin talking. A moment later, the elegant gentleman set the phone back in its cradle.

"Monsieur Bell has agreed to meet you."

"What is his suite number, please?"

The elegant man was shaking his head. "He will meet you here. By the pool. This way, gendarme."

Sourly, Charles accompanied the elegant man to the poolside. Several guests lounging near the pool looked at Charles, in his uniform, with mild interest, then returned to their own activities, or inactivities, as this was mostly the case.

Several minutes later, a man in his early thirties, by the look of him, came marching up to Charles' table.

"What? You're not drinking anything?"

Charles rose. "Monsieur Bell?"

"That's right." He turned, called for a waiter and ordered a coffee with Kahlua. "Nothing for you?"

"Well—" The truth was, Charles had glanced at the menu and been overwhelmed by the extraordinary prices. A beer was four times the price here as it was in one of the local pubs.

"Kahlua Calypso coffee?"

"If you insist."

"Two Calypsos then."

The waiter bowed and left.

"Please, sit, monsieur." Charles studied his subject. Roberto Bell was on the young side and carried himself like an athlete. He had sharp chiseled facial features and an olive colored complexion, spoiled only by a harelip which he attempted to cover up with a thin moustache. Somehow, it only made the image worse.

Roberto Bell straddled his chair and looked at Charles with amusement. "So, you're a cop, eh? First one I've seen here. Not much call for it, I'll bet."

"You're right," admitted Charles. "We've not much crime here on Saint Barthelemy."

Roberto Bell was nodding. "That's what I love about it."

"Have you been coming to the island long?"

"Nope, first time." He clapped his hands with delight as the waiter returned with their drinks.

Whipped cream float atop the coffee, with a brilliant red maraschino cherry at its unsteady peak.

Bell raised his glass. "To your health." He drank.

Charles lifted his own cup to his lips. It was quite hot. He tasted rum mixed with the Kahlua and coffee.

"Say, what's your name, then?"

"Pardon me. Trenet. Charles Trenet." Charles was a bit disconcerted. He was here to interview Monsieur Bell and so far Monsieur Bell had done most of the talking. He needed to correct this. "May I ask what brings you to St. Barts, Monsieur Bell?" Charles carefully spooned a mouthful of decadently sweet cream onto his tongue.

Bell winked. "Came for my honeymoon. Heard it was a

great place." He looked around. "And so far, so good."

"Except for the death of your friend," Charles tossed out the words, using them like a doctor's probe.

"Friend?"

"Monsieur Bobbi Freon."

Roberto Bell was smiling again. "Hey, I don't mind admitting—the guy was no friend of mine. He did recommend St. Barts, though. I'll give him credit for that." He raised his glass and drank some more.

"And yet, you and Monsieur Freon were partners." Charles sipped his own coffee slowly. It was hot and he was perspiring.

"Partners, business associates—call it what you will. I run a capital group that has a significant investment in Bobbi Freon Enterprises. But Bobbi ran things. I spend most of my time in Milan."

"You are Italian? The name sounds more English."

"Half Italian, half American. My father is from Massachusetts, one of the fifty states. And my mother was born in Milan. They live in Italy most of the year, also. I only get to the States on business."

"I see. In fact, you had a meeting here in St. Barts with Bobbi Freon on the very morning he was murdered."

Roberto Bell's smile disappeared into his face. He leaned across the table and whispered harshly. "Who told you that?" His lip quivered like a hare about to jump.

"I cannot say," replied Charles cooly.

"Well, it's a lie." Bell slammed his cup down on its saucer and coffee spilled over the white tablecloth. "Shit." He daubed it with his linen napkin.

"Please, monsieur."

"I'm sorry." He called to the waiter who removed the cup and saucer. "I need something stronger. Get me a brandy, would you? Anything for you, Trenet?"

Charles declined. "I still have my coffee."

The waiter left.

Charles tried again. "You had an appointment with Bobbi Freon the morning of his death. At his villa. What happened?"

Bell's hands twisted the soiled napkin as if he would wring out a pint of blood. "Nothing. I'm telling you. I never went. Somebody's trying to set me up." His voice was rising once more. "Trying to set me up for murder!"

Charles tried a small lie. Bell was very distraught. Too much so. Charles shook his head sadly. "Let us end this charade. You were seen entering Villa Onyx, Monsieur Bell."

Bell's hands tightened around the napkin. It tore. Bell looked embarrassed. "What's the use? Listen, Trenet, I did have a meeting with Bobbi, but so what? That doesn't mean I killed him!"

"Quite so, Monsieur Bell. So why lie?"

"To avoid trouble. I'm on my honeymoon, just like I told you. That's no lie. You can check with my wife, if you like."

"I believe you, monsieur," replied Charles.

"Yes, well," Bell wiped his damp forehead with the torn napkin, "Bobbi and I weren't exactly the best of friends, Trenet. In fact, it's no secret I despised him. Not to mention what happened last week."

"What happened last week?"

Bell swallowed half his brandy and leaned back in his chair. "We had a little party here, at the hotel, you know? A little celebration of the marriage. Anyway, that prick Bobbi made a pass at Angelica."

"Your wife?"

Bell nodded. "And on our honeymoon, no less! Can you beat that?"

Charles was not gaining a high opinion of the very man he was being asked to find justice for. "What happened, exactly?"

"Well, he hit on her, you know? Tried to get her up to our room." He shook his head. "The little weasel."

"Did you witness this, monsieur?"

"No, Angelica told me afterwards. Lucky thing. If she'd told me while he was still here, there's no telling what I might have done." Bell stopped suddenly, eyeing the gendarme nervously; obviously realizing what he'd too quickly said and its unspoken implications.

"I see." Charles finished his coffee. "I know such a revelation would make me quite angry. I suspect it would make any normal man angry."

Bell let out a nervous laugh. "I know what you're getting at, Trenet. But I didn't kill Bobbi. He was alive when I left that villa."

"And what time would that have been, monsieur?"

"Eleven a.m., precisely. I remember looking at my watch just as I was leaving the hotel. An associate of mine was flying in from Saint Martin at eleven-fifteen and I had just enough time to pick him up."

"I would like the name and address, even a telephone number for this associate of yours, monsieur."

"Sure," said Bell, with confidence. "Give me your pen."

Charles handed Bell his ink pen and pushed across his notebook. "Please, jot it down in my book for me."

Bell wrote and shoved the pad back across the table. "Is there anything else? Angelica and I are going boating this afternoon."

"For now, no, there is nothing. Except, did you see anyone else enter or leave Villa Onyx during the time you were there?"

"Nope. No one."

"Are you certain of this, monsieur?"

Bell spread his hands. "Believe me, Trenet, if I could give you another name to go chasing after, I would. Wouldn't I?"

Charles nodded. It was only human nature to offer up another for sacrifice when one's own life and freedom were threatened. "Please call me if you think of anything else that would help the investigation."

"Sure," said Bell, sounding none too enthusiastic. He rose. "Look, this isn't going to impact on me, is it?"

"How do you mean?"

"Like I said, I'm on my honeymoon." Bell winked.

"I understand, monsieur. If you are guilty of nothing, you've nothing to fear."

Bell nodded and quickly finished his drink.

Being close to the harbor, Charles decided his next move was one of crucial importance. He wanted to finish sanding down the galley. Once he finished refurbishing the tiny cooking area, he'd be able to make his own meals. This would be quite a financial savings. On a gendarme's wages, a few Euros here and there soon added up.

Remembering the envelope stuffed in his shirt, he first coasted up to the Poste at the corner of Rue du Centenaire and his own street, Rue Jeanne d'Arc, and deposited a letter for his parents back home.

Afterward, parking his Vespa alongside the road in front of the otherwise empty lot where he kept his sailboat, Charles spotted someone beneath his boat doing something to the hull. He jumped off his bike and hurried across the grass. "Hey, you, there! What do you think you are doing? Quit that!"

"What?"

Charles stopped dead in his tracks. "Oh, it's you!"

"Of course it is me," said Thor. "Who else would be working on your boat for you? The Minister of Eyesores?"

Ignoring the jab, Charles ducked under the boat and joined the old man. "What are you doing?"

Thor, dressed in a frayed, yellow guayabera-styled shirt and cut-off gabardines, held a paintbrush in one hand and a fair-sized trowel in the other. At his bare feet stood the bucket of whatever it was that he had previously left for Charles. "Fixing up your hull for you, son. What does it look like I'm doing?"

He spat, barely missing Charles recently polished shoes. Charles took a judicious step back and to the left.

"I noticed you ain't done any work lately."

Charles crossed his arms. "I have been busy with my duties. With an important investigation. Besides," he said with a huff, "I've managed to do some work."

Thor snorted with derision. "Not much by my reckoning. Why, at the rate you're moving, Charles, you'll be lucky to get this old girl in the water by summer."

Charles frowned. The old man was right.

Thor seemed to read his mind and smiled. He laid the paint brush to the hull. "That's why I've decided to help you out. I've been sealing the hull all morning. By myself."

"I had enquiries to make," Charles said by way of defense, though he was not sure why he needed one. Was it his fault he had official duties? No, it was not. So why and how could Per Ravelson make him squirm with guilt?

Charles shook his head and vowed not to let the old man get under his skin, the way he'd gotten under his boat.

"Oh, yes, enquiries. Into the murder of that rich American."

"Why do you say rich?"

Thor laughed. "They're all rich who come here, aren't they then? Nobody poor can afford to be here on this island, unless they were born here. Like me. Or have some other subsidized reason for being here." He pointed the sharp ended trowel at Charles. "Like you."

It was a bitter truth, realized Charles. To the permanent residents of Saint Barthelemy it must be frustrating and awe-inspiring all in the same breath to see the rich jetsetters that appeared during the winter season at the island's gates, landing like gold-plated parakeets, bearing their designer luggage, filling her small luxury hotels and overflowing her harbor with their luxury megayachts, spending exorbitant sums of money for the least of baubles.

But then, this wealth they brought contributed much to the island's own success. Where would the locals be without the riches that these powerful and famous visitors brought?

"Yes, well. It is not an easy case."

Thor spat again. This time he managed to clip Charles' left heel with a wad of chewing tobacco. "Murder's never easy. Unless you're the murderer."

Charles wiped his shoe in the dirt. "How do you mean?"

Thor shrugged. "What's so hard about killing someone?" A mosquito clinging to the hull met Thor's palm. Bam! He wiped his palm on his shirt, leaving a tiny trace of black and red. "See?"

Charles nodded. "That's what Dr. Duclos said."

"That quack?"

"Quack?"

"Martin Duclos? Went to see him a few years back about a cough I was having. Wife kept nagging me to go. Know what he said?"

Charles shook his head.

"Told me to stop drinking and smoking." Thor's laugh

turned into a cough that turned into a sharp wheeze. When he settled down, he said, "Can you believe that?"

"Incredible," said Charles, diplomatically. "Dr. Duclos said anyone could have killed Bobbi Freon, even a woman."

Thor stuck his trowel in the bucket, scooped up some whitish paste and applied a heavy layer to the boards. "You've got to lay this stuff on thick in some places." He worked some goo into the cracks with the edge of the steel trowel. "Why not a woman? Still, if you ask me, woman or not, it was a foreigner that done it. Not one of us."

Charles looked dubiously at Thor's homemade sealant. Would it hold? "What makes you think that?" He knew what the old man meant about 'us'. To the islanders, the foreigners, though very welcome, were not one of them.

"You don't kill the goose that lays the golden egg, do you?" He looked at his now empty pail. "Gonna have to make another batch for you, Charles." He picked up his bucket. "I'll be back tomorrow, then."

Charles waved and watched Thor work his way up the hill, skirting between the tightly placed apartment dwellings to the southwest. The old man's words stayed with him. No, you don't kill the goose that lays the golden egg—unless you've a bigger goose, laying bigger eggs, inside.

There were two passions, Charles knew, that played heavily in murders like the one he was commissioned to solve—sex and money. As far as the sex went, there were almost too many possibilities on this front for any of them to make sense.

Then again, Bobbie Freon had immense sums of money at his disposal. "Fool!" cried Charles, smacking himself in the head. "You should be looking to see who will benefit most from the designer's death!"

Cheered by this new revelation and new tack to follow,

Charles applied himself to the task of sanding down the galley. A little simple labor was always good for the thought process.

Back at headquarters, Charles ran straight into Adjutant Bruyer who was supervising the return of his cluttered little wood desk to his freshly painted office.

"Trenet," shouted the adjutant. "You've created quite a stink."

"Pardon me?" said Charles, somewhat taken aback.

Adjutant Bruyer laid a hand on Charles' shoulder. "Come into my office." He shooed the other gendarmes off and deposited himself behind his desk which now faced out the window.

Charles sat opposite. "Is something wrong, adjutant?"

"Wrong, he says!" The adjutant ran his fingers through his hair. "A Monsieur Jorge Pena has been screaming my ears off. Came down here looking for you and found me instead—lucky for you, Charles."

"What did he say? I have been trying to interview Monsieur Pena."

"Yes, well, you interviewed his wife and he says you all but accused her of murdering Bobbi Freon." He leaned over the desk, his big chest squashing his papers. "Is that so, Charles?"

'Non, Monsieur Adjutant. Not at all." Charles squirmed in his chair. "I did no such thing."

"He says you upset his wife."

"But adjutant—"

Adjutant Bruyer raised a hand to stop him. "You know what else he did?"

Charles shook his head.

"He telephoned Paris." The adjutant's eyes focused in on

Charles'. "He had a word with Georges Carreau."

"Georges Carreau?"

"The procureur, Charles," said Adjutant Bruyer heavily. "And the procureur called me on the telephone from Paris and he in turn had a word with me." The adjutant was shaking his head at the memory. "And it was not a pleasant word, Charles. Not a pleasant word at all."

The adjutant laced his thick fingers together like a bowl full of sausages. "We simply cannot go about infuriating and upsetting Saint Barthelemy's important guests. These are the words of Monsieur Carreau, not myself, Charles."

"But, adjutant, how can I conduct my investigation—the investigation you have charged me with—if I do not pose questions to the suspects?"

"So," said Adjutant Bruyer, "you suspect the Penas?"

Charles shrugged. "I don't know. I have not yet narrowed my list of suspects at this time."

The adjutant's eyes narrowed and he glanced out his open door being certain none of the other gendarmes were hanging about. "Who are your major suspects?"

"Well," said Charles, stalling for time as his mind busily searched for suspects, "the Penas are certainly suspect. Jorge Pena had a business relationship with Bobbi Freon and his wife may have had yet another relationship with him herself."

Charles carefully watched for his superior's response, but Adjutant Bruyer's face remained a mask. This made him nervous. "But I'm not saying either of them did it. I mean, I cannot be certain at this time," Charles added hastily.

"Are you suggesting that Pena's wife had an affair with Bobbi Freon?"

"That is a possibility." Charles related what he had learned of Bobbi's last night.

"Interesting," agreed the adjutant, "but not enough to

hang a murder on."

"*Oui*, adjutant. I also spoke with Roberto Bell who was himself a business associate of Bobbi Freon. I believe there was much animosity between the two men. Monsieur Bell is here on his honeymoon and Bobbi Freon made a play for his wife."

The adjutant shook his head in disbelief. "An amazing fellow our Bobbi Freon."

"Yes, adjutant. He does not seem to have many friends on the island, excepting his fiancée, of course."

"So, at least you have removed one suspect!" the adjutant said cheerily.

"Unfortunately, no, adjutant. Mademoiselle Patterson is carrying Bobbi Freon's child—"

"All the more reason she'd not kill the man."

Charles told Adjutant Bruyer what Lily had told him about Mademoiselle Patterson and Madame Pena and what had passed between them on the night before Bobbi's death. "So, if she suspected Bobbi of cheating on her—" Charles spread his hands. "Well. . ."

"I see." Adjutant Bruyer opened his bottom left hand drawer and removed a bottle of Chabbaneau XO and two small glasses. He filled them both and handed one to the gendarme.

They drank.

"Is there anything else, adjutant?" asked Charles, setting his glass carefully on the edge of his boss' desk.

Adjutant Bruyer poured himself a refill. "Only this," he said in quiet but ominous tones, "go very carefully, Charles. Monsieur Carreau is aroused. He has suggested returning to Saint Barthelemy himself to take over the investigation."

Charles didn't think this such a bad thing. Life for himself could get back to a more blissful, peaceful norm. But a moment later these thoughts were shattered.

"If that happens," said Adjutant Bruyer, between sips, "we can both say *au revoir* to our lovely little island, Charles."

"Adjutant?"

"Monsieur Carreau can be most unpleasant. I have had to deal with him in the past. If he comes back from holiday early, believing we are incompetent of solving so much as a simple murder—"

Adjutant Bruyer's arm swept across his big desk, sending a cluster of papers flying like paper yellow butterflies in a storm. "He will be the broom that sweeps us clean. We, you and I," the adjutant said, pointing his glass in Charles' direction, "may find our next posting to be Kabul."

Charles pushed his glass away from the desk's edge. It appeared to be near to falling and crashing to the floor. A metaphor for his own career. "Kabul? Afghanistan?"

"I've been to Afghanistan. Some years ago. I shouldn't care to return."

"No, adjutant."

"See that you bring this murder investigation to a close, quickly and quietly. If you need any help or more men, you've only to ask."

"Yes, adjutant." Charles retreated to his makeshift desk. He wrote up a list of those persons he'd interviewed and beside this, in a separate column, he wrote out his thoughts about each. Lost in thought, it was with surprise that he noticed he'd scratched the word Afghanistan in the margin.

The adjutant had made it clear that if he did not bring this investigation to a successful conclusion soon it would soon be the end of his nascent career. What would his parents think then? He'd already given up a university position to become a gendarme instead, much to his mother and father's chagrin. How would they feel if the next postcard he sent them was postmarked Kabul?

II

"There's something I forgot to tell you," said Dr. Martin Duclos.

"Yes?" said Charles, holding the phone close to his ear. He stood at the reception counter of the Gendarmerie's headquarters where he'd been summoned by one of his mates, Gendarme Ronalph Sadjan. "What is it?"

"Your dead man had sex prior to his death," said the doctor, matter-of-factly.

"Yes, I know," said Charles. "This is nothing new, I'm afraid. Monsieur Freon had sex with his fiancée, Mademoiselle Linda Patterson, the evening before his death. And it is very likely that he had sex again that night with yet another woman."

"Ah," said Duclos, "so I suppose you know that Bobbi Freon had sex not an hour before he was stabbed to his death?"

"Well, I did not—"

"And I suppose you also knew that this sex he'd had was with a man?"

"A man!?" Charles dropped the phone. He pulled it back

quickly by the cord. "Excuse me, but are you sure?"

"Am I sure of what? That Monsieur Freon had sex? Yes, I am. There are signs, you know, gendarme. Perhaps you are unaware?"

Charles flushed. "Believe me, doctor. I am fully aware of the signs. But are you certain it was with a man?"

The doctor explained his findings in no uncertain terms. "I take it this will satisfy your curiosity?"

"Yes, doctor."

"Because if you like, I can send over a report. Perhaps even some photo documentation."

"That-that will not be necessary," said Charles. He thanked the doctor for this new information and broke the connection.

Bobbi Freon had had sex with a man not an hour, according to Duclos, before his death. Was there anything or anybody that the American designer did not bed?

Charles frowned. The list of suspects was growing longer, not shorter. Somewhere out there was Bobbi Freon's last partner. How would he ever find this man? Was it Roberto Bell?

"Problem, Charles?" said Gendarme Sadjan.

"No, Ronalph," replied Charles. "No problem at all. Tell me, have you ever been to Afghanistan?"

Gendarme Sadjan watched as Charles turned and headed out the door to his Vespa without so much as waiting for a reply. "What an odd fellow," he muttered. "What an odd, odd fellow."

Charles went straight to the Idyllique Hotel and Villas. He needed some help and Lily was just the girl for the job. Striding eagerly into the lobby, he was disappointed to find Denown hovering over Lily's empty desk.

"Gendarme Trenet, good to see you again." Denown quickly typed some keys on Lily's computer keyboard and turned off the monitor. "How can I assist you?"

"Well. . ." Charles looked about. There was no sign of Lily. The manager smelled of cheap lime cologne. "I was hoping to speak to Lily."

"She's got the afternoon off, I'm afraid. She's playing tennis. Can I be of service?"

Charles covered his disappointment. "Lily, Mademoiselle Vineuil, told me you checked Monsieur Jorge Pena in on the night prior to Bobbi Freon's death. Is that so?"

"Yes," said Denown, scratching his belly. "I seem to remember doing so. It was quite late. I was watching television. Tennis matches being rebroadcast from Marseille, as a matter of fact. It was a women's doubles match. Do you play tennis, Trenet?"

"*Non.* Was there anything unusual that you can remember about Monsieur Pena?"

Denown sat himself down atop Lily's desk. "Unusual? No, I can't say I can." The manager rubbed his fingers together. "He paid cash. I remember that."

"Isn't that unusual? Such a large sum of money?"

Denown smiled. "A large sum of money? For you and I, maybe, Trenet, but not for the Idyllique's clients."

Of course, thought Charles. "Tell me, monsieur, did you ever see Bobbi Freon with another man?"

"With another man? How do you mean?"

Charles hesitated. How could he phrase this? "Did you ever see Bobbi Freon with another man in an intimate—that is, in what might appear to be an intimate moment?" Charles felt his face growing warm.

Denown let out a loud laugh. "Bobbi was a wild fellow, I'll grant you that. But as to his sexual escapades, I am afraid

I was not privy. He could have been having orgies for all I know."

"So there was no one man in particular, then?" pressed Charles.

Denown rose and draped his hand over Charles shoulder. "*Mon Dieu*, Charles, there wasn't even one woman in particular!"

Charles left. He'd interview the guests next, door to door, but first he'd say hello to Lily. He followed the signs to the tennis courts.

As Denown had said, Lily was there. Her playing partner, much to Charles' chagrin, was a shirtless young man in white tennis trunks, with a well-chiseled body tanned the color of a copper penny.

Charles felt suddenly small. A tall, wood slat fence, painted green to match the playing surfaces, surrounded the four courts. Charles held back near the entrance and watched the ball sail effortlessly back and forth.

Lily had on one of those sexy little tennis outfits like Charles had seen on television and in magazines. The pleated skirt, white with a thin blue stripe running along the outside of each thigh, rose, showing wonderful long leg, as she ran and jumped. Her matching shirt, with a round neck collar, fit snugly. And though the fellow was obviously the stronger of the two, Lily held her ground remarkably well.

As an overhead shot came over the net, Lily's head turned in Charles' direction as she reached for the ball. "Oh, *bonjour*, Charles!"

The ball smacked into the wall beside Charles and he stooped to pick it up. Lily ran over. "Hi."

He handed her the yellow tennis ball. "Hi."

Lily turned to her playing partner and shouted, "Let's take a break, okay?"

He nodded, waved his racket and took a chair in an umbrella covered sitting area that featured drink machines and a rack of white towels.

Lily looked at Charles. "Don't tell me you've come to play tennis, Charles?"

"Uh, no."

Lily grinned and wiped the perspiration from her brow with her pink wrist band. "That's good," she said, glancing at the gun on his belt. "I'm not certain they allow firearms on the court."

"Too bad," replied Charles, "I think it would improve my game."

She grabbed his wrist and pulled him closer to the wall, out of the sun. "So, why are you here?"

"I need to question the guests, room by room. To see if anyone can remember anything that might help find Bobbi Freon's murderer."

Lily nodded. "Yes, I think that is a good idea." She looked at him expectantly.

"Ready?" called the handsome, half naked savage, waving his tennis racket in the air. He'd wrapped a towel around his neck.

Something in Charles made him want to tighten it a bit.

"One moment!" Lily cried. She turned back to Charles. "I have to get back to my match with Jean-Marc. Was there something else, Charles?"

"Well," Charles rubbed his toe on the painted surface, "I thought perhaps you would join me for dinner tonight? But if you are busy with your friend, or. . ." He avoided looking into her eyes.

What he didn't see was Lily's surprise. She was beaming. "Why, that would be nice. Thank you, Charles."

"Alright, then," said Charles. "I will see you tonight." He

turned stiffly.

"Wait," called Lily. "What time? And where should we meet?"

"Oh." Charles cursed himself for being an idiot. "I will pick you up here at, say, eight?"

"*Bien*," said Lily, lightly covering Charles' hand with her own. "I'll see you at eight." She ran towards her playing partner, stopped mid-court and turned. "I'll meet you in the lobby!"

Charles nodded and stepped out. He paused several meters away. Idiot! Perhaps he should ask Lily where she might like to have dinner? He retraced his steps.

Looking across the court, he watched Lily run up to this Jean-Marc fellow and give him a hug. Charles frowned and did an about face. So, he thought, that's the way she plays it.

He dug his notebook out of his pocket and headed for the villas nearest Bobbi Freon's.

As far as Lily Vineuil was concerned, he would play it cool. He didn't know what had possessed him to invite her to dinner in the first place! He hadn't intended to do so. It was just something about seeing her with that under-dressed show off that had set him off.

There was no answer at the first villa, nor the second. An elderly woman, with whitish blue hair that curved along the edges of her cheekbones, holding a fawn colored Pekingese to her ample bosoms, watched him through a black iron gate.

He waved.

She returned the gesture. "Is something wrong, young man?" she asked in English, though her accent was unusual to Charles.

He approached the gate which opened onto a courtyard of a villa not very dissimilar from the one Bobbi Freon occupied. "No, madame. You are English, perhaps?"

"Close," said the plump woman. She wore a flowing, Bessea orchid print lounging dress and orange espadrilles covered her feet. "I'm Canadian. From Windsor, Ontario."

"Ah," said Charles, "that explains the British accent."

"It's nice to find someone who speaks the language."

Charles smiled and held out his hand. "Charles Trenet.

"I am Kristine Schaeffer." She scratched the dog's nose. "This is Foofy." She sat the dog on the ground. "Go on, now, Foofy. Would you care to come in for an iced tea, young man? It's terribly hot this time of day."

"Well, I have much to do," he replied, visions of Afghanistan floating through his mind. "Tell me, have you been staying in Saint Barthelemy long, Madame Schaeffer?"

"Close to a month now. We'll be staying through the New Year."

"And you have been staying at the Idyllique all this time?"

"That's correct. Except for an overnight trip we took to Saint Martin about a fortnight past."

"In that case," said Charles, "I think an iced tea is in order."

The old woman unlatched the gate and Charles followed her to a large square table under the loggia. She went inside, telling Charles to take a seat.

The villa had a private swimming pool exactly the same size and shape of the one at Villa Onyx. The old woman was obviously extremely well off. Foofy must be eating steak and fresh fish for dinner.

Madame Schaeffer returned with a cork tray bearing a pitcher of iced tea, two very tall glasses and a basket of pastries. "Help yourself, Charles."

Charles poured two glassed of iced tea and helped himself to a *pain au chocolat*. "*Merci.*" He examined the flaky crust. The pastry was light and golden, with a buttery rich dough, crunchy on the outside, almost like a croissant, wrapped about a mouth-watering chocolate center. This one looked and smelled as good as his mother's own.

Foofy raced about between their feet, no doubt expecting a few crumbs to fall. Charles obliged him, hoping his mistress wouldn't mind.

"Are you a policeman, then, Charles?"

"A gendarme, madame." Charles explained the difference. "The municipal police handle the day to day affairs and we in the Gendarmerie deal with more important crimes."

"Like catching the murderer of that American?"

"*Oui*, madame." Charles bit into the middle of his pastry, luxuriating in the taste of fresh, baked chocolate. "A most baffling case."

"If you ask me," said Madame Schaeffer, breaking apart a croissant with her fingers, "it was that man in the suit."

"Man in the suit?"

"Yes, I mean, who goes about in a suit and trousers in St. Barts? And during the day on top of that!"

"Where did you see this man?"

"Leaving Villa Onyx, of course. It's only three doors up and the side gate faces out on the little road here."

Charles craned his neck and looked out through the gate. Sure enough, the courtyard entrance to Villa Onyx was clearly visible. "And you saw this man the morning that Monsieur Freon was killed?"

"Sure as I see the sun come up everyday."

Charles flipped open his notebook. "Can you describe this gentleman for me?" She was an old woman and Charles wondered how much useful information he could expect from her. He couldn't expect much. "Was he young? Old? Do you recall the color of his suit? Was it light or dark?"

Madame Schaeffer peeled open a sugar cube and dropped it into her glass. "He was young. Had dark greasy hair and dark skin. The suit was medium blue. And he had a white shirt. But no tie."

"That's quite good." It sounded to Charles like Roberto Bell, who'd already admitted meeting with Freon. "Tell me, did he have any other distinguishing characteristics?" The question remained in Charles' mind: Did Roberto Bell harbor homosexual or bisexual tendencies? Had all Bell's talk of animosity and distrust towards Bobbi Freon been nothing more than a clever smokescreen meant to mislead him?

"Hmm. No, not that I can recall."

So, she hadn't noticed the harelip. Charles looked out the gate once more. Still, it was some distance away that she'd probably seen him. Such a defect might not be clear and her eyesight may not be what it may once have been. "What time might this have been?"

Madame Schaeffer did some more thinking. "It must have been nine-thirty or ten, as best I can remember. I believe Nicolas was reading the paper."

"Nicolas?"

The old lady nodded. "That's my husband. Always reads the papers in the late morning with a cup of coffee." She leaned in closer. "He's always telling me I talk too much. Tells me I should mind my own business." She sat back and chuckled. "Oh, I suppose he's right. But what fun is there in that?"

Charles agreed.

"I hear some mighty interesting things just listening." She wagged a rheumatic finger. "Not snooping or spying, mind you, Charles. Just listening."

"I understand, madame." he said, diplomatically. Charles set his glass aside and decided it was time to look up some more witnesses.

"I could tell you stories about that Bobbi Freon, for instance."

Charles retook his seat. "Oh?"

"Oh, yes," said Madame Schaeffer with a telling roll of her eyes. "The comings and goings in that place. The parties, the fights."

"Fights?"

"Why, yes, Charles. Like the one between that man in the suit and himself."

"The man in the suit fought with Bobbi Freon?"

"Yes, I told you, Charles. Now, it wasn't like it was fisticuffs, but I could hear them shouting, clear as church bells."

Charles refrained from correcting Madame Schaeffer on her testimony. "I'm sorry, I forgot. What did they fight about?"

She shrugged. "I don't know. All I know is they were both shouting to beat the devil. These courtyards are like big speaker cabinets, so Nicolas says, and words and sounds sort of vibrate about and carry over the walls."

"And you're certain it was Bobbi Freon that this man was arguing with? Did you see Monsieur Freon?"

She shook her head. "No. No, I didn't. But the man in the blue suit went in and a little while later I heard the shouting. And I've spoken to Monsieur Freon a time or two myself, Charles—he'd say an occasional word of hello to me or Foofy in passing—so I recognized his voice.

"It was Bobbi Freon, for sure. He was good to Foofy. Whenever Monsieur Freon saw him he used to stop and give him a pat. Yes, It was Freon, alright. Nicolas was here, like I said. The pool boy was here and he heard them, too. You can ask them both, if you want. If you don't believe me."

"That won't be necessary," Charles assured her. "So this man argued with Bobbi Freon and then left?"

"Left in a huff, he did. All red faced. His hands balled up in tight fists." Madame Schaeffer lifted her arms and demonstrated.

"And did you see Monsieur Freon any time after this?"

She thought. "No. Nicolas told me to mind my own business and to get away from the gate. Said I shouldn't be poking my nose into other folks' lives." She rubbed her hands together, dropping crumbs of light pastry on her plate. "I went inside then."

"And you didn't see anyone else come or go? Think, this is important."

Time seemed to stand still as Charles waited for the old woman's answer.

"Well, I took Foofy out for a walk about an hour later. But I didn't see anyone. Except for Mademoiselle Somers' boy."

"Thanks, anyway. Well, I'd best be going. And thank you for the tea, madame."

"Nice, boy, but a little reckless."

"I see, well—"

"Yes, he had a surfboard under his arm and looked like he'd hurt himself. I asked him if I could help but he said he was alright and went on his way. Foofy finished her business and I went inside." She shook her head. "Sorry. That's all. Oh, except for a couple of the housekeeping staff that went by as I was chatting with the boy. A man and a woman."

"Do you know their names, madame?"

"No, sorry. I'd never seen them before."

"Yet you are certain they were with the hotel?"

"Yes, they wore Idyllique uniforms at any rate."

"I see." Charles rose before Madame Schaeffer could find

another topic. She was charming, yet he had his duties to fulfill. "Believe me, madame, that's plenty."

12

As Charles left Madame Schaeffer's, he heard voices coming from Villa Onyx. That was odd considering the villa was off limits. Approaching the pool gate, he saw a child, a young boy, calling to his smaller sister to bring him a pole.

Charles opened the gate. He recognized the children now. They were the children he'd seen at the beach on his first day on the case. They belonged to Sofie Somers. The boy threw a stone at the roof.

"Children!" he shouted.

They turned their heads. The boy was shirtless and wore a pair of bright red trunks that ended just above his knees. The girl had on a pink and green one-piece suit with a skirted waist.

"You are Mademoiselle Somers' children, no?"

They nodded.

"What are you doing in here? Don't you know that no one is allowed to be in the villa now?"

The girl, an unsteady grip on a long pole to which was attached a pool leaf-skimming net, looked at him blankly. The boy shrugged. "I've lost my disc. I'm trying to knock it down."

Charles followed the boy's pointing arm. There on the roof lay a red flying disc. Charles crossed his arms and said sternly. "Well, in the first place, you both should not be playing here. In the second place—" They watched him with wide-eyed curiosity and maybe just a little fear. Charles really didn't want to scare them. "In the second place, let me see that pole. I think I can manage it."

The little girl handed Charles the long pole. It was an extension pole, and he pushed it out to the end of its length and tightened it back up. Standing back from the roof to get a clear view, he could see right away that he'd never reach.

"One minute." He picked up the poolside table and brought it close to the wall. "Hold it steady, for me, will you?"

The children gripped the edges of the table and Charles climbed up via a chair. Carefully stepping on the tabletop he reached again. Yes, he could just about get it. He pushed out and up.

"*Zut!*" he muttered. All he'd succeeded in doing was pushing the toy further up the sloping tile roof. "Let me think. Watch out."

Charles jumped down and laid the pole against the roof's edge. He paced from one side of the patio to the other. This was not going to be so easy.

"Can you get it?" asked the girl.

The boy made a face. "No way. Can't you see?" He kicked the ground. "We've lost it."

"Not so fast," said Charles. "Not so fast. Maybe there is another way."

"What way?" demanded the boy.

"Well," said Charles, with no clear idea, "let's just think. Is there a way up to the roof? Through an attic, perhaps?"

"I've never seen one," the boy said.

"You could climb," suggested the little girl.

"Well," said Charles, looking up unhappily at the high, steep roof, "I suppose I could. But then, I'd need a ladder and, unfortunately, I don't have one of those so—"

"There's one on the side of the house," interrupted the girl.

"One what, mademoiselle?"

"One ladder."

"Ladder?"

"Yeah, that's right!" said the boy, kicking up his heels and running towards the side of the house. "Come on!"

Reluctantly, Charles allowed the little girl to take his hand and lead him on.

Hidden behind a tangle of bushes, Charles discovered the pool filtering equipment and a tired, bowlegged wooden ladder lying on its side, as if wanting nothing more than to rest.

"You see?" said the girl, happily. She pulled at the ladder's steps. "It's perfect."

"Uh, yes," said Charles, "perfect."

The boy helped Charles pull the ladder from the ground. Insects, upset at seeing their family home uprooted, packed their little bags and took flight.

Charles opened up the stepladder and admonished the children. "Now, please, you must hold her steady."

The children nodded.

Charles climbed the first two steps, paused as he heard a frightening creak as he laid his foot on the third rung and said, "Hold very steady."

He had to climb to the very top of the ladder to reach the roof, well beyond the 'Do no stand on or beyond this point' sign glued to the sixth step of the ladder.

The old ladder shook like a victim of Parkinson's as he himself tottered at the precipice and hoisted himself up onto the hot roof. He took a step and his shoe slipped. "Whoa!"

Charles looked down at the kids and instantly regretted it. They'd moved away from the ladder now and were looking up at him expectantly.

"Did you get it?" asked the little brown haired girl.

"Not yet," called Charles. "Don't forget the ladder!" He climbed up to the flying disc, using his hands to help steady himself. The barrel tiles were hard to walk over. The toy was near the peak. Slowly, Charles bent over, picked up the disc and shouted, "Got it! Here it comes!"

Charles cocked his arms and sent the disc sailing through the air. It cleared the roof, soared over the childrens' heads and landed in the pool. They clapped with delight.

"Cool!" said the boy, as he ran to collect his toy.

"Now don't go anywhere," said Charles. "You must hold the ladder for me as I come down, children." Charles looked across the roof. He was at the peak of the main house. The sun was beginning its descent, turning the western sky a brilliant orange. It was a wonderful view, but one he could live without.

And now that he was on top, he wondered just how easy it was going to be making it back down again—in one piece, anyway. One slip and he'd go crashing to the unyielding ground.

Perhaps there was an easier way? He scanned the roof, looking for a low point. It was useless. He'd have to go back the way he'd come. Face forwards he started down, sliding on his rear end, afraid to walk down, lest he tumble head over heels.

A brown pelican landed several meters away, giving him a glum look.

"Just what are you looking at?" demanded the sweat-soaked gendarme.

The big bird shuffled its feet and flew off.

"Good riddance," uttered Charles. "Hey, *un moment.*" There was something there, near where the pelican had landed at the conjunction of the main roof with the roof of the master suite. Something dark. "One minute, children," Charles cried. "Children?"

Charles shrugged and side-scooted over the roof to the spot where the two Vs jointed. It was a black sock. A match to the single sock in Bobbi Freon's dresser drawer, perhaps? "How on earth—"

Charles reached out to pick it up. He might as well throw it down while he was up there. He'd gone to all the trouble of getting there in the first place.

"*Q'est-ce que c'est?*" Charles held the sock out in his extended arm. It was much too heavy for a stocking. He laid the sock out on the tiles and slowing rolled it down. Inside lay a gold cross. He pulled the sock loose by the toes.

The cross glowed in the sun, yellow and bright and deadly. For this was not simply a gold cross. Its opposite end was sharp and its sides beveled. A letter opener.

A letter opener with something dried and dark along its edges.

Using the sock, Charles carefully lifted the letter opener, holding it protectively in one hand, working his way down the roof, fastidiously.

There was no sign of the children. More trouble for him with the ladder, but at least he wouldn't have to explain to them what he'd found.

He crawled to the edge of the roof and looked down.

Sofie Somers was looking up at him. Her hands held the warped and sagging ladder. "*Bonjour*, Charles."

"Mademoiselle Somers," exclaimed Charles. He hurriedly descended the ladder. *"Merci."* Charles quickly dusted himself off.

"You're welcome. And it's Sofie, remember?"

"Oui." Not for the first time, Charles noticed how striking a woman she was, dressed now in a loose-fitting, white cotton djelleba through which he could further see she wore a simple white bikini. Her hair was rich and brown, the color of roasted coffee beans. An aura emanated from her that suggested more high society hostess than house-keeper/assistant.

Mademoiselle Somers folded the ladder.

"Here, let me." Charles grabbed the stepladder and tucked it back along the side of the house where it might rest in peace.

"So," said Sofie, "what brings you to my roof?" She laughed. "I never thought I'd be asking someone that question."

"Your children," said Charles. "I heard them on the patio. They were playing with a flying disc."

Sofie was shaking her head. "Don't tell me. And it got stuck on the roof. Sounds just like them."

"You know, they really should not be on the grounds. The area has been officially sealed."

"Didn't you hear? According to Monsieur Denown, we are allowed to move back in."

"Really?"

"Yes. The hotel is quite full and I believe he exerted some pressure on the local authorities. I'm told they'd finished with Villa Onyx. The only place we are restricted from going into is Bobbi's room. They've still got that taped off." She wrapped her arms around herself. "Not that the children or I have any interest in going up there." Her gaze drifted towards Freon's upstairs bedroom.

"I see."

"So, what's that?" She pointed to Charles' side. "Have you come to do your laundry as well?"

"What? Oh." Charles' face turned serious. The black sock was sticking out of his pant pocket. In sotto voce, he said, "I believe I have discovered the murder weapon, mademoiselle."

"What?! Where?"

"Shh. I don't want to alarm your children." Sofie Somers' children had returned from wherever it was that small children disappeared to and were frolicking in the swimming pool.

"Of course." Sofie pulled Charles aside. "What is it? A knife?"

"A letter opener," said Charles. "I must take it to headquarters. They will want to send it for analysis, no doubt."

"Where did you discover it?"

"It was on the rooftop. Between the master suite and the main house."

"You are brilliant, Charles." She laid a soft hand on his chest. "I have great confidence in you, Charles. You will solve this horrible crime. I am certain."

"I only wish I could be as certain as you."

There was a shout of exhilaration as the boy bounced off the low diving board and cannon-balled into the crystal clear water.

"Hey! Watch out!" cried Sofie. "Are you alright, Charles?"

Charles kicked his damp shoes. "Yes, it's nothing." Checking himself over, he was relieved to see the black sock had not been hit.

"Children can be a handful. Have you any children, Charles?"

"No, not yet. One day, I hope."

She nodded. "They are wonderful in spite of themselves. You've never been formally introduced have you?"

Charles said he had not.

Sofie waved. "Children, come here!"

The children waded to the edge of the pool and climbed out. "This is Cleo."

Cleo said hi in a quiet voice, then quickly ran off, hiding behind a chair in the shade.

"And this is Tony."

Charles stuck out his hand. "*Bonjour*, Tony."

"Hi." Tony returned the grip.

"Say, that's quite a scratch you've got there. I hadn't really noticed it earlier. We had more important things on our minds, didn't we? Like flying saucers." A circle of red marks covered the boy's right elbow. "And some bruise," Charles added, noting a fading yellow tinge on the boy's right cheek.

Tony blinked.

"What happened," joked Charles, "did your sister sock you?"

"Are you kidding?" Tony drew himself up. "Cleo's nothing but a weakling. She's not strong enough to sock me and leave a mark like this I've got."

Charles laughed. "Well, I have two sisters myself and, when I was younger, they used to pound on me mercilessly. So there is no shame in taking a good punch."

"Aw, this is nothing," answered Tony, bravely. "And I didn't get it like that."

"Yes. Nothing. That's what you say," Sofie replied in motherly tones to her son. Then, redirecting her speech to Charles, she said, "Tony insisted on trying surfing. He's never done it before but insisted on trying anyway. I told him I didn't like the idea and that he should start with something simpler like one of those Boogie Boards, but he begged me and begged me."

"I see," said Charles.

"So we rented him a surfboard—against my better judgment—" she added, once more facing her son, "and what happens?"

"An accident?" suggested Charles.

"Yes, an accident. Tony ran right into the rocks." She grabbed her son affectionately by the head. "Lucky you didn't kill yourself, young man."

"Aw, I can take care of myself, Mom." Tony twisted free.

"There are some rocky beaches here. But many others are safe," Charles intoned. "Flamands, for one," he added, remembering fondly the great open beach visible from the Pena's villa.

"But the best ones for surfing are where the rocks are," put in Tony. "Like Manapany."

"I see. I'm afraid I don't know much about surfing," confessed Charles.

"I could teach you," said Tony.

"Oh, please," said Sofie, "that's just what I need, two patients!" She gave Tony a push. "Run off, now. I want to speak to Charles."

"Nice children," Charles said.

"Thank you. Sometimes it gets difficult, raising them alone."

Charles nodded.

"Listen, would you care to stay for dinner, Charles?"

"Well, I have to take the letter opener in. It might be nothing, but then again, it may be important. And then I could be tied up for hours. In either case, I'll have to write up a report for the adjutant. . ."

Sofie frowned. "Yes, of course. I'd almost forgotten

about that. Too bad you can't have someone come and collect it for you. I'm making fresh fettuccine with grilled vegetables which I've been marinating in herbs all afternoon long. Peppers, eggplant, zucchini. . ."

Charles found himself salivating. "Perhaps I might make a call?"

Sofie smiled. White teeth shined on him like diamonds. "There's an extension in the kitchen." She grabbed Charles' arm. "Come, I'll show you."

While Charles dialed headquarters, Sofie poured them each a glass of Cabernet.

"I hope you like it," she said, tipping a glass up to Charles' lips.

He sipped. "It's delicious." She smiled as he took the slender-stemmed glass from her hand.

"How do I know this will work?"

"You don't," said Jorge Pena. "Neither do we." He shook his glass irritably, cubes of ice danced for him. "That's what friggin' lawyers are for."

Pena stared off the bow, looking down on the crowd milling its way through the narrow streets of Gustavia. It was getting late. Everyone was on his or her way to dinner. He looked impatiently at his new watch, a JB Blancpain chronograph that Elina had picked out for him in one of the shops here in St. Barts. If they didn't end this damn talk soon, he and Elina would be late for their dinner reservations at L'Orchidee which was all the way out in Pointe Milou.

"Listen, Linda," put in Bell, the calm voice of reason, "we all want what's best for Bobbi Freon Enterprises."

Linda Patterson laughed. "Please. I'm a big girl. We all want what's best for ourselves. And," she added, patting her stomach, "I want what's best for my child."

"Of course you do," answered Roberto Bell. "It is only natural." He rose from his deck chair, fighting off the urge to toss Pena, who stood perilously close to the edge, overboard. He laid on his best smile. "Look, if Jorge and I can bury the hatchet, as it were, why can't you?" One of the worst things about his investment in BFE was Jorge Pena. The Ecuadoran was even more a lout than that gangster Martinelli whom Bobbi—in a moment of cash-strapped desperation—had let in for ten percent.

"Yeah?" demanded Pena. "What's your problem?"

Linda swirled her margarita gently, licking crystals of salt from the sides. Soon, she feared she'd have to cut back on drinking, perhaps cut out alcohol all together. Being pregnant and carrying a child was not going to be easy. And even though Bobbi was gone, she was determined that he was going to pay. "I can only repeat what I said when we began this conversation: I think that Bobbi's child should be given a controlling interest in BF Enterprises."

Pena snorted. "Oh, sure. With you in charge of running things, I suppose?"

Linda shrugged. "I don't have a problem with that," she said with a deadly smile.

"Well, I do," returned Pena, tossing his ice cubes, and then his empty glass, over the side.

"I think," said Bell, rubbing his harelip, a nervous habit he was always fighting, "that there must be a compromise that we can all live with. But first, we have to agree to work as a team. To unite."

Bell paced the deck. "We both know there are other forces at work here." He banged his hand on the rail. "I've invested a fortune in this company and I'll be damned if I am going to watch it all get pissed away!"

Pena couldn't resist laughing. "You invested a fortune?"

He thumped his chest with his thumb. "What about me? I've invested not only my own money but my very own, very precious, sweat and blood!"

Bell's lip turned down, yet he held his tongue. He needed this deal to work. If things at BF Enterprises came undone he stood to lose his entire investment. The state of the company needed to be firmed up and quickly. But Pena's sweat and blood? The only sweat or blood that man had ever seen was the sweat and blood that dripped off his underpaid, undernourished workers! "Yes, Jorge. We know."

But Pena was not giving up so easily. "So, if you think I am going to let that broad take over my company, well, you've both got another thing coming!" He plucked an open pack of cigarettes from his jacket, lit one up, took two furious puffs then stamped it out under his foot.

"Like Bobbi did?" Linda asked.

"Now, Linda," interjected Bell, "there's no need for accusations here."

Pena stomped to the table and leaned over the woman. "If I were you, I'd keep my big mouth shut."

Mademoiselle Patterson stared him down. "I have a child to raise as a single mother. Bobbi promised me that our child would be taken care of. I expect his wishes to be honored."

"Yes, well, we shall see what the will has to say," Pena replied ominously.

Linda shrugged. "Bobbi promised. Besides, even if the will does not reflect his wishes, I will fight it. I will fight it in court."

Pena growled.

Bell pushed his way between them. "That's why we are here—to try and avoid all this. Listen, I believe that between the three of us—with the help of the attorneys—we can maintain control of BF Enterprises. You both know that

Bobbi was spending like crazy. All this lavish living. Costs were up. Bobbi's cachet was going down. The name Bobbi Freon does not mean what it used to. People aren't buying."

"The fool had become passé," said Pena. "I tried to warn the bastard, but he wouldn't listen. I told him we needed to come up with something new. And curb the expenses. But Bobbi wouldn't have any of it. You wouldn't believe how much money he owes me."

Pena poured himself a third scotch and checked his watch again. "How about this?" he said. "Bell becomes president, runs things on a day to day basis. You," he continued, pointing at the woman, "become, I don't know, vice president—"

"I don't think that's suffi—"

Pena cut her off. "With a seat on the board. And the kid gets to be chairman when he or she is all grown up and wearing long pants."

Linda frowned. "And just what do you get out of this, Jorge?"

He grinned, reminding her of the cat who'd just cornered the mouse.

"Acting chairman of the board."

"What?!" She bit her nails.

"It's only until your kid takes over. Gives me time to get my money back."

"And then some," added Bell, cynically.

Jorge only shrugged. "Then you can name me chief operating officer."

Linda shot a look at Bell.

"Sounds good to me," Bell said, smiling, as if to let up would cost him his life—at least his good life. "So long as we share the financials equally. . ." He glanced meaningfully at Pena.

The Ecuadoran grumbled. "Just so long as I get an equal say in how things are run."

"Of course," said Bell, quickly.

"And an unbreakable contract for BF's goods to be manufactured solely by my company."

Bell didn't look happy but he nodded and held out his hand. "What do you say, Linda?"

She rose, looking satisfied, though her brow was creased with obvious concern. "I say you-know-who is not going to like it. But what the hell," she extended her hand, "I'm in."

"Great," responded Pena, twisting his watch around his wrist. "I'm late for dinner." He made his way to the edge of the yacht and paused on the gangplank. "Now get the lawyers on this and make it work! None of us can afford to lose."

13

"*Bonsoir, mademoiselle. Charles est là?*"

"*Oui.*" Sofie smiled at the redheaded boy in blue uniform and raised a finger. "*Un moment.*"

Charles quickly came to the door of Villa Onyx, pulled Gendarme Sadjan outside by the arm and said, "You made excellent time, Ronalph." He looked over his shoulder to see that Sofie was gone. He heard her lilting voice singing in the distance.

"So," said Gendarme Sadjan, pulling off his cap, and scratching his skull, "what have you called me out here for then?"

Charles held out the paper sack into which he had carefully deposited the letter opener and sock. He cracked it open.

Sadjan peered inside. "What the devil is that supposed to be?"

"I'm not certain. But I believe the letter opener may be our murder weapon."

"*Incroyable!*" Sadjan grabbed for the bag.

Charles held it back. "Be careful, man. This could be

evidence." He looked up—Ronalph was a good head taller than he—and stared into his comrade's eyes. "Crucial evidence." Charles explained the circumstances of his discovery.

"You found that thing on this roof? So what are you hanging around here for, Trenet? Why haven't you taken this to the adjutant?"

"Well, I—" He found himself looking over his shoulder. "I might have missed something. I thought I would stay here at Villa Onyx and search. That's why I need you to transport this possible evidence to headquarters."

"I don't get it," complained Ronalph. "You make me come all the way out here, when you could have simply driven back with it yourself? Why didn't you tell Bruyer right away?"

The gendarme stopped as suddenly as he'd started. A sly grin appeared on his face. "Oh," Ronalph said, slowly, "I get it." Through the open draperies, Sofie Somers was busily setting the dining table for four. Tall, tapering candles flickered warmly. "I get it, indeed, Charles."

"It's not what you think—"

Ronalph patted Charles' on the shoulder. "Oh, sure." He winked. "Official business, right?"

"Yes, I told you. There could be more to this."

"I'm sure there is."

"I mean to say there could be more evidence to uncover." Charles felt his face reddening.

"Don't worry," said Ronalph gaily. "I'll take this to Bruyer and explain to him that you are detained with interrogating a most promising suspect." He popped his cap back on his head, leaving his freckles in shadow.

"This is work!" shouted Charles as Sadjan headed up the garden path towards the parking lot. "Nothing more!"

"You owe me!" came his comrade's faraway reply.

Charles shut the door. He pursed his lips. Sadjan was right, he owed him. What had he gotten himself into?

Sofie appeared in the foyer holding the half empty bottle of wine. She'd changed into a clinging silk dress, the color of palest jade. Its neckline ventured seductively along her perfectly proportioned chest. "Is your friend joining us?"

"No," replied Charles, his tongue suddenly dry. "He has taken the letter opener for examination."

"Do you suppose they'll find out anything soon?"

"I don't know," answered Charles. "There are no flights out of here at night. As you must know, the airport is not equipped for night flights. So I suppose that tomorrow the adjutant will have it sent to St. Martin. We haven't the facilities here for such an examination. Though I expect Duclos will want to have a look at it."

"Well, then," said Sofie, taking Charles by the hand, "there is nothing further to be done tonight but to enjoy ourselves. Isn't that so, Charles?" Her emerald eyes tugged on him like a magnetic pull.

"Yes," said Charles, allowing Sofie to pull him along, "I suppose that is so."

Lily studied her reflection closely and carefully in the bathroom mirror. She wanted to look perfect for Charles tonight. She'd chosen a sleeveless, lavender wraparound dress that fell just above the knee. She hoped Charles would like it. She hoped it wasn't too formal or too casual for whatever restaurant he had in mind.

She squeezed some toothpaste over her brush and scrubbed her teeth for the second time that evening. Having done so, she reapplied her lipstick, also lavender, and checked her smile.

Lily stepped back from the mirror and turned around slowly. Should she add the pearl necklace? She tried it on. Perfect. *"Bonsoir,* Charles," she practiced. *"Bonsoir."*

She checked her watch. Eight o'clock. *"Mon Dieu!"* she cried. "Charles will be waiting." She grabbed her low heeled open-toed white sandals and ran out the door.

Lily, like much of the staff, had a small room at the Idyllique. The room was meant to make up for the meager wages. It wasn't bad, but normally she was forced to share her limited quarters with a roommate. Fortunately, her current roommate, Josette, was in France for three weeks holiday and Lily had the room to herself.

She hurried down the hill towards the main building.

The hotel manager, who was sitting in his office behind reception, looked out from the open door in surprise. "Lily, what are you doing here?"

"Oh, Monsieur Denown. Good evening."

"Good evening." He was grinning. "Don't you look lovely." He rose from his desk and leaned in close to the girl. "Come to keep me company?" He snaked his hand around her waist and pressed his lips to her hair. "Why don't you join me for dinner?"

Lily pushed him off. He smelled of drink. Heavens, what if Charles saw?! "Please, monsieur. I have a date."

Denown backed off but he was still grinning. "A date? Well, well." He folded his arms over his chest. "So, who is the lucky fellow?"

Lily sighed. She didn't particularly want to discuss her personal life with Denown, but didn't see much choice in the matter. Not if she wanted to hold her job. "It's the gendarme."

Denown's eyes lit up. "The one who's been bumbling around investigating Bobbi Freon's murder?"

"Yes," said Lily, haughtily, "and he has not been bumbling about. Charles has been making much progress."

"Has he now?" Denown clicked his fingers four times. "Who would have thought?"

"That's right. Despite what you may think, Charles knows what he is doing and he will identify and capture the perpetrator of this horrible crime. Soon." She looked anxiously over her shoulder, hoping that Charles would appear and save her from continuing.

"So, tell me, Lily," said Denown, who'd made himself comfortable on a wooden bench along the wall opposite, "who does Trenet think killed Bobbi Freon?"

"I-I am not at liberty to say." Hoping to cut off her superior's questions, Lily crossed quickly to the entryway and looked out for sign of Charles' approach. Nothing. She frowned. Wait, wasn't that Charles' Vespa parked there near the gate?

She turned back to Denown who had stretched his legs out on the bench. "Have you seen Charles?"

Denown wiggled his feet playfully and said, "Not lately."

"Not lately? What do you mean?"

Denown shrugged. "He was in here earlier this afternoon, doing some of his world-famous sleuthing. I haven't seen him since."

"That's odd," Lily said under her breath.

"What?"

"Nothing." Lily wondered: Had the motorscooter been there when she ran down the hill or had it only recently appeared since her arrival in the lobby? She looked at her watch. Eight-twenty.

He was late.

What should she do? She could go look for him, but what if he then came here to the lobby while she was gone? He would think she wasn't coming and depart.

"So," said Denown, "where's the loverboy?"

Lily said frostily, "I am early." She tapped her foot. "Charles will be here soon. Very soon." Please, she thought, miserable at the thought of having to hang around the lobby with Denown, be here soon, Charles. Be here soon.

"I hope you don't mind the meal," Sofie said, leaning over Charles and filling his plate with noodles and fresh, colorful vegetables, "but since the children and I are vegan, there is no meat."

"What?" replied Charles, as he picked up his fork. "That is remarkable. I, too, am vegetarian."

Sofie rested her hand just briefly across his, like a butterfly testing a flower petal. "What a lovely coincidence."

"Yes," agreed Charles, staring into Sofie's eyes, admiring the scent of her neck. Was it patchouli? He caught the children looking at him and cleared his throat. "My, the food smells wonderful."

"I hope you enjoy it." Sofie took the seat beside Charles. For a moment, her knee brushed his.

"You're really a vegan?" asked Tony. He sat directly opposite Charles. The candle's flame bounced as he spoke.

"That's right," said Charles, digging into his noodles.

"But you carry a gun."

"Tony," said Sofie. "What's that got to do with anything?"

Tony ignored his mother and pressed on. "That means you shoot people, right? People are animals of a sort, aren't they? Do you shoot animals?"

"Animals?" said Charles.

"Yes, cows, chickens."

"Oooh," cried Cleo. "You shoot chickens? They're so

pretty!"

"Cleo!" admonished Sofie. "Eat your dinner. You, too, Tony. Your questions are inappropriate. Charles is our guest. Can't you think of anything else to talk about? Something pleasant?"

"That's alright," said Charles, careful to maintain a smile. "I don't mind." He leaned his elbows on the table. "I do carry a gun, Tony. I have to. It is my job. But, to tell you the truth, I have never used it."

"What's it for then?"

"What's it for?" Charles scratched his head. "Well, it is for the monsters."

"Monsters?" Cleo said weakly.

Tony asked, "You believe in monsters?"

"Yes," said Charles, nodding, "I do."

Tony sneered. "Like Frankenstein, Count Dracula and the Wolf Man?"

"No," said Charles, somberly. "Human monsters."

"Human monsters, Charles?" Cleo set down her water glass, scrunched up her face.

"Yes," said Charles, evenly. "The only real monsters are human."

Tony said quietly. "I believe in monsters, too."

With a forced laugh, Sofie lifted her wine glass. "Well, this is the most interesting dinner I've had in sometime. Now, I insist we change the subject. Tell us more about you, Charles."

It was warm. Lily went to the ladies restroom directly off the lobby and checked her makeup. Charles was an hour late. Even Denown had given up on him and gone off, smirking, to the bar.

There had not been a single phone call either. Where

could he be? She went out and checked the Vespa again. She was certain it belonged to Charles. So his scooter was here, but he was not.

She frowned. The sun had disappeared hours ago. In the dark, it was easy to imagine that something bad, something horrible had happened to Charles.

Perhaps he had confronted Bobbi Freon's killer? Perhaps the killer had attacked Charles? Charles could be hurt. He might be lying bleeding somewhere in the hills in a pool of his own blood.

Poor Charles!

Lily went back to the office, her mind made up. She retrieved the island phone book from the cupboard in Denown's office, found the number for the Gendarmerie and dialed.

"Yes?" The voice on the other end crackled.

"*Bonsoir*. I am trying to reach Gendarme Charles Trenet," Lily said, careful to sound as official as possible. She didn't want to get Charles in trouble for receiving a personal call.

"*Un moment.*"

Lily bit her nails waiting for the speaker on the other end to return.

"Trenet is not here."

"Can you tell me where I might find him?" She tried a small fib. "It's urgent." Well, it was, sort of.

The voice at the other end sighed, then shouted, "Hey, Sadjan, where did you say Trenet was?"

There was a pause. Lily heard the somewhat removed voice saying, "Uh-huh, Uh-huh." She heard a second voice in the distance, but couldn't make out what was being said.

The voice came back louder. "He's at the Idyllique Hotel and Villas down in the Village de St. Jean."

"What? But that's not possible. I mean, I'm—Oh, never

mind."

"Shall I tell him who was calling for him? I can leave him a message. He'll get it in the morning."

"No, never mind."

"Suit yourself."

There was a click at the other end and Lily laid down the receiver. She realized she'd have sounded like a fool if she'd said that Charles might be dying somewhere.

Besides, Charles was probably okay. Certainly he was okay. If she'd raised a fuss at the Gendarmerie for nothing, it might have gotten Charles in trouble.

Drained and worried, she flopped down on the bench, with a sigh, to wait.

Charles' head sank into the deep pillow. He tilted his head up to the ceiling, watching the ceiling fan—visible by candlelight—go round and round. Beside him, Sofie slept, her hair spread out like an angel's. Her left arm lay across his bare chest.

Slowly, he lifted her arm and pulled the covers up over her resting form. He tiptoed to the chair in the corner and retrieved his clothes, dressing in the dark.

He found a hotel pad near the bedside table and left Sofie a note telling her that he would phone her in the morning. Charles feared it would not do to be discovered in Sofie's bed in the morning, not by her children—who slept down the hall—at any rate.

Charles paused in the foyer and checked his watch. It was past midnight. He left, locking the door behind him.

Lily woke with a start. She sat up and rubbed her neck. For a moment, she'd forgotten where she was and looked about in confusion. Then she remembered: Charles.

A glance at the clock told her the story. Midnight. She'd been stood up. Though Charles may have had good reason.

The hotel's doors were closed. Denown must have locked them without bothering to wake her. She was surprised by this. It would be more in character for him to wake her up and chide her some more about her missing date.

She let herself out, facing the brilliant and silent night sky alone. Charles' motorscooter was still there. Lily couldn't get over how strange that was as she headed towards her room above the hill.

Coming down the path, she heard a sound and peeked around the corner. Someone was coming out of Bobbi Freon's villa! She hugged the wall and clutched the edge with her fingertips. This could be the killer!

Lily held her breath and watched as the lanky figure tucked in his shirt tails and turned in her direction. He was coming this way. If she stayed in the shadows, perhaps he wouldn't see her.

The man, for it was obviously a man, walked slowly down the path towards her. Passing into a clearing between villas, the moon lit up his face.

"Charles!"

"What?" Charles froze.

Merde, thought Lily, wishing she hadn't burst out. She pressed herself against the wall as if she might squeeze herself through, then gave up.

She stepped into the light.

"Lily!" Charles came forward. "What are you doing here?"

Lily's glare drove into the gendarme like long, sharp icicles. "I'm going to bed." She pointed. "My room lies that way."

"Oh."

"I see you are fine."

"Yes," Charles replied slowly. The girl looked awfully upset. "Is everything alright?"

"Alright?" Lily exclaimed. "We had a date!"

"A date?" Charles slapped himself. "Oh, *mon Dieu!*" How could he have forgotten?

"I waited hours for you!" she shouted.

"Lily, please, lower your voice," begged Charles. "You will wake the guests."

She was too angry to listen to reason. "I thought you might have been hurt—killed even!"

"Lily, please—"

"Tell me, Charles, just what have you been doing?" She tapped her foot furiously.

"I-I was working!"

"Working! Ha!"

"Really, Lily," Charles held out his hands, "I'm very sorry. I was busy. I discovered some important evidence. I forgot about our date. Please, I'm sorry."

Lily felt her breath catch in her throat. He did look sorry.

"Is everything alright, Charles?"

Lily's head swivelled towards the front door of Villa Onyx. Sofie Somers had appeared. The slut, wearing nothing more than a thin bathrobe that barely covered the upper half of her thighs, approached Charles and laced her fingers through his.

Sofie looked from Charles to Lily. "What's going on? I heard shouting."

"So this is your discovery!"

"I don't understand," said Sofie.

Lily, fighting back the tears that threatened to overwhelm her, said, "It's nothing. I was walking back to my room." She glared at Charles. "I saw a snake."

"A snake?" said Sofie. "I hate those."

"So do I," hissed Lily. She hitched up her skirt and pushed passed Charles. "Excuse me, I'm tired and going to bed now."

"But, Lily—" began Charles.

Lily never slowed her step, disappearing into the night.

"I know that girl. She works here, doesn't she?"

"Yes," said Charles.

"Don't worry. I'm sure she'll be fine now. Lucky you were here to help her."

"Yes, that was luck, all right." Of the worst kind. "I'm sorry we woke you."

Sofie kissed his cheek. "I'm glad you did. Why are you leaving?"

"I thought it best. I'll need to report to the adjutant first thing tomorrow—today."

"Call me?"

Charles nodded.

"Good night, Charles." She kissed him again, this time on the lips, and returned to the villa.

Charles stood there on the path, pushing his palms into his eyeballs. He almost wished he was dead, like Bobbie Freon.

Feeling like a heel, he considered going after Lily but realized that would be useless. Even if he could find her, she would not want to talk to him.

Charles slumped over his Vespa. He'd done a terrible deed and had no idea how to undo it.

14

Charles cleared his throat.

The naked man, stretched out in the sand, without so much as a towel between himself and nature, opened an eye. "Oh, it's you." He sat up.

The equally nude young man beside him turned his head and looked in Charles' direction. "Who is this, then?"

"Friend of Lily's."

"I see." The second man yawned, stretching out his limbs, then settled back down. "I'm Henri. And you are?"

"Gendarme Trenet."

"Well, have a seat, Gendarme Trenet—unless you've come to arrest us?" he added playfully.

The man Charles had come to see came to his feet and stood uncomfortably close to him. Charles, uncertain which way to look, stared out at the incredibly blue sea of Anse de Grande Saline. It was perhaps the most spectacular beach he had ever seen. The sky was as brilliant as any azure and in it a couple of puffy white clouds seemed to be holding hands as playfully as a pair of damselfish.

Charles had crossed along La Grande Saline, a former salt

processing region, that had ceased production in nineteen-seventy. Then, leaving his motorscooter in the parking area some distance away, he'd had to trudge up and down the tall, soft dunes that sheltered the beach from the inland. It was hot, thirst-raising work.

Now, standing on the remarkably beautiful beach, in uniform, he felt conspicuous and overdressed. Most beachgoers that he could see were nude, though some wore bits of clothing or swimwear, apparently meant more for show than decency. Nonetheless, they were in the minority here. Charles had heard from his comrades that there were a great number of nudists at Anse de Grande Saline. It had been no exaggeration.

"You are Jean-Marc Bouton?" Charles asked.

"That's me. You're Charles, right?"

"Yes."

Jean-Marc held out his hand and gripped Charles' in a firm handshake. He seemed to notice Charles' expression of surprise. "I saw you at the tennis court yesterday." He tapped Charles on the shoulder with his brown knuckles. "Lily can't stop talking about you." He pointed to his friend. "That's Henri Leclerc."

The fellow, who'd rolled over onto his stomach, waved his hand in the air. "Hello, again, Charles."

The effect of looking at the man's buttocks while he said hello was disquieting to Charles. He directed his gaze to the jumble of dark gray rocks at the far side of the beach. Lily spoke of him to this Jean-Marc fellow? And apparently favorably so.

Merde, he had screwed up badly. Jean-Marc was no competition, only a friend of hers. Would it be possible to broach the subject of what she might have said about him?

"So, what brings you out here, Charles? You don't seem

to have the proper attire for a dip."

"I was looking for you."

"For me, why? How did you find me?"

"I found you by going to your home. I saw your roommate. Carl, I believe?"

Jean-Marc nodded. "That's him."

"He told me you had come to Anse de Grande Saline. That answers the how. And why? I need to speak with you regarding Bobbi Freon's death, Monsieur Bouton."

"Really?"

Charles nodded.

"Why me?"

"I am told you overheard him arguing on the morning of his death."

"Funny, I don't remember."

"I have a witness who says she was with you. In fact, she and her husband were present with you during this argument."

"Oh, alright. You're describing Kristine and Nicolas Schaeffer, aren't you?"

Charles said nothing.

"Yeah, I remember. I was brushing the pool at the Schaeffer's villa. We heard the shouting. Freon and some other dude were going at it pretty good. But so what?"

"Why would you deny it?"

"I didn't. I forgot, that's all." Jean-Marc shrugged. "Besides, it's none of my business now, is it?" His voice had taken on a hard, cautious edge.

"Did you see anyone else coming or going that morning?"

Jean-Marc replied without hesitation. "No one."

"You are certain?"

"I just said so, didn't I?"

"Jean," cautioned Henri, "play nice."

Charles wiped his brow to no avail. The sweat beaded up again as quickly as he swept it away. "Is there anything else you can remember about that day?"

"It was hot," said Jean-Marc, crossing his well-muscled arms over his chest.

Charles nodded. It was always hot.

Charles made his way once more up and over the dunes which threatened to suck the shoes right off his feet. He climbed back on his Vespa and began the long drive back to town.

He'd gone a few hundred meters up the twisting road before changing his mind. There had been a restaurant at the edge of the parking area near the beach. The least he could do was to throw them some business by having a cool drink.

He turned around.

Charles stepped up onto the covered porch, across which an inviting breeze wafted cooly by on its journey across St. Barts.

A familiar looking fellow, with thick jowls and a short, thick moustache that was streaked with gray, sat alone at a small table. He waved to Charles. "Trenet! *Quelle surprise!*"

"Chief Lebon?" Oh, no, groaned Charles. He was in for another browbeating for sure, like the one the adjutant had given him the other day.

"That's right." The chief rose. "Come, have a seat, Charles." Chief Lebon pulled out the chair next to his own. "What will you have? A beer?"

"Sure. Thanks." Charles sat. "I didn't recognize you out of uniform, sir."

"Bah." He laid a friendly hand on Charles' shoulder. "No need to be calling anyone 'sir' around here. Call me Didier."

"Yes, sir—Didier."

"Besides," added the chief, "this is my day off and I've come here to La Belle Saline to escape the wife for a few moments." He winked at the gendarme. "A married man needs a few moments to himself. A good wife understands this."

Charles could only agree.

The chief ordered two more beers from a passing girl in a gingham apron. "So," he said, with a look to Charles' filthy shoes and sand-speckled calves, "what's happened to you?"

"I was interviewing someone related to the murder."

Chief Lebon leaned in. "A suspect?"

Charles shook his head. "Only a witness. Jean-Marc Bouton. He works at the Idyllique as a pool man. He was cleaning a pool at a nearby villa and overheard Bobbi Freon arguing with another man on the morning in question. I was told I could find him sunbathing at the Anse de Grande Saline."

Chief Lebon laughed and swigged his beer. "I see. Got more than you bargained for, did you, Charles?"

Charles flushed.

The chief laced his fingers and used them to prop up his neck. "The Grande Saline is a fascinating region of Saint Barthelemy. You are familiar with it, Charles?"

"Not very."

"My family has lived here, in the shadow of the Morn de Grand Fond, for many generations. My father worked the salt marsh. So did I," he said proudly, "as a boy. We all helped out then. Had to, if we wanted to survive."

Charles nodded.

"The salt marsh had been formed in a natural lowland between the hills. Locals had built a canal three hundred meters long from the ocean to the low region in which they had built squares to contain the saltwater."

Chief Lebon gestured with his glass-filled hand. "The canal was opened to the sea at high tide and closed every low tide. When the marsh was filled with seawater, all the locals in the countryside were asked to pitch in to collect the salt. This was done with baskets called gabaras, flat boxes installed within the squares."

He paused, as if to let this information sink into Charles brain. "It was back breaking work, son. The salt was collected on the walls until each square was finished. Afterwards, the harvested salt was moved to high ground near the beach where it was drained and washed clean by the rain.

"A schooner then made the trip from Gustavia to Saline to collect the salt for markets in Guadaloupe and Martinique. The salt had to be hauled out to the schooner in canoes."

"Why did they stop?"

The chief shrugged. "Economics. The cost had become too great and the profits too small."

"I see."

Chief Lebon rose. "Well, I must go. We are having a little dinner party Sunday evening—my wife's idea—and I've promised to help prepare the house and clean up the yard." He shook his head sadly. "Sometimes I wish I had a son to help out." He held out his hand. "Good luck with your investigation, Charles. Please, keep me informed and if there is anything you need the assistance of my men for, do not hesitate to request it."

"Yes, sir."

The chief trod down the concrete steps and stopped. "Say, here's a thought. Why don't you come by for dinner on Sunday afternoon, Charles?"

"Me, sir?"

The chief made a face.

"I mean, Didier."

"That's better. See you Sunday, Charles. Come early. We'll have a drink. Third turn-off on the right." He pointed. "It is the house at the end of the road."

Well, thought Charles, the chief was an awfully decent fellow.

No sooner had Chief Lebon disappeared from sight when Jean-Marc Bouton and his mate, Henri Leclerc, showed up on the steps of *La Belle Saline*.

"Hey, hey!" called Henri, "look who's here, monsieur *le gendarme. Bonjour*, Charles."

"Hello," replied Charles, rather stiffly. He was much relieved to see the two men wore shirts and pants.

"Having a beer, eh?" Henri pulled up a chair at Charles' table. "Great minds think alike, don't they, JM?"

Jean-Marc unlocked a smile. "Yes. Mind if we join you?"

"Actually, I was about to leave," said Charles. "I am pressed for time."

"Oh, come on, it's only one more beer. Who doesn't have time for that?"

"Sure," said Jean-Marc, taking the seat on the opposite side of the gendarme. "Besides, I feel like I owe you."

"Owe me?"

"Sure," said Jean-Marc. He turned to the waitress and ordered three beers. "I wasn't very pleasant back there. I apologize. I'm just not used to the police interrogating me, you know? I reacted badly."

"That's all right," answered Charles. "It is an understandable reaction."

"*Oui*," added Henri. "Especially when a fellow is hanging out at the beach on his day off. JM's got a bit of a short temper at times, but he's usually a laid back kind of guy. Live and let live, you know what I mean, Charles?"

Charles nodded.

"Guilty, as charged," Jean-Marc admitted, raising his right hand. When he lifted it again it held a beer which he drained quickly. He ordered another round, though Charles had barely touched his drink.

"Go ahead," said Henri to his buddy, "tell Charles what you told me."

"Well, it may be nothing," Jean-Marc said, laying his hands across the table. "And I don't want to get anyone in trouble. . ."

"Yes?"

"Come on," urged Henri. "Spill it."

"Well, it's like this, Charles. I got to thinking back there after you left." He nervously pushed his fingers through his sun-bleached hair. "And there is someone else that I remember seeing around the villa the morning of Bobbi Freon's death."

"Yes?"

"*Oui*. It was that housekeeper of his."

Charles' choked on his beer. "Housekeeper?"

"Yeah," he snapped his fingers. "What's her name?" Jean-Marc looked at Henri for help. Henri could only shrug.

"Sofie Somers?" asked Charles, the corners of his eyes narrowing.

"Yes, that's her. But I'm sure she didn't have anything to do with Freon's murder," Jean-Marc quickly added.

"When precisely did you see Mademoiselle Somers?" Charles asked slowly.

"Well," Jean-Marc scratched his chin, "it must have been a bit after that other fellow left."

"Roberto Bell?"

Jean-Marc nodded.

"And how did you see her exactly?"

"I was headed up the hill. Saw her come out the front of

Villa Onyx. Holding a beachbag."

"I see," said Charles. The words came out like the sound of air leaving a balloon. "You are certain it was she?"

"Oh, yeah. I even said hello." He sipped from his second glass, then said, "It was her, all right."

Charles thanked the two men for the beer and departed.

"Now," said Henri, "that wasn't so hard, was it? Don't you feel better?"

Jean-Marc was all smiles. "*Oui.* I do."

"You've kept your end of the bargain. Now make sure she keeps up her end."

"I intend to," Jean-Marc said firmly.

Henri laughed and raised his mug. "To success!"

Jean-Marc joined him in a toast. Good fortune was coming his way.

Charles stopped for gas at the filling station in L'Orient, near the cemetery. There were only two gas stations on Saint Barthelemy and the other, nearer the airport, would be closed for the afternoon, like most shops and businesses.

What Jean-Marc had told Charles troubled him immensely. He was certain Sofie had had nothing to do with her employer's death, but if she had been in the villa, why had she not told him? Perhaps, like Jean-Marc, she simply wanted to avoid any uncomfortable implications. He seemed to be running into a lot of that.

It was certainly possible that she could have popped into the villa briefly and never even been aware of what was going on in Freon's separate suite. It wasn't directly visible from her room. Then again, she may have simply forgotten that she'd been in the villa near the time of Freon's murder. She was in and out of Villa Onyx perhaps dozens of times per day.

Returning to his boat, Charles found Thor sitting on an

overturned bucket at the curb, much like a forlorn pet waiting to be fed.

"Hello, Thor," said Charles.

"*Bonjour*, Charles," Thor replied with a twinge of sadness.

"What's up? Something wrong?"

Thor shrugged. "It's my cat."

"Elephant?" Charles joined the old man at the curb.

"Yes. The veterinarian, Coont, tells me my *petit chat* is dying."

"Dying? I'm sorry. What's wrong with him?"

"It's his kidneys. I don't know exactly what's going on. Thieving doctor uses every fancy word he can think of or think up." Thor shook his head. "Something to do with Elephant's kidneys. Says he won't last more than a few months."

"Isn't there anything you can do?"

"*Non, rien.*" Thor squeezed his knees. "If only I could. If only I had the funds."

"Funds for what?"

"The operation that Coont says will keep Elephant alive." Thor shot to his feet. "Twelve hundred Euros? Can you believe that?"

Charles whistled. "That's a lot of money."

Thor nodded. "Damn cat. I never wanted no cat anyway. The useless beast thing followed me home from the harbor one afternoon. He wasn't no more than a kitten."

Thor held out his hands. "This big, he was. Followed me all the way up the hill to my house. I told him not to. I told him a hundred times that I didn't have much. That I couldn't take care of him proper. Couldn't feed him right.

"But that conniving cat followed me all the way to my door. Probably figured me for an easy touch, you know? Trying to get some food out of me." Thor shrugged. "What could I do?"

Charles said nothing.

"I mean, I had to let him in, didn't I? What choice did I have."

"None, I suppose," said Charles.

"None. That's right. I fed him scraps of tuna. I didn't have anything else. Gave him some warm milk. I had to go out on a charter, so I chased him out the door. You know what I told him?"

Charles shook his head.

"I told him, 'Listen, I've got to go, but if you're here when I get back, you can stay. If you're gone, well, good luck.' Then I went to work. When I came home it was dark. I didn't see the cat. And I figured he'd gone off in search of richer pastures. But you know what?"

Charles could only shake his head again.

"The minute I opened my door, that cat ran inside." Thor laughed and rubbed the corner of his eye. "Like he owned the place! Haven't been able to get rid of that damn cat since." Thor stepped into the street. "See you, Charles."

"*Au revoir*." Charles watched as the old man shuffled to the other side of Rue Jeanne d'Arc. The old sailor's story had touched him. "Wait a moment."

Thor stopped. A driver honked her horn.

Charles pulled Thor out of the street. "I'll give you the money."

"What?"

"I will give you the money for Elephant's operation."

"No, you're joking." Thor grabbed Charles' arms.

"No, I wouldn't joke about a thing like this. I have the money. That is, I can get it at the bank Monday." Twelve hundred Euros, it was practically all the savings Charles possessed.

Thor was crying. "You are very generous, my son. Very generous. I will never forget you. Elephant will never forget you. Wait until I tell him!" Thor raced across the street and started up the hill. Turning back, he hollered. "I'm going to pay you back for this, Charles! Pay you back with interest!"

15

Linda Patterson lay sunning herself beside the pool, completely unprepared for Sofie Somers' attack.

"Just what do you think you are doing?"

Linda opened one eye and looked at the fuming woman. "Taking some sun. Relaxing. You should try it, Sofie."

"Try it?" Sofie clenched her hands. "I've had a call from one of Bobbi's lawyers. He tells me that you and the others are planning to take over the company."

"Shit." Linda sat up and put on her shirt. She rose and crossed to the bar.

Sofie followed. "Is it true?"

Linda ordered a glass of wine. "I ask you, what sort of a world is this we are living in when you can't even trust a friggin' shark? Who was it?"

Sofie Somers said nothing.

"Baker? He always did have a thing for you, didn't he?"

"Never mind. It doesn't matter who it was. Is what I've heard true?"

Linda drummed her nails on the bar. This was accompanied by a sigh. "Listen, Sofie, it's nothing personal.

But I have to look out for myself—for my child." Then, more firmly she said, "For Bobbi's child."

"Bobbi promised me that he would take care of me—provide for me and the children, no matter what."

"And now Bobbi is dead. Rest his soul. And it's everyone for his or her self. Now, if I were you, I'd be thinking about packing up. Bobbi Freon Enterprises isn't going to be keeping up the tab on Villa Onyx for you indefinitely, you know."

But Sofie wasn't through with her yet. "It isn't going to be that easy, Linda. I can get lawyers, too. It may take time, but I'm going to fight you on this. Bobbi promised me!"

"If you need any help with your bags, let me know. I'll send a bellman." With that, Linda turned her back on the other woman.

Sofie glared at the back of Linda's head as if it would cause it to explode. When it did not, she turned heel and departed. No, Linda Patterson and the others were not going to get away with it.

Not without a fight.

Linda Patterson hollered at the bartender. "Get me a telephone, would you!"

He hurriedly placed a phone beside her.

She dialed the Carl Gustaf and demanded to be put through to Robert Bell's room.

"Yes?"

"It's me."

"What are you calling here for?" asked Bell.

"She's heard about our deal."

"What! How?"

"That's right. Heard it from some lawyer friend of hers in the company, if you want my opinion."

"Damn."

"Damn is right. You can tell your buddy Pena all about it. And tell him to put some muscle into this thing. We need to get everything all legal-like before all hell breaks loose."

There was a pause at the other end.

"Are you there, Bell?"

"Yes, I'm here."

"Well?" There was a current of exasperation running through her voice.

"I'm thinking. Everything is getting screwed up on this thing. Nothing is going like it's supposed to."

"Yes, well, while you're thinking, do some doing. Like do something about Sofie Somers. And find out who's leaking our secrets."

Linda hung up, leaving Bell to stare at the dead receiver with nothing but his own agitated and angry thoughts to bear his company.

Not having a telephone attached to his boat, Charles walked to the corner. He placed a call to the Villa Onyx. There was no answer. He left a message for Sofie to call him. He hoped she'd be free for dinner.

Next, he telephoned the Gendarmerie Nationale headquarters. "*Bonjour*, Ronalphe. It's me, Charles."

Gendarme Sadjan began laughing. "So, loverboy, have a good night?"

"Oh, cut it out," replied Charles.

"Now, now. I know. You are only doing your duty. The adjutant is always telling us we should be nice to the tourists, make them welcome. Tell me, Charles—how many times did you make the Mademoiselle Somers welcome last night?" With that, the gendarme let loose an annoying guffaw, sounding much like a braying donkey.

Charles ignored his comrade's jests. "Is Adjutant Bruyer

about? I need to speak with him."

"About what? Don't you know how everything works? Need help figuring out the plumbing?"

Charles could hear the others giggling in the background and making animalish noises. He pushed the phone away from his ear until they ceased. "Listen, Ronalph. This is a murder investigation. That's all. I'm trying to determine whether or not the letter opener I gave you is the murder weapon."

Gendarme Sadjan sighed. "Oh, alright. I'd say it probably is, Charles. At least, that's the initial word. Adjutant Bruyer is not here. He's gone to St. Martin. He left word that he would return late in the afternoon tomorrow. He wants to see you then."

"But that's Sunday."

"That's your problem, monsieur detective. The adjutant said you are to make yourself available to him for dinner."

"But I'm having dinner with Chief Lebon—"

"Did you say Chief Lebon?"

"Yes."

"That is where you are to meet the adjutant. He's dining with the chief of police as well. Sounds like you're moving up in the world, Charles. Leaving us poor, lowly gendarmes behind. Until then, don't forget, you are due to stand duty tonight."

"Tonight? I'm not scheduled to be at headquarters tonight. I've made plans." At least, he intended to make plans.

"No, but I am."

"So?"

"Aren't you forgetting?"

"Forgetting what?"

"You owe me. It's Saturday and I plan on having some

fun of my own. You're not the only one who knows how to have a good time."

Charles reluctantly acceded.

"Oh, and there is one other thing, Charles," added Ronalph. "The adjutant said to tell you to be very careful when handling evidence."

"I'm always careful," grumbled Charles.

"Yes, well, next time," sniggered Sadjan, before ringing off, "use a condom!"

"Hi, Lily!" Jean-Marc sauntered into the lobby like he owned the place, rather than cleaned its swimming pools.

Lily, who was polishing the ornamental mirrors to fill the hours during an unusually slow time, turned around. "Hello, Jean-Marc. What brings you here on your day off?"

"Lily!" Jean-Marc ran to Lily and grabbed her gently by the shoulders. "What has happened to you?"

"Nothing." Lily extricated herself from Jean-Marc's grasp.

"*Pardonnes-moi* for saying so, but you look terrible—awful!"

She scowled. "Gee, thanks so much." She looked away.

He pulled her around by the chin and looked into her eyes. "You've been crying."

"No." She grabbed his hand to push it away but he didn't let go.

"Yes." Jean-Marc pulled her to the bench against the wall and forced her to sit. "Tell me, what's wrong? What's happened?"

"Nothing. It's only—" She bit her nails. "Oh, it's nothing. Just man trouble. What is it with men, anyway, Jean-Marc?"

He patted her leg. "Don't tell me. Something went wrong with Charles last evening?"

"Everything went wrong with Charles last evening. He is

a beast. I hate him."

"What?" Jean-Marc grinned. "I cannot believe it. I saw him only this afternoon. He seemed quite pleasant to me."

"You saw Charles?"

"Yes, that's correct."

"Where?"

"At the Grande Saline."

"What on earth was he doing there? Sunbathing?"

Jean-Marc laughed. "Hardly. He had some questions for me about Bobbi Freon's death."

"For you? Whatever for?"

Jean-Marc shrugged. "He's questioning everybody around here. It's his job, I guess."

Lily sighed.

"He spoke quite highly of you." He patted her thigh once more. "I think he's really quite fond of you, Lily." Jean-Marc believed a small white lie was not a sin but a duty if it resulted in or reinforced another's happiness. Truthfully, the gendarme had said little about Lily, but how could the fellow not be fond of her? She was such a lovely, sweet girl.

"He did?" Her voice was filled with disbelief.

"He did."

"Humph. And did he also tell you that he slept with Sofie Somers last night?"

"*Nom de Dieu!*" Jean-Marc shook his head. "I don't believe it. After his date with you?"

"He never showed up for his date with me," replied Lily, her voice as cutting as battery acid.

"And you know for a fact that he slept with Sofie Somers?" This would be interesting news indeed.

"Well—"

"Yes?"

"I saw him coming out of Villa Onyx quite late."

Jean-Marc looked unconvinced. "Did Charles see you also?"

"*Oui.*"

"And what did he say?"

She shrugged her soft shoulders. "He said he was working."

Jean-Marc clutched his bare knees. "So. He was interrogating the woman, Lily. His job, *non?*"

"I suppose." She sounded reluctant to agree. "But what about our broken date?"

Jean-Marc nodded. "That is another thing. He should have apologized. A man must treat a woman with respect. If he does not, he is a cad. Gendarme or not, I will not let him insult you so. I will speak with him for you."

"Well, he did say he was sorry."

"Ah. Then you must forgive him and give him a second chance."

Lily was shaking her head. "I don't know."

"Come, Lily, you like him, don't you?"

She shrugged.

"Think he is handsome?"

She grinned, then lowered her eyes as if embarrassed by her unspoken admission.

"Then you must give your man a second chance."

She hesitated, then said, "I'll think about it."

"That's a girl," said Jean-Marc. He gave her a peck on the cheek. He rose. "Now, I must go. I am searching for Mademoiselle Somers, myself, in fact. She is not in her villa. Have you seen her?"

"That woman?" Lily's voice frosted over once more. "*Non,* I have not. What do you want with her, anyway, Jean-Marc? She is not your type."

Jean-Marc helped himself to a small, wrapped candy on

Lily's desk and tossed the cellophane in the trash. "I only want to chat her up a bit. Keep on her good side." He rolled the little pastille around on his tongue.

"Whatever for?"

"You know I want to be a fashion model. She has contacts. She can help me. I will not," Jean-Marc said adamantly, "clean swimming pools for a living the rest of my life. I want a chance to model." He ran his hands down his sides. "While I've got the looks for it."

"Well, I haven't seen her all day," Lily replied. "And I hope I never see her again."

"Now, now, Lily. Your jealousy is unbecoming. And," he added, "completely unnecessary. Go. Talk to Charles. Give him a second chance."

Jean-Marc stopped outside the door and spun on his heels. He held up a finger. "One more chance. No more, no less."

Lily nodded.

Jean-Marc completed his circle and disappeared.

Charles sat at his makeshift desk, poring through his notes. There really was not much new. He was grasping at straws. And a bed of straw, under the stars of Afghanistan, was in his future, he feared.

However, with luck, there would be some fingerprints found on the letter opener. If there were traces of blood that then matched Bobbi Freon's, the case would conclude quickly and simply and he could go back to concentrating on completing the work on his sailboat.

All he could do was to hope for the best. He looked at the clock over the counter. It was nearly seven. Sofie would be arriving soon. He'd finally reached her at the hotel and she had promised to drop by as Charles himself was unable to get away.

Charles was grateful that he was the only officer on duty. Technically, three men were required to reside at the Gendarmerie at all times, and this usually led to several of his comrades being in attendance at all times. Sometimes with their wives or girlfriends. But, as the adjutant was away and one of their mates was having a party at his girlfriend's house up in L'Oignon, this was not a time for technicalities.

Charles turned his head at the sound of the front door being opened. It was Sofie. His pulse quickened.

"*Bonsoir.*"

"Good evening," replied Charles, letting Sofie through to the back. She smelled as if she belonged on the seventh cloud of Heaven and looked alluring in a sparkling blue gown with matching open-toe heels.

She kissed his cheek. "So, this is where you work."

"Yes," said Charles. "It isn't much, I know. We are renovating at the moment."

Sofie nodded and ran her hand along a yellow bar erected in the corner. It had blue painted trim and a thick, nautical rope ran along the top edge. There was a reasonable painting of a diving swordfish on the front of the bar, beside a compass point. Behind this, the image of the island of Saint Barthelemy was itself outlined in blue.

Over the bar, a fishing net with a life preserver resting inside it had been hung on carpenter's nails. The caption on the white life preserver read, *Bienvenue A Bord.* The French flag hung from the left end of the bar. "Interesting."

"It was the adjutant's idea. Something to cheer up the men."

"I'll bet," Sofie said. "Can I get a drink, barkeep?"

Charles found a bottle and poured two glasses of wine. Sofie had gone into one of the two small jail cells which were part of the building. "The light doesn't seem to work," she said, flipping the switch back and forth.

"No, the bulbs are out. Part of the renovation." He handed Sofie her drink.

The dimly lit cell had a small, double row of glass blocks, three across. Below this was a cement sleeping platform with a wooden slat mattress. The walls were white. The floor was gray. "Not too cozy."

"No," concurred Charles, standing closely behind her, admiring the curve of her neck.

She sat on the sleeping platform. "I wouldn't want to spend a night on this thing."

"There are pads, I believe. Mattresses. We don't often have guests."

Sofie laughed. "With accommodations like these, I am not surprised." She set her glass down on the crude bed. "Come, sit beside me, Charles."

Charles joined her.

"You know, it's almost romantic here." She laced her fingers through his.

"You think so?" Charles had never thought of the jail cells in quite that way.

"Umm-hmm. Especially the lovely glow from those glass bricks. It's very romantic. But you should really add some curtains. Red, I would suggest. And candles. You must have candles."

Charles laughed.

Sofie looked up at Charles with eyes that stopped his heart. "Or perhaps," she said, pulling herself closer, "it is only you that make it seem so romantic."

She placed her warm lips on his and Charles felt himself on fire. He pushed his hand up under her dress, sliding up her silken thigh. She gently but surely pushed him away. "The children are with a sitter. We have all night, Charles."

Charles gulped, feeling he'd made a fool of himself.

Sofie held up her glass. "Bring me another, please?"

Charles returned, with the bottle this time. He refilled their glasses.

"And how goes your investigation?"

"I am awaiting word on the letter opener discovered at Villa Onyx. You know, it would never have been discovered if it had not been for Tony and his toy. If it turns out to be the murder weapon, Tony will have helped to 'crack the case' as you Americans say."

"I'll tell him you said so. He'll be happy to hear it. He likes you, you know."

"I like him. Cleo, too."

They were silent for several minutes and then Sofie said, "I worry about you, Charles."

"Worry?"

"Yes. Do you ever think about the future? You work so hard. Will you always be a gendarme?"

"I don't know. I suppose I haven't really thought that far off." He shook his head. "I don't know."

"Don't you want to get married someday? Have children?"

"Yes. I think so."

"But aren't you always moving about, going from one country to another on your assignments?"

"*Oui*," Charles said with a sigh, "three years here and then three years there. That's the life of a gendarme."

Sofie leaned her head against his chest. "That could get lonely."

Yes, thought Charles, it could.

Lily packed a picnic basket with wine, cheese, bread, and

fruit. She borrowed linen napkins and fine silverware from the Idyllique's kitchen, promising to return it the next day.

"Go, help yourself, Lily," said the chef, a fatherly fellow who enjoyed eating as much as he enjoyed cooking. And he was not immune to the bliss of amour. He insisted she take two cherry tarts for dessert.

"Thank you, Stefan." She kissed the head chef on his cheek and he flushed with joy.

Lily strapped the picnic basket to her motorscooter and sped off towards the Gendarmerie. She'd asked around and heard that it was on the road between Corossol and Public. Going quickly, she'd managed to miss it the first time she swept down the long, narrow, unlit road.

Coming back more slowly, Lily caught sight of a military-looking blue vehicle with a blue light on its roof, parked in a concrete drive leading up to a two-storied building and pulled in.

Beside the official vehicle sat a sedan, a rental from one of the agencies down at the airport, no doubt, by the look of it. She'd noticed Charles' motorscooter parked along the side of the Gendarmerie as she rolled to a stop.

She unhooked her basket, checked her face in the little mirror she kept in her purse and went to the door. The rooms out front were dark, but she could see some lights on further back. The door was not locked.

Lily smiled. Imagine Charles' surprise when he sees me, she thought, slowly inching open the door and tiptoeing inside.

She leaned over the counter. There was no one in view and she heard nothing. Just maybe some faint sounds coming from somewhere further back. Perhaps Charles was here alone. It was perfect.

And Jean-Marc had been right. She should not have

prejudged Charles. Perhaps he had only been working, questioning Mademoiselle Somers. The woman obviously had something to hide. And even if she didn't, well, she certainly wasn't Charles' type. Besides all that, Jean-Marc had said that Charles told him that he was fond of her!

Lily let herself behind the front counter, her purse over her left shoulder, clutching the basket in her right hand. Where on earth was everyone?

Lily crept further in. Each office she passed was empty. A faint rustling sound caught her attention. It came from the direction of the light further back. Perhaps Charles' office was back there. She unbuttoned the top two buttons of her blouse and fluffed up her hair, hung a smile on her face. She wanted Charles' impression of her to be pleasant and alluring. Definitely alluring.

Lily squeezed the handle of her picnic basket and turned the corner. Her mouth went dry. Charles was sitting in the dark, wrapped in an embrace with Sofie Somers who looked to have her tongue down his throat.

"Charles!" Lily raised the picnic basket and hurled it with all her heart and all her might.

Charles opened his eyes just in time to see the basket explode against the cell wall, spilling bread, cheese and fruit into the air and over the floor. A bottle of wine clattered against the floor then popped, leaking red wine like it was blood from a dying man. "Lily!"

Lily gripped the door and slammed it. "I hate you!"

"Lily!" He pulled the door. "Hey, Lily, the door is stuck." He kicked the base of the door. "Lily, come on!"

"Well, well," said Sofie.

Charles spun around.

"What was that all about?" She rose. "Don't tell me you have a girlfriend, Charles?"

Charles pulled his hair, banged his head against the cell door. The stuck door chose that moment to pop loose and Charles tumbled to the ground on his behind, slipping in a puddle of wine and soggy French bread.

"Cheer up, Charles. It could have been worse."

He looked at Sofie with eyes filled with expectation.

"We could have still been locked up in here when your fellow gendarmes and even your adjutant himself returned." She stepped over Charles and headed for the exit.

"Where are you going?"

"I think I'd better leave. Call me when you have an explanation for—" she waved her hand in the air, grasping for words, "this."

"But Lily—"

Sofie placed her hands on her hips and glared at him.

"I mean, Sofie." Charles struggled to rise, grabbing a chair for support.

"Goodnight, Charles."

Charles nodded and hung his head, listening to the sounds of Sofie fading away. His uniform was ruined. His night was ruined. And how will I explain this mess, he thought, shaking his head sadly. He touched his head. There was cherry tart in his hair.

He headed to the broom closet where the towels and mops were kept. Saturday night in paradise and here he stood, mopping up one mess; unsure of how to deal with yet another.

And all because he was charged to solve a murder case that he had no business or interest in pursuing.

16

Charles stifled a yawn. It had been a long, difficult night. Ronalphe and the other gendarmes had returned to headquarters so late that Charles had ended up sleeping at his makeshift desk. His back was resentful and shot him little reminders of pain with each bounce in the road.

Rolling to a stop, he found Thor standing under his sailboat, a gaping hole in its side. "What's happened?" cried Charles.

"Not to worry. Thor held a saw in his hands. I noticed a few loose boards. I'll have her fixed up in no time. Mixed up a fresh batch of my special sealant for you, as well."

"But—"

"You know, you really should get this old girl in the water." He patted the sailboat affectionately. "She needs it. Not good to leave a boat grounded too long."

"Yes, I'm certain you're right, Thor, but I've still got an awful lot of work to do on her."

"That may be, that may be. But let's seal her up and get her in the water. Then you can take your time on the rest of it. Trust me, it's the thing to do."

Charles scratched his chin and yawned yet again. "I suppose you're right."

"Of course, I'm right. Trust me. I know the sea and I know boats."

Charles nodded.

"Once I've got these boards refitted I'll seal her up. I'd give it three days and then we can rechristen this old girl." Thor dropped his saw and grabbed up a bottle of water that lay against the fence. He took a long drink. "Have you got a name in mind for her, Charles?"

Charles twisted his lips. "No. No, I haven't really given it any thought." However, Afghan Bound, sounded like it might be appropriate.

"Well, just you let me know, Charles. I noticed the stern's pretty clean. When you've thought up a proper name, I'll paint her on for you." He laid his hand on Charles' shoulder. "A boat's got to have a proper name."

"I know," Charles said, his voice tired. His eyes sore as the sunlight dried them out like grapes on their way to becoming raisins.

"It's unlucky not to."

"Why are you doing all this, Thor? I mean, it's an awful lot of work and trouble. I should be doing all this myself."

Thor grinned, revealing two rows of uneven, nicotine stained teeth. "I want to. Besides, you've been good to me. I want to repay you with more than money. This is the least I can do for you."

"It really isn't necessary, Thor. And don't worry about the money. I've no use for it. Not right now."

A tear came to the old man's eye. "You're a gentleman, Charles. A gentleman. Elephant and I will never forget what you've done for us."

Charles couldn't help thinking just how untrue those

words of Thor's were—all one had to do was to ask Sofie Somers or Lily Vineuil. They'd have a difference of opinion to be sure. "How is Elephant?"

Thor grinned. "He's at the vet's now, poor thing. Coonts says he wants to fill him up with fluids, vitamins and the such before the operation." Thor's face took on a sober look. "That's tomorrow morning."

Charles expressed his good wishes for a successful operation.

Thor shrugged off his concern. "Coont may be a *canard*, but I've heard he knows what he's doing. Old lady Marigot told me her cat had a similar problem three years ago and that old tabby of hers is still running around the island leaving his disgusting hairballs wherever he goes."

Charles allowed himself a laugh. It felt good.

"Say," said Thor, "what happened to your uniform? And what's that in your hair, blood?"

Charles touched his scalp. "No, cherries."

"Cherries?"

"I had a little trouble with some food," Charles replied rather cryptically, hoping Thor would let the subject drop.

"What sort of trouble? Did your dinner attack you or did you simply forget how to hold your fork?"

"Very funny. Actually, if you must know, it was woman trouble."

Thor smiled. "Ah. Now I understand. It looks like you have found yourself a very passionate woman. Trust me, Charles, that is a good thing. A very, very good thing. A woman who is passionate in her life is passionate in her bed."

"Yes, well, I wouldn't know about that. Besides, this involved two women!"

"*Nom de Dieu!*" cried Thor. "You are the scamp!"

"No, no. It was nothing like that." Charles relieved

himself of his story. And he had to admit, it felt good having someone to express himself to, even when that person was an eccentric old seadog.

Thor listened carefully and did not reply until Charles had finished. "Sounds like you've screwed up big time."

"What do you think I should do?"

Thor shrugged. "What do you want to do?"

"Crawl in a hole and cover myself up."

Thor chuckled. "I don't blame you. But that won't work. Someone would only dig you out again. No, Charles, what you must do is apologize."

"Sure," said Charles, "but to whom?"

"To them both, Charles. To Mademoiselle Vineuil for what you did to her and to Mademoiselle Somers for what you put her through."

"Yes, you're right. But then what?"

"Then?" Thor patted Charles on the back. "We must let hearts beat."

"What's that supposed to mean?"

"It means that hearts will go the way they go. We cannot control their beating. Each heart follows its own destiny."

"That's true." Thor was wiser than he looked. Charles could only do his best to make things up with both women. After that, things must go the way they will. "That's good advice. Thank you. Once I've cleaned up, I will do just that."

"Excellent," said Thor. "Oh, and there is one other thing."

"Yes?"

"After you've apologized to the Mademoiselle Vineuil—"

"Yes?"

"Duck."

Charles left Thor doubled over with laughter and climbed up into his sailboat for a change of uniform.

"What is it with women?" Jorge exhorted, slamming down the phone, picking up his drink and slamming down his whiskey.

Elina pressed her hands down on her husband's shoulders, loosening the knots that threatened to strangle him. "What's gone wrong now?"

"Bell tells me that Somers woman is causing trouble."

"What sort of trouble could she cause?"

Jorge twisted his neck and glared at his wife. "All sorts of trouble. She's threatening to bring in lawyers of her own."

"Darling, I'm sure you can out-lawyer her any day of the week."

He pushed free of his wife and rose. "Yes, but you know how these things go. The more lawyers get involved the more things get complicated, strung out. And the more things get drawn out, the more screwed up they get until no one ends up getting what they want."

Elina wrapped her arms around her husband's portly waist. One hand fell between his legs. "And just what do you want, baby?"

Jorge ignored her earthly supplications. "I want that bitch out of the way."

"And just how will you manage that trick? By killing her?"

Jorge smiled an evil smile. "No. That might only complicate matters all the more."

Elina raised an eyebrow.

"I'll pay her off. She wants money and I'll give it to her. Just so long as she plays the game my way." He chewed on his lips a moment. "I'll need cash. No one can resist cold, hard cash. I'll have to fly to the Caymans to get it."

"Now?" Elena's hand stroked the inside of his thigh.

He lowered his eyes to his crotch. "Now? Oh no," he said, softly stroking his wife's hair, "I never leave in the middle of a game."

Looking smug, Elina pressed her lips to his as her hand looked for something to hold onto.

With great trepidation, Charles tiptoed into the lobby of the Idyllique, picnic basket in hand. Its handle was broken and one corner had caved in. Charles had tossed out the food. The basket contained linen and silver. The linen, which he he had tried unsuccessfully to wash, were wine and cherry stained.

Lily looked up at him from her desk and he winced as if expecting a sharp blow. She pulled some sort of fashion magazine from her side drawer and began furiously turning the pages.

Charles set the picnic basket down soundlessly on the desk. "I wanted to return your basket."

Flip-flip-thwack went the pages, flying by as if she was watching a nickelodeon.

Lily looked at the basket with disgust. "Not in very good shape, is it?" she said sharply.

Charles opened his mouth to respond that it was not at all his fault, but quickly realized that reminding Lily that her throwing the basket at the cell wall was the reason it was broken was perhaps not a good idea. "I'm sorry. I tried washing out the napkins. I'm afraid the stains would not come out."

Lily picked up a pen and, using the tip, lifted one of the serviettes from the basket. The white napkin was blotchy and red, as if it had caught a poisonous rash. "Lovely."

Flip-flip-thwack. She returned to her magazine. "Well, if there is nothing else, gendarme, I am quite busy."

Charles fiddled with the broken basket handle, wishing somehow he could fix it. Wishing he could somehow fix things between Lily and himself.

But he could not.

He turned to leave.

"She doesn't love you, you know."

Charles twirled. "What?"

"She doesn't love you. She could never love you. Not a woman like that."

Charles turned about, stepped into the sun.

Lily's words followed him like an extra shadow. "A woman like that would never fall for a lowly gendarme!"

These words echoed in his ears long after he'd gone, left Lily far behind.

Charles found Chief Lebon's residence without much difficulty. The chief's home was a rambling affair set back against the hills. Wide gardens buffeted it along each side. The walls had been painted bright yellow. The wooden shutters were blue and red.

It was not at all the type of house Charles had been expecting it to be. Adjutant Bruyer's was parked on the dirt drive. Charles left his motorscooter beside it and crossed to the expansive front porch which boasted a settee, two chairs and a rocker. All were empty.

He heard voices inside and knocked on the edge of the screen door. The scent of lobster and bouillabaisse wafted through the screen.

A man's voice called from within, "Come! Come!"

Charles entered.

Chief Lebon stuck his head around the corner. "*Bonjour*, Charles." He stepped forward and shook the gendarme's hand. His other held a beer. "Welcome to my home."

"It's quite lovely," said Charles.

"Speaking of lovely," Chief Lebon placed a guiding hand

on Charles shoulder and led him through to the living room, "I would like you to meet my daughters."

Entering the large room bursting with comfortable, utilitarian looking furniture, Charles first caught sight of his adjutant. "*Bonsoir*, monsieur."

"Hello," said the adjutant, rising slowly from his chair and squeezing Charles' hand. Adjutant Bruyer's eyes were slightly glassy. No doubt he'd been enjoying himself. There was an empty glass of beer on the table beside his chair.

"How was your trip, monsieur?"

"*Tres bien*," replied Adjutant Bruyer, slowly releasing his grip on Charles. "You did well discovering that letter opener, Trenet."

"It was the murder weapon, then?"

"Oh, yes," said the adjutant with a nod of his head.

Charles brightened. "Then perhaps this entire investigation will come to a close quickly?"

Adjutant Bruyer was shaking his head. "I'm afraid there are no prints on the thing. At least, no usable ones. It had been wiped fairly clean—with the sock you found it in."

"So the letter opener does us no good," said Charles, crestfallen.

"It tells us precisely how Monsieur Freon was killed. That's something." He pulled Charles aside. "You'll have to go back to Villa Onyx. Maybe climb up on the roof again, see what else might have been missed."

Charles didn't look forward to standing on that high, sharply angled rooftop again, but understood he had no choice in the matter. "I will do it right away, adjutant."

"You'll do it tomorrow," said Chief Lebon, cutting into the conversation. "Now," he pulled Charles along, "let me introduce you to my lovely daughter, Rose."

The young woman resting on the sofa beside a uniformed

municipal officer smiled and held out her hand.

"It is a pleasure to meet you," said Charles.

"Thank you, monsieur."

"And this is my husband, Pisar."

Charles shook the gentleman's hand. "We've met, have we not?"

"Yes," said Pisar, "I am Pisar Mercer. Our paths crossed at the Idyllique."

"Ah, yes," Charles replied. "I remember."

A herd of small children stampeded past Charles, nearly knocking him to the ground.

"Our children," said Pisar, smiling weakly.

Rose called out, "Children, behave! You want someone to get hurt?"

Chief Lebon laughed. "Such youth! Such animation! It is a wonderful thing, is it not, Charles?"

Charles smiled in response. "How many children do you have, Pisar?"

The officer opened his mouth to speak but the chief jumped in. "Come along, Charles. I'll introduce you to my wife." He patted his well-spoiled gut. "She's prepared quite a meal for us. A true feast!"

They crossed a small hall and entered the kitchen. Steam rose from the stove.

"Elisabeth, I'd like you to meet Charles Trenet of the Gendarmerie."

A well-trimmed woman in a formal looking pink dress, covered for practical purposes with a gingham apron, turned, ladle in hand. She laid the spoon down atop a yellow trivet, wiped her hands carefully on her apron and said hello. "It is a pleasure to meet you, Charles."

"You also." Charles sniffed the air. "Dinner smells wonderful."

"*Merci.* It will be ready soon. Has Didier offered you a drink?"

"I was just about to," interjected the chief. "What will you have, Charles?"

"A beer would be fine."

"Beer it is." The chief pulled a bottle of beer from the fridge and filled two glasses. "To your health."

"And yours," replied Charles.

Elisabeth Lebon squeezed past her husband. "Now, if you don't mind, why don't you men go join the others and let me work." She patted her husband on the back. "You're getting in my way."

"Ah," beamed the chief, "I would not want to get in your way, especially when you are preparing such wonderful cuisine. My wife is an excellent cook, Charles and she teaches the girls as well." The chief kissed his fingertips. "They cook like angels, all of them."

"All of them?" said Charles. "I only saw the one."

"Yes, I have two daughters. The other—" The chief turned to his wife. "Say, where is Violette?"

"I think she's still upstairs," said Madame Lebon, tossing salt into a pot of boiling water.

"Upstairs, whatever for? We've company."

"She said she needed something in her room."

"Well," said the chief, "not to worry, she'll be down presently. He lowered his voice as they crossed the hall leading back to the living room. "Violette is even more lovely than my wife. But don't tell her I said that. I am surprised that no young man has snatched her up."

Charles didn't know what to say.

"Violette is very particular in the type of man she wants. Very discerning."

"I see." Charles was beginning to feel uncomfortable with

the direction of their conversation and was relieved when they were all seated back in the living room.

Adjutant Bruyer was relating a tale from his younger days, when he was in the *Groupe de Sécurité de la Présidence de la République*. He'd been assigned to protect the prime minister himself.

Charles chose a chair to one side of the room and listened with amusement. He'd heard the tale before but the adjutant never failed to give it a new twist. Charles wondered what new twist it might receive this evening. There was the sound of footsteps on the wooden stairs and, between the rails, Charles caught sight of a lovely pair of legs descending.

Chief Lebon rose. "Ah, my daughter, Violette."

Charles hastened to rise.

The young woman came fully into view.

"You!" she screamed.

Charles bowed; partly as a courtesy, partly to hide his pink face. The chief's daughter! He'd been barely civil to the girl when she'd delivered papers to him. He groaned. Why hadn't she said who she was? He forced himself to meet her gaze. After all, this was partly her fault. "*Bonjour*, mademoiselle."

Violette crossed the room and clutched her father. "What is *he* doing here?"

Chief Lebon looked from his daughter to Charles and back again, completely bewildered. "What is wrong, *ma petite fleur?*"

Violette broke free of her father and ran from the sitting room crying, "*Maman!*"

"What is the meaning of this, Trenet?" demanded Chief Lebon. "Have you defiled my daughter?"

"No, of course not!"

Adjutant Bruyer rose to Charles' defense. "Now, now, Didier, relax." He laid a calming hand on the chief's stiff shoulder. "Now, what's this all about, Charles?"

Charles frowned, sat. "It's nothing, really. I mean, she came to the Gendarmerie to bring some papers. I didn't know who she was." He turned to the chief. "She didn't say she was your daughter. She didn't even give me her name."

"Ahhh." Pisar was chuckling and Rose yelled at him to hush up. He did so quickly.

"Did you ask my daughter her name?" The chief stood above Charles like a skyscraper ready to fall on him with all its weight.

"*Non*, monsieur. I didn't think to. There was so much to do—" He turned to the adjutant for moral support. "I have been doing my best to solve this most difficult case."

"I still do not understand why her reaction to you is so strong—"

"I must say, Charles," said the adjutant, "neither do I."

"I-I may have been rather brusque with her," admitted Charles.

"Brusque?" Chief Lebon repeated with rising indignation.

Charles nodded forlornly. If only the hand of God would reach down and pluck him from here—set him down somewhere different, someplace safe; the beach per-haps—he'd promise to go to services every Sunday. He closed his eyes for a moment and prayed.

"Well," said the chief. He paced.

The room seemed suddenly small to Charles.

The chief stopped, stared at the gendarme. Everyone, even the adjutant himself, seemed to be holding their breath. Chief Lebon's right hand shot out. Charles braced himself for a blow to the face.

Would it be an open hand or a closed fist?

With great shock, Charles held still as the chief rubbed his head fondly. "You'd better apologize to Violette, don't you think, young man? Violette is not named for a flower for no reason. Both my daughters are as beautiful as they are delicate and, like the honeybee when she nears, we must touch them lightly and with respect."

Charles gulped. "*Oui,* monsieur." He rose and glanced at the adjutant who nodded. Charles knew where his duty lay. As he walked past the sofa he heard Pisar mumble. "*Pardon?*"

Pisar said, "Huh?"

"You said—"

Rose was glaring at her husband as if her face contained twice the heat of the sun. Sweat was beading up on the poor man's collar.

"I said nothing," Pisar responded quickly.

Charles took one last look at the others and then took off in search of Violette. He shook his head. He'd have sworn Pisar had said something like '*welcome to the family.*' In fact, he was certain of it. But what an odd thing for him to say.

He found Violette in the kitchen with her mother. She was chopping tomatoes with her back to him. He cleared his throat. "*Pardonnez-moi.*" Even to Charles, his voice sounded hesitant, unsure of itself.

Charles was relieved to see the girl's mother take the exquisitely sharp looking knife from her hand.

"Why don't you show Charles the garden before dinner, dear?"

"But, *Maman,*" complained Violette.

"Go," said Madame Lebon, giving her daughter a loving push out the door. "Charles is our guest." She turned to Charles with a smile. "And I'm sure he'd love to see the gardens before it gets dark. Wouldn't you, Charles?"

"Yes, of course," he replied.

Madame Lebon checked the cuckoo clock on the wall. The case had been handcrafted by an artisan from Monserrat who himself imported the inner mechanisms from a cousin in Switzerland. "Wonderful. There's still time before dinner. Off you go, now!"

Charles, reluctant as a herded calf separated from his mother, followed Violette out the kitchen door and onto the back porch. The chief's daughter wore a blue and white polka-dot dress with matching low-heeled blue shoes. The pearls around her neck made her look sophisticated beyond her obviously young years. She was a lovely kid. There was no doubt about that.

She seemed to have a bit of a temper though. A delicate flower or a thin-skinned, spoiled little daddy's girl? wondered Charles.

"Well," said Violette, without turning around to face him, "we might as well get this over with." She hopped off the porch to the garden path.

"Come on," she said wearily.

17

"What is it, Anna?" snapped Jorge Pena. The house-keeper hovered at the edge of the master suite, looking nervous.

"There's a gentleman to see you."

"So? Who is it? And what's he want? You know I don't like to be disturbed this late in the day."

"I know, monsieur, but he was quite insistent." Anna looked over her shoulder and wrung her hands.

"What is it, darling?" Elina called from the bath.

Jorge pulled his towel tighter about his waist. "Anna says we've a caller. I suppose I'll have to see who it is."

"Didn't he give a name?"

Jorge shot the housekeeper a scolding look. "Apparently not." He grabbed his bathrobe and tied it about his waist as he headed off. "I'll be right back, Elina." He addressed Anna. "Where is he?"

"In the entry hall, monsieur."

Jorge stomped off, barefooted, his feet slapping along the tiles like an overgrown baby's. Anna retreated to the kitchen.

A stranger in a dark suit was fingering an Ethiopian

statuette on a tall stand beside the main door. Nobody wears a suit in St. Barts. And this guy wasn't even sweating. What was his game?

"Can I help you?" demanded Jorge.

The tall man turned, apparently unfazed. His face was clean-shaven and his jaw looked hard. The fine cut of his suit couldn't conceal the fact that he was in obviously top physical condition. Jorge recognized the cut—the Brioni label—if he was not mistaken. It paid to know his competitors. "Mr. Martinelli wishes to see you."

"What?" Jorge took a step backwards. "Martinelli is here?"

The tall man nodded.

"In St. Barts?"

"He wishes to speak with you." The tall man gestured toward the door.

"Now?" Jorge eyed the henchman suspiciously.

"Yes, Mr. Pena. He is waiting on his yacht. Entertaining. He also said you may wish to bring your wife."

Jorge did some thinking. Mitch Martinelli made him look like a Boy Scout. Best to keep his wife out of this. "I'm afraid Elina isn't here."

"Then you will accompany me yourself." The cold, hard eyes made no sign of this having been a question.

"Of course," smiled Jorge. "I'll get changed and drive right down. What is the name of the yacht?"

"She is called Hard Luck. But it is not necessary for you to drive. I have brought a car and Mr. Martinelli has insisted that I be your chauffeur." The tall man was smiling, a chilling, lipless smile. "Mr. Martinelli does not want to cause you any inconvenience."

Jorge nodded. "That's very nice of him." He tugged at his bathrobe. "Give me a minute then to change. I'll be right with you."

"Of course." Martinelli's henchman crossed his arms over his ridiculously broad chest and leaned against the door.

Jorge suspected this move was more than just casual. He returned to the master suite and quietly locked the door behind him.

His wife rose from the tub, shimmering like a goddess. Frothy white soap bubbles clung to her dark skin in all the right places. "Mmmm," she purred and threw her arms around Jorge's neck. "I missed you."

"Not now, baby," whispered Jorge. "I've got to go."

"What? Why?" Elina withdrew her hands. A puddle of warm bath water encircled her feet.

"Martinelli's here. He wants a meeting."

"Now?"

"Yes. Keep your voice down."

"What for?"

Jorge explained the henchman outside the door.

Elina looked concerned.

"Don't worry," said Jorge. "I'll be fine. After I'm gone, call Bell and tell him where I'm at and what's going on."

Elina did some thinking of her own. "He may be there himself."

"That's true. Look, the name of the yacht is Hard Luck. Give me twenty minutes, then take the car and come down to the harbor. Keep an eye on the situation. If you don't see me in an hour, sound the alarm."

"You mean the police?" Elina wiped herself quickly with a towel.

Jorge hesitated. "Damn. Yes, the police. We'll have no choice." He grabbed his wife by the arm. "But only as a last resort. You understand?"

"Yes, darling."

He kissed her sloppily on the cheek. "I'd better get dressed before Muscles out there gets suspicious."

Elina had a sudden fantasy of this Muscles bursting into her bedroom and catching her alone, naked and wet as she stepped from the bath. Would it be such a terrible thing?

She groaned. Coitus interruptus was such a bitch.

"These are my favorites," said Violette, "the hibiscus."

Charles stooped for a closer look and was rewarded with a peck on the cheek by the troublesome white chicken who'd taken to following him around as the chief's young daughter took him on a walking tour of the expansive flower gardens surrounding their country home.

"Ouch! *Mon Dieu*! Shoo! Go away! Fly away, chicken, will you?" Charles waved the red-headed bird off. She responded by pecking at his feet.

Violette giggled. "Chou-chou likes you."

"The beast has a name?"

"Yes, of course. We've a dozen hens. They've all got names. There's Chou-chou and Cacki, Two Toe. . ." She proceeded to name all twelve of the fowl.

"Yes, well I hope the others are locked up behind a chicken wire somewhere." He looked nervously about.

"There's no need," replied Violette, giving Chou-chou a scratch along the side of her head. "They never go far."

Charles wished Chou-chou would go far. Very far. One good kick ought to do it.

"Over here is the vegetable garden," explained Violette. "We grow much of our own vegetables right here. Carrots, peas, radishes. Just about everything."

Charles nodded. "My mother does the same."

Half the garden hung in the shade of a large wooden barn. A horse stuck its head out one of the side windows.

"That's my horse, Champagne."

"Champagne? That's an interesting name for a horse."

"I call her that because of her color—that and because she gets all bubbly when she sees we're going off for a ride." Violette led Charles to her horse and stroked her lovingly. "I missed her when I was off at school, didn't I, Champagne?"

Violette turned to Charles. "You can pet her, if you like. It's okay."

"Oh," said Charles, who'd until then had no intention of laying his hands on the beast, "sure." He stuck a finger on the horse's wheat-colored head.

Champagne twisted her neck and whinnied.

Charles jumped back with a cry.

Violette laughed. "It's alright. There's nothing to be afraid of." She pet her horse's side. "I told you she gets all bubbly. She's only excited. Go ahead," she urged Charles, "try again."

Charles recovered his dignity and approached the beast who stood taller than he did. He gave her a gentle slap on the side. "Good girl."

"Care to ride her?"

"Now? Won't we be eating soon? And isn't it getting too dark to ride? Won't it be dangerous—for Champagne, I mean?" Charles felt he could go on thinking up excuses all evening if forced to, anything to keep from getting up on that horse's backside. He had a fear of horses and didn't even know why. Didn't care to figure it out either.

"Well, I suppose you're right. But Champagne knows her way around here as well as anyone." The chief's daughter pulled a sugar cube from a pocket of her dress and Champagne eagerly swallowed it up. "You can ride her some other time."

Charles quickly agreed, having no intention of ever returning or doing such a thing. "Ouch!" He looked down.

The miserable hen had pecked him in the calf.

"Chou-chou!" scolded Violette. "Bad girl." She picked up the white hen. "Naughty girl. What's gotten into you?"

Chou-chou nipped Violette's pinky and fluttered off.

"Ow." Violette stuck her finger in her mouth and sucked.

"Are you alright?" asked Charles. "Let me see that."

Violette held out her finger. "It's nothing really. Only a scratch."

Several meters away, Chou-chou was dancing in circles. Charles couldn't help wondering if this was some sort of chicken victory dance or war dance. Personally, he was praying it was the chicken victory dance, because if Chou-chou was only getting started, he was getting going.

Keeping one eye on the aberrant hen, he checked out Violette's wound. "You're bleeding," he said.

Holding onto her hand, he led the chief's daughter to a narrow stone bench at the edge of the garden. "Maybe you should put something on it. An antiseptic, perhaps?"

"It's okay, really," Violette said softly, her soft shoulder rubbing against the fabric of his uniform.

Inside, from the vantage point of the kitchen window, Chief Lebon smiled. "You see, Elisabeth. I told you they were meant for each other. They're holding hands."

Standing at her husband's side, Elisabeth couldn't resist a small smile herself. "Let's not get ahead of ourselves just yet, Didier." She wrapped an arm around his waist. "It's far too soon to say." She stood on her tiptoes to get a better view. Charles and her daughter were sitting close together on the garden bench. He held her hand delicately.

"Look at them. They are like two little lovebirds," Didier said.

"Nevertheless, I suggest you postpone calling him 'son'

until they at least become engaged. And I would not go counting on that just yet, either."

"You're right," Didier said, turning to his wife. He kissed her squarely on her forehead. "Still, Charles would make a fine son-in-law."

"Are you forgetting that he is a gendarme, my husband? If he marries Violette, she will be gone in three years. Think about that. We may never see our daughter again."

"Oh, but I have already thought about this," said the chief.

"Didier! Whatever do you mean? You want Violette to leave us?"

"No," said the chief, taking his wife's hands in his, "of course not. I will offer him a job with the municipal police."

Elisabeth smiled. "You can do this? There is an opening?"

Chief Lebon held himself erect. "I am the chief of police. Leave it to me."

Elisabeth gently kissed her husband's nose. "*Bien.* Now we must eat. Call Violette and Charles, would you? And not a word about marriage!"

"Of course, *ma chérie.* As you say, we must be patient."

Elisabeth nodded and began counting out the dinner plates. Yes, one must be patient. Still, she thought, pulling the best silver from the hutch, perhaps she should begin looking through the bridal catalogues for an appropriate wedding gown for her youngest daughter. The design and creation of a fitting wedding outfit took time, after all. If the two married in Spring, this was not so far off.

After dinner, when the guests had gone, she would look in the chest at the foot of the bed. She was certain she kept her wedding materials there, having last been used for Rose's nuptials.

The chief's wife laid the plates around the dining table, her eyes glancing at the walls. They would definitely need to repaint if the wedding reception was to be held here. Definitely. And perhaps some new curtains would liven things up.

Mitch Martinelli was fat, hairless and mean. Oh, and he was short. And that pissed him off. Jorge and Mitch's nameless henchman had been taken out to the Hard Luck in a small motorboat by a querulous little man with a frightening habit of snuffing out his smokes on a rusting gas can beside the hot, stinking engine.

There were a lot of folks onboard. Among them—as Elina had suggested—was Roberto Bell and his cute, little wife, Angelina, showing off her wares in a blue pareo and matching bustier.

"Hello, Angie," Jorge said, sidling up to Bell's wife and planting a wet kiss on her cheek before she or her weasly husband could raise a protest. He eyed her chest with unrestrained lust. "Nice view. Don't you think, Bell?"

Bell, wine glass in hand, fumed but held his temper in check. "If you'll get your hands off my bride, Martinelli is belowdecks and waiting for us."

Jorge chuckled, a display of bravado that did not have its equal in reality. "Let me get a drink first." He reached out for one of several open bottles on a serving tray.

Muscles interjected, laying his grip on Pena's forearm. "Talk first. Drink later."

Jorge nodded.

Bell snickered at Pena's discomfiture and Jorge's continence turned ugly. "Don't worry, baby," he said loudly to Angelina, "you and I can get some alone time later. Once I'm through with you, you'll be able to tell the difference between men and boys."

Bell rushed him. Muscles intervened. "No fighting," he said softly. "Mr. Martinelli does not wish anything to disturb the enjoyment of his guests."

Jorge's eyes darted about the suddenly quiet crowd. They were all looking at him like he was some sort of animal. They could all go to hell. Still, once more he nodded.

Looking at Jorge, Bell deliberately downed the rest of his drink, set his glass on the rail, kissed his wife and headed down the steep little steps. Not to be outdone by a man he considered a wuss, Jorge quickly followed.

Mitch Martinelli sprawled like a beached, tuskless Pacific walrus in the middle of his king-size bed, leaving a depression that nothing less than a three hundred pound weight could have equaled. He had on a pair of colorful Hawaiian trunks whose waistband had gone beyond the limits of what elastic was meant to do, and nothing more.

A couple of young bikini girls, twins no less, looking like Hugh Hefner hand-me-downs, stretched out on either side of him—perfect legs, breasts and tans—holding onto his flabby arms like they were fatty life preservers.

"Hi-ya, Mitch," Jorge said. "Good to see you again."

"Yes," said Bell, "welcome to Saint Barthelemy."

"Haven't been there yet. Haven't left the boat."

"I see," said Bell. "You ought to go into Gustavia. There are a number of fine restaurants."

"I've got me a chef. He knows what I like." Martinelli sat up and stuffed an extra pillow behind his back.

Bell nodded. It was awfully hard to share pleasantries with a man as unpleasant as Mitch Martinelli. The air itself seemed to stink down here, as if the fat criminal had gone rancid. Was it possible, wondered Bell?

"Plenty of topnotch shops on the island as well, Mitch.

Maybe the girls would like to go shopping? There are so many boutiques it's like being in friggin' St. Tropez."

Martinelli shrugged. "Perhaps."

The gangster rolled off the bed and Bell could have sworn he felt the boat move.

Martinelli turned to his muscleman. "That's all, Theo. See that everyone is happy." After the big man climbed the steps, Martinelli turned to Bell and Jorge and said, "Tell me, who killed Bobbi?" With his back to them, he removed an eight ounce bottle of soda water from the small fridge beside his bed and twisted off the cap.

"We don't know, Mitch," answered Jorge.

"Yes, the police are investigating. I don't know if they even have any suspects to speak of."

Martinelli strode back and forth at the front of the bed, lumbering like a caged elephant. The bikini girls sat watching, their arms around their knees. Jorge thought he wouldn't mind sharing a bed with those two for an hour.

"Bobbi was like a son to me." He looked hard into Jorge's eyes.

Jorge nodded. "I know, Mitch."

Martinelli lifted the bottle to his lips and drank. Bubbles escaped from the corners of his mouth like a dog with rabies. "He was into me for two mil."

Jorge whistled. "I'm sorry, Mitch. I'm sure his estate is good for it."

"You think I want to screw around with Bobbi's estate and goddam lawyers?"

Jorge swallowed, said nothing.

"Mr. Martinelli, I'm certain that once all this is sorted out, the murder, the division of the company—"

Martinelli cut Bell off. "I want twenty-five percent."

"But, Mr. Martinelli, you already have twelve and a half

percent of Bobbi Freon Enterprises now," Bell replied. "So I want twelve and a half friggin' more." He was talking to Bell but looking at Jorge. "Twelve and a half more and I forgive Bobbi the two million he borrowed from me." He turned to Bell. "And I forgive whoever killed poor Bobbi. Do I make myself clear, Mr. Bell?"

Bell lowered his eyes.

Martinelli smiled. He clapped his hands. "So, do we have a deal, Pena?"

Jorge held out his hand. "We have a deal."

"There are a few problems," interjected Bell.

"Like what?" demanded Martinelli.

"Linda Patterson, Sofie Somers. We've made a deal with Ms. Patterson."

"What the hell do I care about a couple of women?" complained Martinelli.

"Ms. Patterson got herself knocked up by Bobbi," explained Jorge.

"Why that conniving bitch!" But instead of blowing his top, the gangster was laughing. "Alright. What's the deal?"

Jorge, suddenly emboldened, helped himself to a bottle of Mitch's soda water. He winked at the bikini girls. The closest giggled. Jorge figured her for a live one and determined to take a shot at her later. "Roberto here becomes president of BF Enterprises, I become acting chairman of the board and Linda becomes VP."

Martinelli was nodding. "And I get my twenty-five percent and hold my seat on the board. You guys do all the work." He smiled. "I like it. Now what about this other broad?"

"Sofie Somers," said Jorge.

"She's threatening a legal fight. Bobbi promised to take care of her and her children."

"Get rid of her," said Martinelli, having no patience for women, their needs and/or their troubles.

Jorge explained how they were planning to pay her to go away.

"Perfect," replied Martinelli. He went to a bureau drawer, tossing aside socks and underwear like so much trash. He pulled out a bundle of cash and broke it in two.

Martinelli stepped toward Jorge, then, changing his mind, handed the money to Bell. "Should be about two hundred and fifty thousand there, give or take. Make sure Sofie Somers gets it. Tell her to consider it my contribution to her and her kids' retirement fund. If she wants more, you two will have to kick in something yourselves."

Bell nodded and stuffed the money inside the pockets of his sportcoat.

"Can we go shopping now, Mitchie?" begged one of the bikini girls.

"Sure," said Mitch. "Let's celebrate." He turned to Bell and Jorge. "You heard the girls, this meeting is over. Get back to me when you've got something good to report."

Topside, Bell pulled Jorge aside and whispered, "I don't like this one bit. What the hell does he think he's doing muscling in on our company for another twelve and a half percent?"

Jorge smiled. "I don't know, why don't you go and ask him yourself."

Bell frowned. "So what are we going to do?"

Jorge helped himself to a drink. "We are going to do exactly what we told Mitch. We are going to give him his piece of the company and pay off Miss Somers."

"But—"

"We don't have any other choice. Besides, there's still

plenty of money for everybody."

"I suppose," said Bell, though he didn't look happy about it. "I just don't like someone who contributes nothing to get so much. I work hard to keep this business afloat."

"So do I," answered Jorge with a careless shrug, "but this one's out of our hands.

"You didn't tell him everything."

"What do you mean?"

"About how we—you—promised Linda that her child would get control of the company when they reach legal age."

"Big deal. Anything can happen in that time. I could be dead. Mitch could be dead." He tapped Bell on the chest. "You could be dead."

"Mitch won't like it."

"Who's gonna tell him? You?" Jorge left Bell standing there and called out to the little fellow who'd brought him out to the Hard Luck. "Hey, you, Popeye! Get me off this tub!"

Sitting at a harborside bar and coddling a dry martini, Elina Pena watched as the boatman returned Jorge to the dock. He flagged down a nearby taxi driver and drove off. The boatman returned to the yacht, only to head back to shore once more, this time with a broad-shouldered, dark haired fellow in sunglasses. This must have been the one who'd come to the villa.

She passed a pleasant moment considering the bulging muscles which must lie beneath the well-built man's clothes. Perhaps she'd have a drink with him. Jorge would be pleased if she learned something.

Elina smiled. She'd be pleased even if she did not. She paid for her drink, rose and proceeded to follow a path sure to intersect with that of her prey.

The guests were gone, the dishes cleared. Rose and Pisar—taking their young hoard with them—had departed hours before. Charles and Adjutant Bruyer had left together.

As was her habit, Madame Lebon brushed Violette's hair in the bathroom mirror before sending her off to bed. "What a wonderful evening," said Madame Lebon, in an attempt to test the waters of her daughter's mind.

"Yes," sighed Violette, lightly scrubbing her face with a pad.

"Charles seemed quite nice, didn't he?"

Violette's eyes sparkled. "Yes."

"He seemed to like you."

Violette turned. "You think so?"

"Oh, yes," said Madame Lebon. "I think he was quite taken with you. But then again, what young man would not be?"

"Oh, *Maman*." She pulled the brush out of her mother's hand. "You know, he seemed like such a-a jerk when I first met him."

Madame Lebon chuckled. "I felt the same way when I met your father."

"You did?" Violette's eyes grew wide.

"Oh, yes. He was throwing stones at me and one of my girlfriends."

"Papa did that?"

"Yes, of course, he was only sixteen and, looking back, I can see that he was only trying to get my attention."

"I see," said Violette, rather thoughtfully.

"Men are like that, you know," continued Madame Lebon, "they sometimes have a difficult time expressing themselves."

"You can say that again."

"They have trouble with their emotions. Often they don't

even know how they truly feel," Madame Lebon patted her heart, "on the inside. It is up to us as women to help them to know their true feelings."

"*Oui, Maman.*"

"Come," said Madame Lebon, "time for bed." She pulled back the bedspread and switched on the bedside lamp. "Men are merely big children, you know."

Violette nodded. Charles had seemed rather awkward. She would have to nurture him along.

18

Charles was sweating. Why were there never any clouds when you needed them? He stood on the roof of Villa Onyx. With him were Gendarme Ronalph Sadjan and Officer Pisar Mercer.

Half an hour of searching and they hadn't found a thing, unless the adjutant was interested in a variety of bird droppings, many of which stained Charles shorts by this time. About to give up and call off the search, he heard a commotion and froze.

Jean-Marc, the hotel pool man, a rolled up length of pool hose in one hand and a long pool brush in the other, had entered by the courtyard gate and was hollering at Sofie, who lay sunning herself while the children swam.

Charles sighed. He'd barely had a word with Sofie since Saturday night. She seemed to be avoiding him. And there had been no one home when they'd climbed the roof.

Sadjan was leaning over the edge of the roof, getting a good look. "Hey, isn't that your girlfriend, Charles?"

Pisar who, though married, wasn't immune to the charms of a bare-breasted beauty, was caught by surprise. "Your what?" He arched his neck, lost his footing and slid down the tiles. Charles caught him.

"Quiet," hissed Sadjan. "I'm trying to hear what they're talking about." He ignored Charles and the officer's troubles. But it was too late. Sofie Somers had heard the commotion on the roof and pulled Jean-Marc indoors. Nothing but two kids splashing about now. The pool cleaning equipment lay on the ground by the table. "*Merde*. You fellows all right?"

He helped lift Pisar who, despite his near death experience, was grinning.

"What's so funny?" asked Sadjan. "You some kind of thrill seeker, Pisar?"

"No, no," answered the municipal officer, dusting himself off. "Just thought of something funny."

"So let us in on the joke," pushed Sadjan.

"Sorry. It's nothing really. You wouldn't find it funny." He stepped to the edge of the roof. "So, that was your girlfriend, eh, Charles?"

Charles shrugged. "She's a friend."

Sadjan hooted. "Some friend. Charles had a bit of a slumber party with her the other night."

Officer Pisar whistled long and low. If the chief should find out. . .

What a quandary. Should he tell Charles so the poor fellow could save himself, or should he tell the chief so that Charles couldn't break out of the same trap that had snared him? Misery does love company.

"I'd say you've got yourself some competition there, Charles. Stiff competition," he said, nudging Charles with his elbow, "if you get my meaning."

Charles scowled. "That's only Jean-Marc Bouton. He's the pool maintenance man."

"I'd say he's cleaning more than her swimming pool, if

you asked me," chided Gendarme Sadjan.

Officer Pisar snickered.

"Oh, grow up, will you?" Charles stamped his feet. "Let's get down from here. There's nothing more to be found."

"Sure," said Sadjan, not done with his ribbing so soon, "maybe you want us to search the courtyard so you can keep an eye on—" he winked, "things."

Charles ignored the bait, found the ladder, grabbed a rundle and headed down. He made a point of skirting clear of the courtyard. He sent Pisar and Sadjan up the hill beyond the villa to cover the ground once more.

After they'd gone, he snuck back into the courtyard for a quick peek. Not that he was jealous. Only curious. The children were nowhere in sight.

Sofie and Jean-Marc were in the sitting room. Charles noted with satisfaction that the two were not locked in a passionate embrace. Sofie sat in an overstuffed leather chair. Jean-Marc, who seemed incapable of wearing a shirt, was pacing. Neither appeared happy.

Feeling foolish, he turned to go before someone discovered him. How would he explain to Sofie that he was hiding in her bushes? As for Sadjan, if he found out, well, such a thing must not occur.

The sliding doors were open. Charles heard Sofie shout. He turned back around. "What can she be yelling at the pool man about?" he wondered aloud. Overcome with curiosity, Charles approached the side of the house, careful to keep himself between the wall and the shrubbery. He pressed up against the chalky wall and listened.

"It's not fair," Jean-Marc was saying. "This is my chance."

"It's my chance, too, Jean-Marc. I'm doing all I can. You must have patience."

"I'm too old to have patience. You promised me. I risked

everything for you. And you know how short a life a model has. My time's running out."

"Please, Jean-Marc, just a little longer?"

Charles peeked around the corner. Sofie's hand was on Jean-Marc's arm.

"Please, give me a little more time. We can work this out. We both know—"

Charles heard Tony and Cleo coming. There was no cover where he stood and he'd be exposed. Without hesitation, Charles placed his hands on the wall and threw himself over. He landed in a flower bed on the other side.

Unfortunately, Lily was standing on the walk. She looked down at the smashed and mangled red and orange wildflowers beneath his feet. "So," she said, folding her arms, "I see your gardening skills are every bit as sharp as your people skills."

Charles opened his mouth. "Oh, Lily, I—"

Jean-Marc appeared at the front door to Villa Onyx, and was heading their way. Lily ran up to him and threw her arms around his fatless and muscled waist.

Charles soured. It wasn't natural not to have at least tiny love handles. It wasn't normal. Besides, all that exercise that a fellow had to do to get like that, it was much too vain a pursuit for him. He had better, more important things to do with his time.

"Jean-Marc, there you are." She kissed his cheek. "I've been looking everywhere for you. Did you forget our date?"

"*Bonjour*, sexy." Jean-Marc looked from Lily to Charles. "What are you two up to?"

"Us?" laughed Lily. "Don't be ridiculous. I was coming down from my apartment to meet you. Charles just," she tapped her cheek, "dropped in. Didn't you, Charles?"

Charles stood and brushed the brown soil from his legs.

"Shouldn't we be going, Jean-Marc?"

Jean-Marc shrugged, swung a proprietary arm around Lily's hips and led her down the path.

Charles knocked on the door.

Sofie herself opened it. "*Bonjour*, Charles," she said. Her tone was flat, noncommital.

"May I come in?"

She stepped aside.

"What did Monsieur Bouton want?"

"Who?"

"Jean-Marc. He seemed angry."

"Oh, you heard."

"Not really. I mean, just a little. We were on the roof. The adjutant wanted us to search for further clues. He thought we might have missed something."

"Did you find anything further?"

Charles shook his head.

The sound of the children carried through the villa.

"The children are out in the pool. I really should keep an eye on them." Sofie crossed the floor. Her bare feet made no sound.

Charles followed her out to the courtyard. He waved to the children and they waved back. They'd put up a volleyball net and were using a multicolored beachball for their match.

Sofie sat. Charles remained standing. "What is your relationship to Jean-Marc?"

Sofie looked amused. "What is your relationship to the hotel's receptionist? What is her name, Lily?"

"I do not have a relationship with Mademoiselle Vineuil," Charles answered strongly.

"Really? So, I suppose you often have tourists come by the Gendarmerie and toss picnic baskets at the walls." She laughed. "It's no wonder you are renovating. In such conditions, you must be doing it constantly."

Charles said nothing but she judged that he actually seemed to be getting angry. "Listen, Charles, I don't have a relationship with Jean-Marc. He cleans the pool, for God's sake." She shrugged. "And he's done me a few other little favors. Nothing untoward. He's not my boyfriend."

"He's gay."

Sofie looked amused. "You think so?"

Charles recalled his visit with the poolman at Grand Saline, soaking up the sun naked with his mate. He nodded.

Sofie shrugged. "I'm sorry I got angry and ran off the other night."

"Me, too. I mean, I'm sorry, too."

Sofie rose and kissed him.

Behind him, Charles heard the children giggling. He gently pushed Sofie away. "Listen, Sofie, it's nothing personal, but I need to ask you about—"

"About what?"

"About something Jean-Marc said when I interviewed him."

Sofie's brows came together. "Exactly what did he say, Charles?"

"He said he saw you coming from Villa Onyx at approximately the time of Bobbi's murder." Charles held his breath.

Sofie's neck bent to one side. Her index finger bounced across her lip. "Let me think." She nodded. "Yes, you know, that's possible. Oh my, I should have remembered earlier, shouldn't I. I'm such an airhead sometimes, I swear. Yes, I did come back to the villa. I was getting some snacks for the children. I'd forgotten them."

"I see." Charles felt relieved. He knew there would be a

simple explanation. "Did you see anything? Anyone?"

Sofie shook her head. "No. But I only came in from the front, went to the kitchen and left again. Even if Bobbi had a visitor up in his room, I'd never have known it."

"Of course," said Charles.

Sofie hugged Charles. "Just think, I might have been here in the house while—" Her eyes drifted up towards Bobbi's room.

The children ran past, dripping wet, disappearing down the corridor leading to their rooms.

"Careful!" shouted Sofie. "Don't fall." She shook her head. "Children. Bobbi was a big child himself, you know." She paused. "I miss him."

"How long did you work for Monsieur Freon?"

"Oh, ten years or so." Sofie grabbed a cigarette from a pack within reach on the outdoor table.

Charles picked up the lighter and lit it for her. "Did you know that Monsieur Freon had sex not long before he was killed?"

"What? No, I didn't know that. I told you. We were at the beach."

"And you didn't see anyone when you returned to the villa?"

"No, like I said, no one at all." She took a strong pull on the cigarette and threw it into the bushes where it smoldered. "You're not accusing me of having sex with him are you?"

"Did you?"

"Of course not." She turned and stuck her foot in the water.

"I know. He had sex with a man, in fact. Did you know that Bobbi slept with men?"

There was a smile on Sofie's face when she turned back around. "He slept with anyone that intrigued him. Bobbi was not very discriminating."

Charles nodded. "Do you have any idea who this man might have been? Was he seeing anyone in particular?"

"No. Only Linda Patterson. You think she could be a transvestite?"

"Not very likely since she's carrying Monsieur Freon's child."

"No, I know that. I was only joking. I'm not fond of that woman."

"She must have her good qualities. After all, Monsieur Freon was in love with her."

"Oh, please. You are too naive, Charles. If Linda hadn't managed to get pregnant—"

"Did Monsieur Freon seem happy about the situation?"

"You mean about the baby?"

"Yes."

Sofie shrugged and took another smoke. "He didn't seem unhappy though I'm sure he would have preferred if she'd gotten rid of it. But Linda is at that age where having a baby becomes a biological crusade for a woman."

"No matter what Bobbi wanted?"

Sofie smiled. "No matter what Bobbi wanted. I'll give credit to Linda for that—she is very strong-willed herself."

"Bobbi may have been quite upset."

"He knew how to deal with things."

"How do you mean?"

Sofie looked at her wristwatch. "Oh dear, I really must be going, Charles. I promised the children I would take them to Shell Beach."

Charles gently yet firmly took her wrist. "I don't think so," he said sadly.

She looked surprised. "What?"

"May I use your telephone?"

She nodded. Charles went to the kitchen and dialed. "This is Trenet," he said. "I need someone to send the car over to the Hotel Idyllique." He looked at Sofie, his expression blank. "And tell Adjutant Bruyer that I am bringing in a suspect. Yes, that's right."

Sofie glared at him.

"I must make one more call." He dialed once more. "*Bonjour*, Lily? I thought you'd gone with Jean-Marc?"

"Something came up," the receptionist replied rather cooly. "He's gone home. What do you want?"

"I need you to do me a favor."

Lily laughed. "I think not."

"I'm serious. I need you to come to Villa Onyx."

Click.

Merde, she'd hung up. Charles redialed. "Listen to me, Lily," he said quickly, "I need you to come to the villa. This is official business. Are you coming or aren't you?"

"You're out of your mind, you know that?" she shouted.

Charles waited. Said nothing.

"*Bien*. I'll be right there."

Charles thanked her and hung up. "You should get dressed, Sofie."

"Why?" said Sofie. "Why are you doing this to me, Charles?"

As much as he longed to hold her, Charles kept his hands to himself. "It is my duty. You were the last one to be seen leaving here. You lied about this. If Jean-Marc had not admitted to having seen you, the truth would have never come out."

"That's it?"

"You said you came back to Villa Onyx to get snacks for the children."

"So? What of it?"

"The first day that I interviewed you, at the beach, you interrupted our conversation to give the children some money."

"And that is a crime, Charles? Goodness, I should have been arrested long ago!"

"You gave them money for lunch. You said they'd had nothing since breakfast." Charles tapped his temple. "I remember."

"Oh."

"Why, Sofie?"

Sofie turned to the door, letting the breeze lift her. "Bobbi was going to throw us out. He said he didn't want us around anymore."

"Because he was getting married?"

"That's right." She spun around. "He didn't even give me any notice. He promised me, Charles. He promised me that the children and I would always have a home. And then he was just going to throw us out like so much trash."

"And so you murdered him?"

She collapsed onto a kitchen chair and spread her hands over the table. Her neck sagged. "I didn't mean to. I only came back to try and talk to him."

"Up in his suite?"

She nodded. "But he wouldn't hear anything I had to say. It made me so angry."

"Maybe you shouldn't say any more. Maybe you should wait, talk to a lawyer, Sofie."

"No, Charles, I want to tell you. I need to get this off my chest. It's been making me crazy. And you, you understand. You care about me, don't you, Charles?"

"Yes."

Sofie sniffled and managed a ghost of a smile. "*Merci*, Charles. Bobbi was never so kind. I didn't ask a lot of him. I only wanted for things to remain the way they'd always been. It wasn't perfect, but the children were happy. That's all that mattered. But Bobbi had made up his mind. He was a selfish bastard. He told me to leave. Gave me until the end of the day to pack our things.

"I pleaded with him—on my knees I got down and begged him—" she said, dredging up fresh sobs. "He told me to get up, that I was making a fool of myself."

"Then what happened?"

"He pulled me up and slapped me."

Charles waited, knowing there was more.

"I stumbled against the desk. You know, the writing desk by the window. I-I picked up the letter opener. It was lying right there, and—"

Sofie paused, as if replaying the scene in her mind's eye. "Bobbi was laughing and I-I just. . .I don't know. . .I just. . .I looked down. I had the letter opener in my hand. I didn't mean to, Charles. I didn't mean to."

She looked into his eyes for support. "After, I grabbed a sock from his drawer. I didn't want to touch the letter opener again. All that blood. I'd never seen anything like it. I wiped the handle and stuck it inside the stocking. And then I didn't know what to do with it." Trembling, she wiped at her tears.

"And so you threw it on the roof."

She nodded. "The window was open. I wasn't thinking. I only wanted to get rid of the awful thing as quickly as I could. I didn't know what I was doing."

"It's all right, now," said Charles. "Everything is all right."

But nothing was.

Sofie Somers collapsed in tears and Charles held onto her until Lily arrived.

19

Charles went to the door. Lily stood on the porch, tapping her feet. "Lily, thank you for coming."

"This had better be good, Charles."

"It is." He reached for the girl. "I need you to watch Sofie's children while I—"

Lily turned and stomped off.

Charles ran after her. "Please, Lily. Listen to me."

"Go away!"

"Won't you, please, stop a moment and listen to me? It's important." He put a hand on her shoulder and she spun around to face him.

"What's important? You have a hot date with Miss Super-model?"

"No, Lily, I—"

"And you expect me to babysit her two children for you two lovebirds? Is that it? You, Monsieur Gendarme," Lily said, stabbing Charles in the center of his chest, "are out of your mind!" Each word had been a thrust.

"Ouch," complained Charles. "Stop a moment." He grabbed her hand tightly and held it before she could inflict any more damage to him. "I need you to watch Cleo and Tony because—"

The pair was interrupted by the sudden appearance of Gendarmes Sadjan and Brin. "What's going on?" asked Simon Brin. "Is this lovely young girl giving you trouble, Charles?"

"*Oui*," said Sadjan, "do you need some assistance?"

"She does look quite strong," said Brin, with a smirk. "If there's going to be a fight, my money's on the girl."

Charles let go of Lily's hand. "Very funny." He straightened his back and tucked in his loose shirttail. "Now, if you two clowns are done with your little jokes, I have a suspect who needs escorting to the Gendarmerie."

Sadjan's eyes widened. "Her?" He was pointing at Lily.

"No, not her." Charles sighed. "Come with me."

Lily hurried to Charles' side and whispered. "What's going on, Charles? Is this about Bobbi Freon's murder? What suspect?"

Charles kept his mouth shut. He led his three irksome companions through the wide-open door of Villa Onyx and out to the kitchen. Sofie was not there. *Merde!* He spun in a circle, looked out at the pool. It was deserted.

"What's wrong with him?" Brin asked Sadjan.

Gendarme Sadjan tapped his skull. "He's touched in the head."

Charles ignored them. "She was here a moment ago."

Brin said, "She who?"

"I hear voices coming from down there," Lily replied, pointing down the hall.

Charles raced down the corridor. Sofie was holding her children's hands, speaking quiet words of comfort to them both. Cleo was crying.

"Don't worry, baby," Sofie said, petting her daughter's

hand. "Mommy will be home soon. And you," she said, giving Tony a firm hug, "remember, you are the man of the house while I am gone. I expect you to take care of your sister for me."

Tony nodded. "I will, Mommy."

Sofie rose. She'd changed into a pair of blue jeans and a white blouse. "All right. I'm ready now, Charles."

"What?" Lily's eyes grew wide. "Her?"

Charles turned to Lily. "I need you to keep an eye on the children. It's only temporary. I'm sure we can make some other arrangements."

Lily nodded. "Okay."

"I'll telephone you or come and let you know once I've found someone appropriate to take care of them. I'm sorry to have to ask you to do this."

"It's alright. I can take care of them as long as you need," Lily replied.

Charles turned to his mates. "Mademoiselle Somers will need a ride to headquarters."

Sadjan and Brin had become quite serious. "The car is up at the entrance," said Sadjan.

"Good. I have my Vespa and will follow you." He squeezed Lily's hand. "Thank you."

Lily felt she might have to take back every bad thought she'd been harboring about Charles Trenet.

Jorge Pena sat in his car watching the scene unfold. On the seat beside him was Elina's Longchamp valise stuffed with Martinelli's quarter of a million U.S. dollars. This was a down payment on her silence. He still had to fly to the Caymans for the rest. Or did he?

Jorge smiled. Sofie didn't look too happy and she had a uniformed gendarme on each arm. That other fellow, Trenet, who had been making a pest of himself, was there, too.

Jorge waited until they'd all driven off. With a little luck, he'd be getting out of this stinking mess more cheaply than he'd expected.

He tapped the brown leather valise. A pity, he'd have to give Martinelli his money back. He'd never get away with keeping it? Would he?

Jorge turned the car about in the parking lot. No, and even if he stood a chance, a lousy quarter million wasn't worth the risk.

He telephoned Linda Patterson from his car. "Where are you?"

"Shopping in Gustavia, why?"

Jorge nodded. He could hear cars in the background. "I'm leaving the Idyllique and guess what I see?"

"I'm not in the mood for games, Jorge."

"Come on, guess."

"Bobbi walking around like a zombie."

Jorge couldn't help laughing. "Would that be funny, or what? God, Bobbi Freon the Zombie. I'd pay to see that. But, no, that's not it."

"So what is it?" said Linda, growing more and more weary of Pena and his games.

"The gendarmes have just taken Sofie off in a squad car."

"What for?" This was getting interesting.

"I don't know," said Jorge. "You think I should have asked them?"

"You think it has to do with Bobbi?"

"I don't think it's about parking tickets."

"What are you going to do?"

Jorge replied. "I'm doing it. I'm calling you. You're a woman. Call and see what's going on." Thick with sarcasm he added, "Express your concern."

Linda sighed. "Fine."

"Call me at this number when you find out what's up." Jorge turned off his cell phone.

Charles followed Sadjan and Brin from a distance. These were troubling times. On the road to Public, Charles turned off and headed for Jean-Marc Bouton's home near the beach. He would catch up with the others in a little while.

He parked his motorscooter and knocked on the door of the little white gingerbread house where Jean-Marc resided.

The door was answered by a comely young woman of no more than twenty years by the look of her. She had very short brown hair, a Roman nose and a high forehead from which shined two bright blue eyes. A swath of freckles across the bridge of her nose gave her added character. She was wearing a white bikini top and a black bottom.

"Can I help you?" She looked at him curiously but with innocence.

"I am Charles Trenet of the Gendarmerie. I wish to speak with Monsieur Bouton." Charles tried to angle a look around the corner into the sitting room. "Is he here?"

"Oh, sure." She held out her hand. "I'm Donna, his roommate."

"His roommate? I thought Carl was his roommate. I met him here the other day."

"Carl is. We've got an extra room."

Charles looked confused.

"Jean-Marc and I have our room and we rent out the other to Carl. The extra money doesn't hurt and Carl's cool. Hardly any trouble at all." Donna was a talkative girl.

"But, I thought Jean-Marc was—"

"Was what? Oh, come on in." She pushed the door open wide and waited for Charles to pass. "Not much, but it's home. So," she studied Charles with amusement, "you thought Jean-Marc was what?"

Charles cleared his throat. "Well, no, it is nothing really."

"What's nothing?" Wearing nothing more than his undershorts, Jean-Marc sauntered into the room, planted a kiss on Donna's lips and said hello to Charles.

"Perhaps I could have a word with you privately?"

"What's wrong? Heavens, you look like you've been through the ringer." Jean-Marc went to the fridge in the small kitchen which occupied the front corner of the room. "Care for a beer?"

"*Non, merci*. I need to speak with you. It is important."

"So," said Jean-Marc, handing Donna an open beer, "what is it?"

"Mademoiselle Somers has been arrested in the case of the murder of Bobbi Freon."

For a moment, Charles thought he saw a look of fear cross the man's countenance, like a deer dodging the headlights in the road—a leap and then it was gone.

There followed an awkward silence. Donna glanced at her boyfriend but he carefully avoided looking in her direction.

"Perhaps we should continue our conversation privately?"

"No, no, that's okay," replied Jean-Marc. "Anything you have to say, you can say to us both."

"There are some awkward questions."

"Go ahead." He took a long swig of beer from his bottle.

"If you insist." Charles stuck his hands in his pockets and paced up and down. "How well do you know Mademoiselle Somers?"

"Not very. I cleaned her pool."

"I recall seeing her speaking with you on several other occasions on the grounds of the Idyllique."

"Lots of people speak to me," answered Jean-Marc. "I'm

a nice guy. Besides, it goes with the job."

Charles nodded. "How well did you know Bobbi Freon?"

There was the slightest of hesitations before the pool man answered. "I knew him. Took care of his pool just like I take care of all the rest."

"Did you ever sleep with him?"

"No."

An electric tension filled the air as if a power line lay broken and twisting on the ground between them.

"There is evidence that Bobbi Freon had sex with a man before he died."

"Good for him."

"There are tests," said Charles, hoping there were and that any evidence remained to be tested—after all, such things were not his specialty— "that can reveal the identity of a person based on their semen."

"Jean-Marc?" Donna laid her hand on his arm.

Jean-Marc cursed and tossed his beer in the open trash bin beside the counter. "Oh, alright. Yes, I had sex with Freon. So what of it?" he said belligerently. "It doesn't mean I killed him? Why would I? Besides," he added, "you say you've already got your murderer."

"Mademoiselle Somers has confessed, *oui*."

"There you have it then. What gives with all the questions?"

"I am trying to get a clearer picture in my head of what occurred on that day. At what time did you see Monsieur Freon?"

"I don't know. It was after that other fellow left. The fellow in the suit."

"Monsieur Bell?"

"If you say so."

"What else can you tell me that you have not already?"

"What?" Jean-Marc was smirking. "Want to hear what the sex was like, Trenet?"

"Jean-Marc!" scolded Donna. "Please."

"Look, I'm not proud of what I did, but if I had to do it all over again, I would in a flash. Freon promised me he'd make me a model. You think I like cleaning swimming pools? You think I want to spend the rest of my life doing it?"

"Bobbi Freon was starting up a new menswear line," put in Donna. "He told Jean-Marc he'd make him a featured model. It would have meant a lot of money."

Jean-Marc bemoaned, "A whole new career."

"You knew about Jean-Marc's activities, then?"

"Yes, I knew. Again, I didn't love the idea, but if making Bobbi happy by having a little sex with the guy could get Jean-Marc a contract," she shrugged, "well, why not?"

Charles could think of a thousand reasons given the time, but voiced none.

"Why do you care, anyway?" asked Jean-Marc. He clutched Donna's hand. "You've got your killer."

"I wonder," said Charles. He turned and left, started up his scooter and was gone.

Donna and Jean-Marc stood looking at one another long after he'd left.

"You put her in a cell?" Charles said. "Was that really necessary?"

"We had no choice. She was adamant," replied Adjutant Bruyer. He pulled Charles into his office. "I tried speaking to her, but you know how bad my English is."

"She speaks some French."

"Well, she's chosen not to use it." The adjutant pulled open his drawer and extracted the Chabbaneau. "Mademoiselle Somers insisted we lock her up."

The adjutant poured two generous glasses and offered one to Charles. "So we did."

"Has she spoken to a lawyer?" Charles took a sip of cognac.

"She doesn't want one."

"What will happen to her now?"

The adjutant shrugged and refilled their glasses. "We'll send her to St. Martin. The case will proceed from there." He smiled. "You've done splendidly, Charles. Wait until the procureur hears about this. He'll be pleased, very, very pleased."

"Well, that's one good thing," agreed Charles, though he didn't look happy.

"What's wrong, Charles? Feeling guilty, yourself?" Adjutant Bruyer rose and rested a fatherly hand on Charles shoulder. "Listen, I've heard the men talking. I know about you and Sofie."

"Monsieur Adjutant, I assure you—"

"Never mind all that," said the adjutant. "I was young once, too, you know. You've done the right thing, that's what counts. What man would not have been seduced by Mademoiselle Somers? She is a beautiful woman. Do not let it trouble you. You've learned a lesson in life—"

The adjutant chuckled. "And women, I dare say. And you've done an admirable job."

Charles was shaking his head. "I don't know."

"What?"

Charles rose. "I feel that something is not right."

"Nonsense, Mademoiselle Somers has given us a confession. I heard it myself. We have witnessed it and have it in writing now." The adjutant pulled a document from his desk and held it out for the gendarme's inspection. Sofie Somers' signature was at the bottom.

"I know, but—"

"But what, Charles?"

"I think she is lying. I think everyone is lying to me."

"Lying? About committing a horrible murder? Really, Charles, why would she do such a thing?"

Charles looked through the doorway to the closed cell. "I don't know."

"You do not feel that Mademoiselle Somers is capable of murder, but many women have committed capital crimes, Charles. She is not the first. And Heaven knows, she will not be the last."

"Oh, I do believe she is capable—even of murder," admitted Charles. "Yet I do not believe she killed Bobbi Freon."

"Maybe she was in a hurry to get her hands on his money."

"What do you mean?"

"Well, she and her children were in his will and—"

"Mademoiselle Somers and her children were in Bobbi Freon's will?"

"*Oui.* Didn't you know this, Charles?"

"No," confessed Charles. "I did not."

The adjutant riffled through his desk and came up with a file. "It's right in here. I thought you'd seen it. I had told Ronalphe to give it to you in my absence. He must have forgotten. He's a good fellow, but. . ." The adjutant let his thoughts trail off. "Anyway, have a look."

Charles read quickly. Robert Frianetti, more recognizably known as Bobbi Freon, had bequeathed practically his entire estate to Sofie Somers and her two children. "How very odd."

Adjutant Bruyer shrugged. "I don't know. Some people leave everything to their cats. Maybe he was simply rewarding the mademoiselle for her loyalty? He had no other family."

Charles thought of Thor and his cat. Yes, he'd definitely leave all his earthly possessions to Elephant if he outlived his wife and had no children. Come to think of it, did Thor have children?

"Think about it, Charles," theorized the adjutant, "Bobbi Freon is rich. Mademoiselle Somers finds out that Freon has left her and the kids everything. She's his housekeeper, maybe she finds a copy of the will lying about someplace. It starts eating at her. She's tired of being a housekeeper." Adjutant Bruyer ran a finger across his throat. "There you have it. Murder. Motive and opportunity. A *fait accompli*. Of course, she'll never get the money now."

Charles rose and started for the door.

"She almost got away with it, too. And she would have if it hadn't been for your cleverness, Charles."

Charles turned in the door. "You're right, Monsieur Adjutant," he said, "Sofie Somers has almost gotten away with it. And if she does, it will be because of me. May I take the car, adjutant? It will be faster than my scooter."

"Of course, Charles, but where are you going?"

Charles grabbed Ronalphe Sadjan and said, "How are your babysitting skills?"

"My what?"

"That's great, come with me." He pulled the gendarme along by his shirt as he raced through the lobby.

"And what's your hurry?"cried Adjutant Bruyer, scratching his head, staring at the back of the door.

20

Charles and Ronalphe went straight to Villa Onyx. Charles knocked. There was no answer. "Where could Lily be?"

"Beats me," said Gendarme Sadjan.

"Let's look around back." They made their way around to the courtyard. All was quiet. The sliding doors leading into the villa were wide open. 'Hello, Lily, are you there?"

"No one's home," said Ronalphe, who'd made a pass through the living area and dining room.

Charles called Lily and the kids' names and checked out the bedrooms. Nothing.

"Now what?" said Ronalphe. "And what's this all about, anyway, Charles?"

"I'm not sure," said Charles. "Come, we'd better go down to the office."

They found Lily at her desk in the lobby. She had one ear to the telephone.

"Lily," called Charles, "what are you doing here? Where are Tony and Cleo?"

Lily pointed to Denown's office. Charles saw Sofie's

children sharing a chair behind the manager's desk.

After a moment, Lily set down the telephone. "Sorry, Charles, Monsieur Denown was having a fit. I had told him I was going to Villa Onyx for a moment and when I did not return quickly, he came looking for me. I had no choice but to bring the children. They seem happy enough. In fact, I think it might have been better for them—to get out of the villa, that is."

Charles nodded. "I believe you are right. Thank you, Lily." He glanced at the children. He heard laughter. "What are they doing?" Philip Denown stood behind them, a computer joystick in hand.

"Playing computer games. Monsieur Denown's got about a dozen of them on his computer. He thinks the staff don't know what he's doing when he shuts the door and draws the blinds. But we get the sound effects through the glass."

The manager looked Charles' way and strode towards him. "*Bonjour*, Trenet. What's going on then?" He lowered his voice. "Lily tells me you've taken Tony and Cleo's mother in for questioning. Is it true? You suspect her of killing Monsieur Freon?"

"I am afraid that is so," admitted Charles. "The mademoiselle has confessed."

The manager was shaking his head. "Still, I do not understand how this is possible."

Gendarme Sadjan said, "She was in his will. We believe she killed him for his money."

"I knew there was something wrong about her," said Lily.

Denown was snapping his fingers. "Still. . ." He walked to the front entry, looked out, then paced back. "I remember that day. Nicholas was out. You remember, Lily? He called in sick."

Lily nodded. "The restaurant was short handed."

"Yes, I helped out all morning. As I recall, Mademoiselle Somers spent the entire morning at the beach, with her children."

"According to her statement, she left the beach some time in the midmorning, stabbed Monsieur Freon and then returned."

Denown was shaking his head again. "Ummm, I don't know about that."

"Why?"

"I just don't remember her being gone, that's all."

"Still, it is possible—" put in Gendarme Sadjan.

"Perhaps you were busy and she was only gone a short while," Charles added.

The manager shrugged. "I suppose. But, a beautiful supermodel like that, it's the sort of thing I notice."

Lily snorted. "That's true, Charles."

"Why does everyone keep calling Sofie Somers a supermodel?" asked Charles. "She is lovely, no doubt."

At this comment, Lily frowned.

"But still," continued Charles, "she was merely Bobbi Freon's housekeeper."

"That's true, Charles," answered Lily, "but in her time, she was quite famous."

"She was?"

"Of course," said Sadjan. "Have you been living under a rock, Charles? Even I know that. Sofie Somers was a famous model. Did all that swimwear and sexy underwear stuff."

Charles gaped.

Lily said, "Sure, there was even a picture of her in one of the fashion magazines recently. At a party somewhere. Bobbi Freon was there, too." She shrugged. "I tried to tell you, Charles."

"What do you mean you tried to tell me?"

"About a woman like that, how she could never really fall for a man like you. I mean, nothing personal, Charles. But she is Sofie Somers, after all." Lily patted Charles' hand. "I could never understand what her interest in you was, now it's clear."

Charles raised an eyebrow.

"She was using you."

"Seducing you," added Sadjan.

Denown laughed. "She's a clever woman. Clever and beautiful."

"Did she work for Bobbi Freon as a model?"

"Sure, she was one of his regulars," replied Lily.

"Then perhaps she is not clever enough." Charles knew there was more to this case left to be revealed. So far, he'd only touched the tip of this particular iceberg. He needed only to keep digging. "Do you have this picture, Lily?"

"I suppose. Back in my room."

"May I see it?"

"All right."

"Hey, what about the kids?" demanded Denown.

"They seem happy where they are," Charles answered.

"But I've an appointment with a supplier in twenty minutes."

"Ronalphe, you stay here with the children then."

The gendarme agreed and Charles and Lily headed up the path to Lily's room.

Lily's room was quite small. There were two twin-size beds separated by a single night table. "My roommate is still away," said Lily. "So I've got the whole place to myself for another week or so."

She was rummaging around in her closet with her back to Charles. When she turned around, her arms were loaded with magazines. She dumped them on her unmade bed. "I'm not sure which magazine it was. I've got a bunch of them here."

Charles picked one up and started flipping through it.

"It was one of those retrospective articles," said Lily. "You know, like showing fashions from ten years ago." She patted the mattress and wiped a stray lock of hair from her forehead. "Have a seat, Charles."

Charles sat down on the edge of the bed and laid the magazine across his knees. Lily had handed him a stack of magazines. There were so many photos, so many advertisements, it seemed impossible that he'd ever find a picture of Sofie Somers. And even if he did, what then?

He sighed, tossed a second magazine to the floor and continued turning pages. All he could do was to keep digging. The truth was there. He was certain.

"Here it is," said Lily.

"Let me see."

Lily nudged up beside him and held the magazine spread out. "See," she placed her finger on a photo in the far right corner. "That's her right there."

Charles nodded. "That's her alright." More than a dozen years younger. Still, she had aged remarkably well. "Who is that fellow?"

Lily laughed. "That's Bobbi Freon, of course."

Charles laid his finger on the page. "This fellow, right here." He jabbed.

"Yes, that's Bobbi Freon, like I said."

"Are you sure?"

Lily sighed. "Look," she grabbed the magazine from Charles lap. "It says right here, Bobbi Freon and Sofie Somers at the BF Spring Fashion Show, New York City."

"He looks very different. I'd never have recognized him."

"You think? It's all that hair, I expect. He wasn't always

bald, you know. This was the late eighties."

"*Mon Dieu*," whispered Charles.

"What? Afraid of what you'll look like if you one day lose your hair, Charles?"

"Look at Bobbi Freon very closely, Lily." He laid his hand on her back and pushed her forward. "What do you see? Do you see who I see?"

"Huh? What do you mean? I see Bobbi Freon."

"Do you see anyone else?"

"Sofie Somers?"

"No."

"No?" Lily stood. "You're making no sense, Charles. No sense at all. What do you see? Who do you see?"

Charles said somberly, "I see Tony Somers."

"Tony Somers?" Lily looked once more at the photo. "You're crazy. I bet he wasn't even born yet."

"No," said Charles, shaking his head. "Look at Bobbie Freon and tell me if you do not also see Tony Somers."

"This is ridiculous." Lily crossed her arms, and reluctantly studied the photo Charles held before her eyes. "All I see is—" She gasped.

"This photo. It is a younger Bobbi Freon. And," said Charles, rolling the magazine up and placing it under his arm, "it is also an older Tony Somers."

"His son?"

Charles nodded. "Yes."

"That's amazing," uttered Lily. "His own son. Cleo must be his daughter, then. I can see the resemblance now." Lily was shaking her head in disbelief. "And yet their mother worked for him as his housekeeper? What sort of monster was Bobbi Freon?"

"One can only imagine."

"Yet, how does this change anything, Charles?" Lily

asked. "Mademoiselle Somers has already confessed to killing Bobbi. This only means that she'd at one time had a deeper relationship with him. All the more motive, so it would seem."

Charles opened the door and waved for Lily to follow. "It changes nothing, Lily. It merely confirms for my mind what my heart has been saying."

Lily looked at the gendarme in bafflement.

Kristine Schaeffer was out with her dog as they retraced their steps. "*Bonjour*, Charles."

"Good afternoon, madame," said Charles.

Lily said hello.

"Is it true what I heard? You've taken Mademoiselle Somers in for the murder of Bobbi Freon?"

"Where did you hear this?"

"Why, the manager mentioned it. I saw him earlier."

"Oh," Charles wished everyone would mind their own business. "Yes, I am afraid it is true."

Kristine said sadly, "It such a shame. And those poor children. Is there anything I can do?"

"Not at the moment, though this may become necessary. Madame, do you recall when I initially interviewed you?"

"Why, yes, we had tea."

"Yes. You told me how you'd seen the man in the suit."

"The blue suit," corrected the old woman.

"That's right," said Charles. "You also mentioned that you'd seen Tony."

"You mean Mademoiselle Somers' boy, Anthony?"

"Yes."

"Of course. He was crying and I felt entirely helpless." She was shaking her head. She raised Foofy to her bosom and squeezed. "Imagine how he must feel now. Both of them.

Those poor, poor children."

Lily, who until then had remained speechless, asked Charles, as he led her down the hill, "What on earth is going on?"

"Have you ever had children, Lily?"

"Of course not. Don't be ridiculous."

"Then perhaps you wouldn't understand."

"Understand what?" asked Lily, as they entered the hotel lobby.

Charles called Sadjan out from Denown's office. The manager was nowhere in sight. The children were wrapped up in their computer game. "We're finished here. We'll have to take the children in to headquarters."

Gendarme Sadjan nodded and Charles heard groans and moans as Sadjan returned to Denown's office and shut off the computer. He brought out the kids.

Charles turned to Lily. "Thank you for your help, Lily." He nodded. "*Au revoir.*"

He got as far as the door when Lily hollered, "Wait just a moment, Charles!"

He turned. Sadjan stood for a moment, a child on each hand. Charles motioned for them to continue but Ronalphe stood his ground.

"You think you can just leave like this?"

"Like what?"

"Like this! Like without telling me what's going on!" Lily's face was red.

"This is police business. You must remain here. I'm sure you have a job to do."

She fumed. "If you think you're going to keep me out of this now after all I have been through, you've got another thing coming, Charles."

"I'm sorry. Please, keep your voice down, the children—"

"Come on, Charles. You owe me an explanation."

"Again, I am sorry. Perhaps, if you telephone the Gendarmerie later—"

Lily strode up to Charles and punched him in the stomach. Not hard, but it got his attention.

"There," she said. "Arrest me."

Charles was flabbergasted, and not a little out of breath. It was a pretty good wallop for a girl. Ronalphe was sniggering. "Take the car and drive Tony and Cleo to headquarters," snapped Charles.

Sadjan hustled the kids outside and disappeared.

"I have one further interview to conduct. Have you a car?"

"I have a scooter."

"Lovely," said Charles, ruing the idea of having to wrap his arms around this assaultive lunatic.

"Don't worry," replied Lily, as if reading Charles' thoughts, "we can take one of the hotel's cars."

Lily sat behind the wheel. "Where are we going?"

"Your boyfriend's house."

"What?"

"Jean-Marc's."

"Very funny." She headed up the road. "What are we going to see Jean-Marc for?"

"We," answered Charles haughtily, "are not going to see Jean-Marc about anything. I am going to interview Monsieur Bouton one more time concerning his previous statements."

"You think he had something to do with Bobbi Freon's death?" Lily turned the wheel sharply to avoid a passing Moke, one of the small topless vehicles common on the island.

Charles hung his right hand out the window, letting the

wind slip through his fingers. "I believe Jean-Marc is part of the lie that has been ensnaring me from the beginning."

Donna, Jean-Marc's young girlfriend was out front, watering her flower garden. She twisted the nozzle, shutting off the water, and stared at them. "*Bonjour*, Lily, what's up? What's he doing here?" She aimed the garden hose in the gendarme's direction as if getting ready to fire.

"Charles would like a word with Jean-Marc. Is he about?"

Donna looked like she was trying to make up her mind about something. Finally, she shrugged. "He's inside. Go on in."

She kept the nozzle targeted at Charles as he passed. Charles stopped Lily at the door. "You wait here."

Lily started to protest but Charles shut the door on her.

Jean-Marc was stretched out on the sofa in his tennis clothes. "You again." He sat up. "What do you want now?"

"I want the truth." Charles loomed over the other man. "Or rather, I want you to confirm the truth."

"I've already said all I have to say. It's the truth. Whether you want to believe it or not."

"Let me tell you what I believe, Monsieur Bouton. I believe you are lying."

Jean-Marc said nothing, folded his arms across his wide chest.

"You said that you saw Mademoiselle Somers leaving Villa Onyx at about the time that Monsieur Freon is estimated to have been killed. This is not so. I have another witness who places the mademoiselle at the beach the entire morning up until the discovery of the body."

Jean-Marc refused to respond.

"So, this means that you are lying to me. But why?"

Jean-Marc broke his silence. He stood. "Exactly. Why

would I lie about a thing like that? Huh? You tell me, *Monsieur le gendarme.*"

"It could be that you are trying to implicate Sofie Somers in the murder." Charles watched the other man's face for his reaction. "Or it may be that you are lying because she asked you to?"

A twitch of Jean-Marc's eyebrows gave him away.

"And why," continued Charles, "would Mademoiselle Somers ask you to claim that you saw her leaving Villa Onyx which would only implicate her in the murder?"

"She wouldn't."

"Unless she was protecting someone else."

"You don't know what you're talking about. Why don't you just leave everything alone, Trenet? You'll only cause more people pain. Sofie's confessed. It's over."

"What did she promise you? The same thing that Bobbi Freon had promised you in exchange for your sexual favors? A well-paid modeling career?"

Charles moved to a low bookshelf and examined a seashell. A colorful conch. "Think about it, Jean-Marc, how will Mademoiselle Somers keep her bargain with you if she spends her life in prison?"

"Get out of my house, will you?"

"I am no judge, but you may be an accessory to the murder after the fact." Charles went to the door. "You would not like prison, I think." He turned the handle. "I am sorry you chose not to cooperate. It might have made things easier on you. I am even more sorry for the boy." Charles opened the door.

"You-you know?"

Charles nodded.

"He's only a kid, Charles—"

"Sadly, this changes little."

21

"Are you okay, Charles? You look pale?"

"I am only weary." He climbed in on the passenger's side. "We can go to the Gendarmerie now."

Lily drove. Charles remained quiet throughout the short trip.

Adjutant Bruyer was waiting for him like a cat ready to pounce on a pesky mouse. "What is going on here, Charles? Why did you have Sadjan bring Mademoiselle Somers' children here? *Mon Dieu*, I've had to keep them occupied. We can't have them seeing their poor mother incarcerated, can we?"

"No, monsieur. I am sorry." He looked toward the cell. The door was closed. "I need to speak with Mademoiselle Somers."

"Very well."

"Perhaps you should be present as well, monsieur."

The adjutant agreed.

"What about me?" Lily asked.

"My child, keep an eye on those two children, won't you? My men are ill-equipped."

Lily reluctantly agreed.

"Wonderful. Take them for a walk. Out the side door there." The adjutant pointed through a corner office where the children sat reading ragged magazines.

Leaving Lily to the children, Charles went to have a word with Sofie. Adjutant Bruyer followed. The door to the cell was not locked and they simply walked in.

Sofie sat on the mattress reading an English novel the adjutant had lent her. It was a Georges Simenon novel left over from his predecessor's reign on the island. She closed the book and looked up expectantly. "Hello, Charles."

Charles nodded. "I'm sorry, Sofie."

"Don't worry, Charles. I know what I did was wrong. And now I must pay the price."

Charles was shaking his head. "No, maybe what you did was not right, but you did it for the right reasons." Charles thought of all the things a parent did for a child. Even Thor had a passion for protecting Elephant, his cat, and would do anything for him. This was only natural.

"What are you talking about, Charles?" demanded Adjutant Bruyer.

"Monsieur, Sofie Somers is innocent of the crime of murdering Bobbi Freon."

"What?"

"Charles, please—"

"You see, she is only protecting Tony, her son."

Tears welled up in Sofie's eyes. "Charles, please, I beg you, stop!"

"The boy?!" Adjutant Bruyer looked dumbstruck.

"Yes, adjutant."

"Are you certain, Charles?" There was a gasp. "*Mon Dieu*, you had better be."

"*Oui*, monsieur. You see, Tony was seen leaving Villa

Onyx by Jean-Marc Bouton, the poolman, at a time that would coincide with the murder. Sofie Somers was herself at the beach, in front of witnesses, and could not have committed this crime. Madame Schaeffer, who has the villa near Bobbi Freon's also stated that she had seen the boy that morning at about the same time."

Sofie was crying, her hands over her face.

"Madame Schaeffer said that Tony was crying and he looked hurt. He told her he was fine. I didn't think anything of it at the time, but now I see. Mademoiselle Somers told me that Tony had injured himself trying to surf. I expect he was hurt in his struggle with Monsieur Freon. Probably struck. That would explain the bruising I noticed on his face as well as any surfing accident."

"Jesus help us all," whispered the adjutant. "The boy. But what possessed him?"

"Tony and Cleo are Monsieur Freon's children."

Sofie looked up. "How did you know?"

"The resemblance is striking." Charles told the adjutant about the old photograph he'd seen. "And then it all came together. Tony's injuries, his being near the scene of the crime. You lying.

"And something you said earlier, about the pyramid being the symbol for Bobbi Freon Enterprises. You told me on the beach that first time I interviewed you. You said how Monsieur Freon was into all things Egyptian."

"What does that have to do with anything, Charles? wondered the adjutant.

"Tony and Cleo. Anthony and Cleopatra."

"The names were Bobbi's idea." Sofie rose. "Oh, I didn't mind. But it wouldn't have mattered even if I had. Everything had to be Bobbi's way. Bobbi's way or no way."

"Why would the boy kill his own father?" asked Adjutant

Bruyer.

Sofie sighed. "It's not his fault, Charles. Please, I've confessed. Can't you just let it be? Adjutant?"

"I'm sorry," said the adjutant. "I am helpless."

"He was a monster. God, how I hated him. Still, all this is my fault. I should never have let him treat me the way he did. Being his housekeeper, lying about the children."

Charles asked, "Tony and Cleo did not know Monsieur Freon was their father?"

"No, not until the other night."

"*Mon Dieu!*" cried the adjutant for the umpteenth time. He made the sign of the cross. "He was a monster, indeed!"

"You see, the night before Bobbi died, we were arguing in the kitchen. What I said before, about him kicking us out, that was true. He was getting married and Linda Patterson made it clear to him that she did not want us around. He promised to take care of us, but I knew that once he pushed us out of the picture he'd soon forget us."

Sofie let out a mournful sigh. "Anyway, Tony, poor Tony, our shouting woke him. He heard us arguing and learned that Bobbi Freon was his father. I didn't know he was listening. Tony told me all this the next day. After."

She paused and let fresh tears run down her patchy red cheeks. "Poor Tony. He went to see Bobbi. He wanted to confront his father. He wanted to find out why his own father would not recognize him as his son. Can you blame him?"

Charles and the adjutant were shaking their heads.

"They fought. Bobbi laughed at him. Bobbi laughed at everybody. He slapped Tony in the face, the bastard. That's when Tony picked up the letter opener and—"

Sofie broke down. When she collected herself she said. "He didn't mean it, Charles. He is only a boy. Rejected by his father while living in his house. Imagine, will you? Growing up thinking he was only a housekeeper's son, his own father dead."

"And you tried to cover up for Tony?"

"Yes, he came to the beach. I could see he was crying, upset. I insisted he tell me what was wrong. He told me what he'd done. I told Tony to stay on the beach and that I would take care of everything. Not to worry. Before reporting the murder, I went upstairs, removed the letter opener—"

Sofie shook visibly at the memory, "then wiped it with a sock and did the first thing I could think of—"

"Throw it on the roof," said Charles.

Sofie nodded.

22

"I will never understand why Sofie Somers let Bobbi Freon treat her and the children like that," remarked Lily.

"As I told you, she had a serious drug problem years before and even spent six months in jail for supervised rehab. And I hear her sexual escapades were equally wild."

"I can believe that."

Charles ignored Lily's last remark. "Sofie didn't want her children to know about her somewhat unsavory past. And she was broke. She had turned her life around and wanted what was best for the children. As a model, Sofie had made a great deal of money, but had wasted it all on drugs, booze, and a lavish lifestyle.

"Bobbi was rich. She needed him. He threatened to tell Tony and Cleo all about her sordid past if she did not go along with his wishes."

"Some wishes. Live with me as my housekeeper and tell everybody the kids' father is dead. Brain dead, I'd say."

"Can we forget all about that now? Grab that line, would you?"

Lily grunted and grabbed her end of the rope.

"Ready, Charles?" cried Thor.

"Ready!" Charles ducked his head under the boat. "Are you ready, adjutant?"

Adjutant Bruyer, rarely out of uniform, wore cut-off shorts and a colorful rayon Hawaiian shirt decorated with yellow pineapples. "Yes, Charles. We're all set here, aren't we, men?"

Charles' mates, Ronalphe Sadjan and Simon Brin, nodded. Their hands were flexed and ready. This was the big day. Charles' sailboat was going in the water. No longer would he be stuck on land, living with the ridicule of a boat that his colleagues and neighbors all whispered to be unseaworthy. "All right, then." Charles kicked out the blocks that held the trailer in place.

Chief Lebon arrived just then, honking the horn of his Daihatsu SUV. "*Bonjour*, Charles. Sorry we're late. Don't you want a tow?"

Charles waved. "No, that's alright. The ramp is around the corner. It's just as easy to push it there."

Chief Lebon parked the SUV and hopped out. His daughter squeezed out the same door. "Violette was able to come. Isn't that wonderful? She was supposed to babysit Rose's children, but Pisar volunteered. That's why he's not here helping with your launch."

"Oh, hello, Violette."

"Hello, Charles." Violette kissed Charles' cheek. She held up her hand. "I brought a picnic. For the boat." She looked smashing in a yellow sundress and leather sandals. She had a cute little sailor's hat on her head.

"Well, isn't that just lovely, Charles," said Lily, who had appeared out of nowhere.

"Violette's made some delicious sandwiches," the chief said proudly. "There's a bottle of champagne in there, too."

Charles nodded awkwardly. He carefully avoided looking at Lily or Violette and kept his eyes on the chief of police. "Well, let's get started, shall we?"

"Fine looking vessel," said Chief Lebon politely, running his hand along the hull.

"*Merci.* Of course, she still needs lots of work."

"But she's seaworthy, that's for sure," put in Thor, rapping the boards with his knuckles.

Together they all gathered around the boat and pushed. The wheels of the trailer resisted for a moment then gave and the tiny sailboat rolled along. With a gentle bump, they cleared the sidewalk.

Chief Lebon stood in the center of Rue Jeanne d'Arc forcing traffic to a halt while they maneuvered Charles' sailboat over to the ramp.

"It's all downhill from here," shouted Thor. "Get in, Charles!"

"Are you sure?"

"Yes, climb in, son. These two sturdy young fellows and I can handle the trailer," he said pointing to Sadjan and Brin. "We'll ease her in gentle like."

"Thank you, Thor."

Thor stuck out his hand and they shook. "Thank you, Charles." A tear welled up in the old man's eye. "Without you, I don't know what I would have done. You saved Elephant for me."

"It's nothing," said Charles. "I'm only glad he's alright."

Thor slapped Charles on the back. "Get on board, then."

"Aren't you coming?"

"No, I want the honor of watching you sail off on your maiden cruise."

"Well, if you say so."

"I say so. And about Elephant, I'm going to pay you back,

don't think I won't!"

"I know." Charles stood on the deck. Chief Lebon helped Violette up with her picnic basket. Adjutant Bruyer had already climbed aboard and helped himself to a beer from the Styrofoam cooler that lay open near the wheel in the cockpit.

"Congratulations," said Adjutant Bruyer.

"*Merci*," said Charles. He gripped the wheel as the boat slowly slid into Gustavia Harbor. He was in the water at last.

Chief Lebon and Lily were unwinding the sails. The adjutant dropped his beer and lent them a hand.

"Maybe we'll take a run around the island?" Charles considered aloud.

"Can I get you anything, Charles?" asked Violette. "Would you care for a sandwich or a drink?"

Charles heard Lily clearing her throat. "Well, perhaps—" There was a deep groan from below and the tiny sailboat shuddered.

"What the hell was that, Charles?" demanded Adjutant Bruyer, running to the gendarme's side. "Have you got some sort of a beast down there?"

"No, I don't know what—" The sound came again, deep and grumbling. This time followed by a loud crack and a rush of water.

Lily cried, "We're sinking!"

"What?" Hands refusing to let go of the wheel, Charles swung his head about side to side. The bow of the boat was pointing down.

Lily ran to the cockpit. They were going down fast. The boat tilted at a forty-five degree angle with water up to the boom. Everyone scrambled to the back of the boat but for Charles who stood waist deep in seawater.

"Come on, Charles," said the adjutant. "She's going down, son."

Chief Lebon and Violette were the first off. Adjutant Bruyer helped Lily over the side. Charles saw Violette's picnic basket go floating by his eyes as the harbor gurgled and swallowed his sailboat, his home.

He waded to shore, wet and shocked. Loose boards floated to the surface. Thor. Thor and his useless, defective glues and sealants. Come to think of it, where was the old man?

Charles stamped his wet feet on the boat ramp. "Is everyone alright?" Everyone was. "Has anyone seen Thor?"

Sadjan and Brin were pointing. Charles followed their arms. The old man was running up the hill between a couple of houses.

"Don't worry, son," said Chief Lebon. "We'll take you back to my house. Violette will fix us up. Get us some dry clothes."

"But everything I own was in that boat." And he'd given all his savings to Thor and his cat. Not only was his boat sunk, Charles was sunk, too.

But Chief Lebon had other plans. He laid a fatherly hand over Charles' damp shoulder. "To tell you the truth, I did think that boat of yours a bit small, Charles. In fact, you've seen what a big place my wife and I have. I've got a spare room just your size, Charles."

Charles stared, his legs felt numb. Was it the cold or the shock?

"We've even got air conditioning." The chief's wet moustache was dripping like a leaky faucet.

Violette retrieved a jacket from her father's car and wrapped it over his shoulders.

"*Merci, ma petite*," said Chief Lebon, escorting the two youngsters to the SUV. "Violette takes such good care of me, Charles. *Oui*, she's going to make some lucky fellow a fine wife someday."

Charles, feeling like the warden was leading him to the executioner's block, squeezed into the hot and cramped back seat. He caught a glimpse of Lily's face as they drove off and feared there would soon be another killing in Saint Barthelemy and that he would not be around to solve it.

"You know," said Chief Lebon, who was behind the wheel, "St. Barts is a lovely place to live. I've spent my entire life here. Elisabeth, also." His eyes met Charles' in the rear view mirror. "Have you ever given any thought to where you'd like to settle down, son?"